A TAMIL MONTH

A TAMIL MONTH

V SANJAY KUMAR

B L O O M S B U R Y
NEW DELHI • LONDON • OXFORD • NEW YORK • SYDNEY

BLOOMSBURY INDIA
Bloomsbury Publishing India Pvt. Ltd
Second Floor, LSC Building No. 4, DDA Complex, Pocket C – 6 & 7,
Vasant Kunj New Delhi 110070

BLOOMSBURY, BLOOMSBURY INDIA and the Diana logo are trademarks of
Bloomsbury Publishing Plc

First published in India 2020
This edition published 2020

ISBN: TPB: 978-93-88630-10-8; eBook: 978-93-88630-12-2

2 4 6 8 10 9 7 5 3 1

Typeset in Adobe Garamond Pro by Manipal Technologies Limited
Printed and bound in India by Replika Press Pvt. Ltd.

To find out more about our authors and books visit www.bloomsbury.com and sign up for our newsletters

I

NADU

The southern state of Tamil Nadu is where the real sun shines. The capital, Chennai, is a sauna by the sea. Every morning, the citizenry toils over tiffin. They pound rice mixed with gram and watch the dough rise, they pour water over -powder and watch the dark Arabica drip. Grinding centres mash the all-important masalas while street dogs stand outside and sneeze.

Ye olde village was a leafy pattinam called Madras. It was a colonial outpost under British administration. The French in nearby Pondicherry had their eye on it and they challenged the British in 1746 and 1758. Dupleix defeated the old rival and ruled Madras briefly. Robert Clive, a young fellow at the time, reportedly fled.

Come the high tide of the Indian Republic and fifty years of erasure followed. Erasure is a national pastime, yet some vestiges remain. I drink to them, these ruins of the Empire. In this Nadu, British Empire is a bottled beer and Napoleon is a brandy.

Mornings I head to Elliots Beach, a sandy Sahara with a sea attached. The fisherfolk look up and the young ones wave. They call me paithyam, a certified loon. The sea is in a churn. Foamy waves crash over each other, in a hurry to get to the shore. Unable to resist the urge,

I walk to the edge, shed my clothes and swim. I return alive, salty and famished, and head to a nearby Udipi whose blackboard proclaims, 'Tiffin Ready'.

In the month of July, there is an urgency in temples. For a couple of hours each morning, loudspeakers door-deliver prayers to homes. What follows is spooky. A vacuum. I step out, right foot first, and tiptoe to the market where an air of uneasy expectation has brought down ~~the~~ prices. 'Aadi has come,' says a shopkeeper, shaking his fist at the stars above.

Aadi is a Tamil month that begins with the ides of July. The sun changes course and nothing is auspicious anymore. I find Aadi alluring. I feel alive. To me, it seems every risk meets its measure in July and every chance is worth taking.

I arrived as a visitor in Tamil Nadu. 'We will cut the cloth to suit you,' the locals said. I wore what they gave me and it was the mantle of the outsider. I wore it well, surviving the language, the slow acquaintance with its mores, the almost shy unravelling of its best-kept secrets. After many years in its embrace, I have understood that this Nadu is a country. Like Bombay, the one I came from. I have withstood the worst, bearing up even with this singular word called 'poramboke'. I am scared of this word. It tells me that there exists a strip of no man's land at the water's edge that people like me belong to.

God knows I have tried to belong. I printed a local calling card that has my local name: Nanban. I married Sharada – she grew up here – and we have a daughter. My daughter has grown and she has two questions.

'Where are we from?' she asks. Adding, a little later, 'Why are we here?'

'I came here from Mumbai,' I tell her.

'Describe the city,' she says, 'since you refuse to go back there.'

Thinking of the city that made me, now far removed, the visuals that come are of sharp contrasts and brittle edges. Mumbai is a stapled narrative, a bandaged muse that hurtles along and somewhere in its sensual disorder (if you search hard enough), there are compelling reasons for its existence.

I tell my daughter, 'If this country is a garden of weeds, Mumbai is its wild flower. It is a posh beautiful ruin.'

'Then, why are we here?'

I carry this question as scientists have before me.

'Why are we here?'

Come evening, I accompany Sharada to a classical music performance at the Kalakshetra auditorium. Under a thatched roof, we sit on cane chairs in the company of elders. Some of them are nodding to the beat, others are just nodding. These elders are vidwans in their own right, a Chennai speciality called an informed audience.

The young singer on the dais is good but the audience raises the bar. She breaks free, soaring to where she has never been. Kalakshetra has me enthralled. I feel small in here, in my place, a comet in an ancient constellation.

A stray thought breaks the spell. Why are we here?

I should have told my daughter that we are here because my mother died here; we cremated her nearby and every morning, I swim in this ocean because her ashes return with the tide.

Sharada sees me fidgeting. 'Go away,' she says.

I leave halfway, alone. I decide to walk home. It is evening and as I stand at a store to buy some soda, cell phones come to life around me, glowing in shirt pockets, vibrating in trousers. People shout out intimate details, gesticulating at imagined relatives and friends. The sun blinks and sinks behind some tamarind trees. Birds are nesting and pet dogs are being walked. Streetlights flicker and strengthen, illuminating the sandy pavements. I walk the length of Tiger Varadachari Road, following two dancers in plaits and half saris. I cross Velankanni Church where, under tremulous entreaty, Yesu is saving the flock. I turn left onto the beachfront where waves are forming and waiting their turn. A peg measure waits for me at home. It is ornamental; I am done with dispensations, small and large. I have learned by now to measure drink by the hour.

TEN YEARS AGO

I am scared of visiting a place. Who can bear the sight of a man held down against his will? They have strapped Veerappan to a gurney and stuck tubes into him. He lies in a spotless room with a fixed smile, hooked up to machines that incessantly beep. On my last visit to this eerie chamber, I saw a nurse lift his naked legs, wipe and powder his arse, medicate a sore; he did not protest. I wish she had wiped that smile off his face.

'Have you reached? I can hear you breathing.'

This is Sharada, whispering through my dangling earpiece.

'I am sweating. There was a sharp stab in my chest just now.'

'Get admitted then,' she says.

'You know I hate these places.'

I hate places where you pass on the baton to a machine, to people who wear masks, hold knives and make deep incisions.

'It is a phobia,' she says. 'It preys on VIPs like you.'

I feel queasy as I approach Apollo, the big hospital off Greams Road. I have parked my car at a distance and I am walking along the crowded road. Hawkers have occupied the pavement and two-wheelers have occupied the kerb. Somebody honks behind me. I walk faster. He honks again. The bastard nudges me aside.

'Get off the middle of the road,' he shouts.

An ambulance floats past, eerily silent, its red light circling slower and slower. I halt at a crossing and people behind bump into me. 'Sorry,' I say.

'Why are you sorry?' Sharada asks.

They stay close, these locals. One fucker is sticking to me like my shirt. 'Excuse me.' I move away. He sidles up again.

'Don't touch.'

He looks up, noticing me for the first time. He scratches his crotch.

'Touch me not,' says another, cowering, mocking me.

They laugh loudly, the lot of them. 'Dai,' they call after me as I walk away. 'Pardesi!' they shout.

I hurry past a line of tightly parked vehicles and suddenly it appears before me, this apparition.

'You should see this hospital, Sharada. It looks like a posh hotel.'

On the side of the large building, there is a neon sign that says 'Emergency'. It is a staging area where they turn you into a patient.

'Don't hang up yet.'

There is security at the entrance and a man in a grey safari suit who welcomes Very Important People. He ignores me. I walk into the crowded foyer where people are milling around. There are signboards, arrows and counters. There is a nervous energy. Forms are being filled, prescriptions are being thrust through the pharmacy window, doctors are being summoned on the PA system and, in the middle of all this, patients are being wheeled through to various parts of the hospital.

'An old man just walked past me towards the entrance. He is barefoot.'

'Patient?'

'He is wearing a smock and an Iyengar sign, nothing else. Oh, he is carrying his saline drip and the tube is trailing behind him. He is trying to get away. He has made it to the revolving door. A nurse is chasing him.'

A nurse grabs him by the arm and ushers him away. I catch his eye as he passes.

'That's how you will behave when your time comes,' says Sharada.

I walk up to the small shrine near the lift. It looks like a carved almirah; inside it, an electronic flame flickers. When I bend low, I can hear a bhajan.

'I have to hang up now. I will call you.'

I fold a currency note, place it before the deity and murmur a prayer. An old crooked woman is watching me, holding on to a walking stick. She has been here for a month.

'For your son,' I tell her.

'He is still asleep,' she says.

I give her room, she joins me and I hold her wizened hand for a while. She squeezes my hand.

'Go now, speak to Veera. I am sure he will listen to you.'

They told me they drilled three holes in his skull, made three cuts and pulled out a triangle. They peeped in and there was blood that was pressing down on his brain. They inserted a tube and sucked and the blood came out and next to it was soft brainy tissue that was loose and willing. That tissue was he, his warmth, his memories – his unspoken thoughts, perhaps. They were very careful. When he awakens, he should recognise me and himself. The question is – when will he awaken?

I walk past the bank of lifts and take the stairs. I avoid the lifts because sometimes they wheel in patients headed to the first floor where the operation theatres are located. I hate seeing terrified people. I reach the fourth-floor landing, a little breathless. There is a nurse station that helms the floor. A matron smiles at me.

'Good morning, sir.'

We walk together down a long corridor to the last room. The door has an inserted card that says Veerappan. It is quiet.

'Remove your shoes please.'

I knock softly and enter.

They have washed him carefully today, dressed him in a pyjama and kurta and propped him up on the bed. They have combed his hair and his cheeks glow. A nurse is examining a chart. She makes careful portions from a boxful of ampoules, writes into the chart, pats Veera on the shoulder and leaves.

I call Sharada. 'He looks normal, like he is sleeping.'

'What are you going to do?'

I pull up a chair and sit next to him.

'Does he know you have come?'

'I would like to think so.'

I lean forward and look into his face, hold a finger under his nose and feel his breath. It is a quiet regular rhythm.

'Talk to him,' says Sharada.

'The party is enthused with our results Veera and the attendance at rallies is soaring. We miss you. We need someone who will take charge. They want me to find someone else till you…'

Veerappan Gounder passes motion. I can hear it and now I can smell it.

'Fuck, he is like a baby.'

I run out of the room, call the nurse and stay outside for a while.

'A nurse has gone in to clean up.'

She wipes him with a damp towel and then, inevitably, powders his arse. Then, she uses a room spray. I sit next to him again.

'They have strapped him down, his hands, his legs. There are all these tubes, so many of them. His eyes are closed. Should I open one?'

'What? Why not? Won't do any harm.'

I open one of his eyes.

'Veera, this is Nanban.'

I imagine a flicker. But, the fact is that the great leader of the middle caste called Gounder is completely unresponsive.

'What happened?' asks Sharada.

'Nothing. It is surreal. You look at him and you feel he will wake up any minute. But he doesn't.'

A nurse walks in without warning and she uses a small towel to mop Veerappan's face. Despite the air-conditioning, Veerappan is sweating. He can really sweat.

It hurts to see him like this. Right now, he is a farce; a force-fed, nappy-wearing farce. Machines are keeping him alive. I wish he had seen what we had achieved. Out of 234 elected assembly seats in the state of Tamil Nadu (one is reserved for an Anglo-Indian), the fledgling Lions Party competed in 75 and won in 50. I had been hired to do this. I had taken up the challenge because interventions like these made me whole; surprising people such as Veera kept me sane, but the job was incomplete without him.

'Veerappan, they are going to appoint an upstart as your successor. Do you want to know who it is?'

He does not react. I crouch over him, cup a palm over his ear and say the one name that should wake him up from his slumber, 'Karivardan.'

'What are you doing?'

'I think he shivered. I can see goosebumps.'

As I leave, I ask the matron to keep a vigil that night. 'Believe me,' I tell her. 'He will come to life.'

'Did you sign the register, sir?' she asks, sounding prim. We look. 'This is so childish. You should write your real name.'

Under 'Visitor's Name' I had signed in as Machiavelli. Previously, it was Ponniyin Selvan. Each was a character that lived between pages.

'You are back to your tricks?' says Sharada. 'Why do you do it?'

Sharada hangs up and after a few minutes, I call Muskaan. She does not answer my calls anymore. Muskaan is my last surviving link to my muse Mumbai, and I the last surviving buccaneer from the financial district of that city, a crowded square kilometre that houses brokerages, investment banks and a clearing house for the nation's money. Muskaan and I were chat room residents for the many months that I was in this southern city, estranged, a man with a cause. We used to chat for long hours until our hands ached.

II

THREE YEARS EARLIER

THE OUTSIDER

If you are dark-skinned, you must be dull, prone to date failure and a reject in the arranged-marriage market. Big data says so. Big data says the only weapon you have against such bias is a fairness cream. You watch the ads and feel powerless. You begin to believe in the message that feeds into your insecurities, a message crafted by clever corporations. Your hand reaches out for that tube of fairness cream.

This is how truth forms. It is what you learn to believe. In a world ruled by advertising, truth is nothing else but a gradual hardening of confirmation bias.

Your ancestors in the southern state of Tamil Nadu were dark, unlike the fair Brahmins. It seems the Brahmins arrived as high-caste pilgrims from Aryan shores and you, in turn, broke away from the Dark Continent. They kept their distance from you. As did the European colonisers. You were powerless against such prejudice. Dark is a native root in your Nadu. Your shade card is from the palette of a Baroque painter called Velasquez who lit up his works to discover the dark.

Your Nadu is a Dravida Nadu. Insulated for centuries from invaders who ravaged the Indo-Aryans in the North. Your ancient culture blossomed, unfettered. You developed an insular nature and an aversion to impositions. Imagine the North imposing on you a national language. Hindi was never meant to lord over Tamil, one of the oldest surviving languages with inscriptions dating as far back as 500 BC. The attempt ended up fanning a resistance.

In the pages of history, a 'resistance' is a beauteous thing. Your resistance drew strength from caste. Caste is a social hierarchy; it has four tiers and is shaped like a pyramid. You, the vast majority, fester at the base of this pyramid, struggling to meet your daily needs, treated by other castes as pariahs and untouchables. At the peak is the Brahmin who is educated and feels entitled. Brahmin priests claim a direct line to the gods, with whom they communicate in Sanskrit, chanting shlokas. They have foisted on you an elaborate system of rituals for which they have to be paid – or else.

You hated this. You were atheist, powerless as you watched the believers pray. Their shlokas and rituals cemented another confirmation bias. When the believers chanted, truth appeared, this time in an exalted form. A truth that they called God.

Nanban arrived in Tamil Nadu with the mantle of the outsider. Your rich culture spoke to him. 'We have our own patriarchy,' it said. 'We have our private cusspedia. And we have our booze bars with our patented stupor that comes from a morning quarter.'

He tried to merge with your ilk. He studied Dravidianism, a political movement you forged through agitation. Tamil was its pride, the Brahmin its hateful object. It was a unique movement that you choreographed using scriptwriters, poets and actors from Tamil cinema. Two Dravidian parties emerged. They took turns and ruled your state for over half a century.

Nanban had stayed for long years in Mumbai, revelling in its commerce and its bluster. He carries two phones with him, each synced to a Bluetooth accessory lodged in his ear. Nanban is not his real name. The word means friend. The fact you locals call him that is surprising. His mother is his accomplice in Chennai.

Nanban broke down barriers by learning your language. He read Tamil literature. He toured the state, shore to temple. He saw rice grow and toddy run. He ate the stem, the flower and the fruit of the banana tree, served to him on plantain leaves. He drank cheap liquor with you in ugly places where men lifted their flapping veshtis and watered the walls. He saw the moon rise in Chennai because he had time enough. It was large when it rose and, up close, its craters were visible, but as the night progressed, it receded into the sky, preferring the company of stars.

'The locals are understated and they underplay their achievements,' he said, after observing you. 'They hide their money and take modesty to bed.'

'And you?' his mother asked.

'Right now I am like them,' he said. 'It is better this way.'

He made a pile of money in his years in Bombay. He began as a day trader hoping to make a quick buck. The trading screen was his gaming console and he became a member of a small-change casino where addicted gamers logged in and wasted their lives. Technical investing followed day trading, a chart and algorithm approach that, on the surface, seemed more scientific. He resisted the slow charm of value investing – that tried and tested game of patience. For a while, he went contrarian, an enterprise that proved bloody. At the end of five years, he was nursing a hidden ulcer. His blood pressure had ruined his arteries.

'You can't walk on water,' he told himself. 'Learn to part the waves.'

He made the big move. He invented a financial instrument that bent a few guidelines. It leveraged his capital hundred-fold. He deployed his 100x in the market and then let the idea loose among the big bulls in the ring. It was an interesting idea, a suspicious one that broke no law in the book. One after the other, the bulls leveraged themselves. Soon, there was a stampede at the buy counter and the market climbed the screen tracing a jagged edge. Nanban sold his portfolio near the peak. He exited wholesale and shifted his money into treasury bonds. The market collapsed when the instrument was banned. He waited for the aftermath, ready for the investigative teams. They came combing, uncovered his modus operandi and declared him an 'economic offender'. The authorities spent long nights trying to make a case. They could not. 'You shouldn't have,' they finally said. They could only admonish him.

It hurt them so they harassed him, days and nights, and they let the press loose on him. He was placed on standby, the case stayed open. Systematically they broke into his life, condemning him to a state of permanent prosecution. The summons came thick and fast and he had to attend hearings. Please wait. He waited. Submit copies, please. He submitted. Clarify this, please, in writing. He did so repeatedly. Sign every page. He broke his wrist signing.

He greyed. His signature changed. He fled the city where he had grown up, taking with him his mother and two suitcases. The fortune he had made, he could not spend, not yet.

'This looks provincial,' said his mother, on her first visit to a temple in Chennai. 'Where have you brought me?' she asked him. 'What will we do here?'

'What are these long eel-like vegetables?' she asked at the market. 'Look, the pumpkin here is white.'

Mostly he read. He read philosophy, biographies of rogue traders and books on theories written by men on crack. The theory that appealed to him was 'random walk'. This theory said, 'Don't bother, and don't look at the past in order to predict the future, because stock price behaviour is truly random, just like the gait of a drunk.'

This mirrored his life. The idea of a random walk was practical as was an evening spent drinking. He explored the city of Chennai under the influence, taking detours, walking down nameless streets, getting lost and meeting people who dropped him home.

'All this comes naturally to you, beta?'

'You don't want to know, mama.'

His mother knew what he was capable of doing. She watched him bide his time in Chennai, a pressure cooker on simmer. The passing months should have ameliorated her dread but they did not. If anything, his inactivity stoked her discomfort. Unknown to her, Nanban had met a man called Veerappan from the Gounder community who had, only a month ago, lost badly in an election.

Veerappan Gounder had, with great enthusiasm, formed a political party and put up 50 candidates in the state assembly elections, touring the state tirelessly and campaigning vigorously on their behalf. People were genuinely curious and attended rallies in large numbers. Veera and his team were optimistic but the results took them by surprise. The candidates did so badly they lost their electoral deposits. Veera too lost and that hurt even more. He took it personally and started spending more and more time alone at a bar, wasted. That is where they met. Nanban was a regular at the same bar; they saw each other for a week, became nodding acquaintances and then got talking.

'Who did you meet in your bar today?' his mother asked.

'A TV reporter and filmmaker called Narsimhan,' he said. 'Narsimhan sits in a corner. It is a gloomy bar that has just two dim lights.'

'And why does he drink?'

This was a substitute question to, 'Why do you drink?'

Nanban knew the answer but he would not accept it, leave alone divulge it. A sullen pessimism afflicted him as it did Narsimhan.

'Which channel does he work for?'

'He has quit his job,' said Nanban. 'Some say he was kicked out for spending too much time drinking at the Press Club. He teaches a television course at the Asian College of Journalism. He freelances. He made a documentary on a politician called Veerappan. For the money it gave him, he said. He is now a provocateur.'

'Who is he provoking?'

'Tamil people. He publishes a sheet by the name *Dai Tamizha*. It is an underground magazine. It has ten pages of reportage and opinion, one cartoon and his stirring editorial.'

'What does dai mean?' asked his mother.

'Dai is a Tamilian alert. It places the recipient on notice. *Dai Tamizha* is a wake-up call for the people of Tamil Nadu.'

'Did he wake up the people?'

'Almost. He called the state a rice-fed fat farm that subsisted on political dole. The Tamil translation for that is a word called dhandasoru.'

'He must be a communist,' said his mother.

After his documentary on Veerappan, Narsimhan wrote a book on the Brahmin precinct called Mylapore. It was part ode, part rant.

'Today, Chennai is a collection of ghettos whose boundaries keep shifting,' began his book. 'The core is missing. It used to be Mylapore. Mylapore, the capital of Brahmin Utopia, came into the crosshairs when the Dravidian movement swept to power. The outnumbered Brahmins were ring-fenced and relegated. The elders retreated, into their spare abodes, to the prayer room where they stood barefoot at the auspicious hour and awaited divine intervention. Nothing happened. They retired, defeated, to the nearby music halls, incestuous sabhas where veenas and violins mourned. Their dominion crumbled outside while the great Semmangudi held Bhairavi to ransom.'

Narsimhan, a keen listener, sat in the front seat of the Mylapore Fine Arts Club during music season, slapping his thigh. When the music touched his soul his sounds of appreciation resembled a gecko's mating call. He was in his 40s, late 40s perhaps, because there were flecks of grey near his temples. His spectacles were plastic, the apertures round and the styling retro. His clear, broad forehead shone in the evenings. He was light on his feet, a yogi when sober.

His wistful moments took place when he stood at the maw of Brahmin Mylapore, a middle-aged mavin watching the next generation study computer science, receive the H1B visa from the US Consulate and disappear thereafter into the cloud in Silicon Valley, Syracuse and Seattle.

'Mylapore was never a large geography,' he wrote. 'Nor is it any more a satisfactory one. I can see people here trying to integrate. It is distressing. Why don't they wear veshtis, naamams, poonals and chappals and declare their ethnicity? I like Muslims and Sikhs for this reason. They walk around looking like cultural hoardings.'

'You like the idea of a ghetto?' Nanban asked him.

'Ghettos are a natural phenomenon,' said his provocative book. 'It is the nature of the human beast to seek commonality in its midst and separate the different. Man was born a statistician first and maths came later. He could group before he could count.'

Nanban read a few issues of *Dai Tamizha*. The sheet had a masthead with a lighthouse as its symbol. Narsimhan stayed near a beach and he liked the idea of a maritime beacon. One editorial began like this:

Welcome to the capital, Singara Chennai. Please pay the toll. Your political masters are your feudal lords and they own this state. They own this cinema, they made this film. They own this college, this hotel and this estate. You are drinking their beer. And you are feeling grateful, receiving their benami charity. Dear Morons, it is your money in their name. You and I stand outside their palaces. Behind their high walls, they are safe, armed with cash-counting machines. Today, the visitor is Changez Khan. Changez has arrived to pay his respects. He wants to learn how personality becomes cult, how a public, whose mortals immolate themselves for their masters, believes that in the southern tip of this country there has never been an invasion.

Nanban told him he was planning to advise Veerappan Gounder. Narsimhan gave him a copy of his documentary film. 'I know him too well,' he said.

'Caste might make a comeback in Tamil Nadu politics and I hope it does. But Veerappan Gounder cannot.'

'Why not?'

'Compare him to the Dravidian parties. Their leader Karunanidhi is a fiery poet with a unique style and diction. His guttural tone is his signature. Their other great leader M G Ramachandran, the cine actor, had charisma and a larger than life image. What does Veerappan have?'

A pertinent question.

'His meetings were boring, the crowds were paid for and the cheering was fake. He was fooled into believing an illusion his cronies created.'

'All debutants are gullible,' said Nanban. 'He would have learnt from his failure.'

'Have you?' said Narsimhan.

Narsimhan was no genius but he was self-obsessed. He stayed in a small flat in Mandaveli where he kept a meticulous record of himself. He brought to bear his journalistic skills on~~in~~ his small life. He cut and pasted every mention, every by-line and every pathetic reference in chronological order. He wrote assiduously into diaries. This was a daily log of the last thirty years – minute observations of the neighbourhood and granular notes on self.

'Anything significant?'

'No,' he said.

He spoke of a typical week in his life, every little detail laid out threadbare. It was simple and utterly true. The honesty glowed. It was a dogged routine prescribed by elders – a unique repeatability followed scrupulously by most Brahmins. This was caste – this chemistry table of beliefs, rituals, abstinences, diet, hygiene and behaviour was Brahmin DNA. At a molecular level, it was unapologetically incompatible with other castes.

Nanban was looking for exceptions, for evidence that Narsimhan had wavered. 'I feel like you are not telling me everything,' he said.

'I fell in love once,' said Narsimhan, shifting in his seat. 'Very badly.'

It sounded like a hamstring injury.

'And I imitated the actor M R Radha in a college skit,' he said. 'Nobody who saw it has forgotten it.'

Narsimhan fell asleep. The music played on and on and the breeze from the fan flipped the pages of his diaries. Nanban read an early page; a few lines seemed to have been written for him.

In Tamil Nadu, nutrition comes from cooking batter called maavu. When it is a day old and it is steamed, you get the round fluffy idly, a day later it is flattened on a hot griddle to make the dosai, and another day later it is a little sour and still useful, spread thicker with a seasoning of cut onions and crisped on a slow fire to make the uthappam.

Smell the batter each day, feel it between your fingers, know that it comes from paddy that stands in knee-deep water for months under a hot sun, travel then to the land that skirts the river Cauvery where the green fields sway and the coconut trees stand, where the white egret flies and the temples rise with their gopurams painted in pista and pink. People get hooked to this Tamil land. It is a sun-soaked utopia with coffee-coloured people.

'I don't understand how a boring life can be engaging,' said Nanban's mother.

'Things can be deceptive,' said Nanban. What he was not mentioning was his discovery of a box file that he had briefly opened. On it was a single word – 'SUMMONS'. Just as he had flipped the cardboard cover, Narsimhan had stirred and he had to leave. However, he had caught a fleeting glimpse of a legal summons. There were many. It was a fat file.

'Who else was there in the bar?' asked his mother.

'The politician called Veerappan who heads a community called Gounder.'

'A politician? In a common bar? What does he want from you?'

'Look at yourself,' Nanban said, pointing to Veerappan's hand. 'You wear a ring on each finger. They have gemstones which have been prescribed.'

Veera looked at his fingers and nodded. The rings were fat and ugly.

'You change the rings often; it means that you are consulting someone who tells you which gemstone works for the day, or week, or month. Is this faith or is it fear? Are you fearful? Why would you, the leader of a community, a prosperous farmer and the head of an extended doting family, be fearful?'

'All this is insurance,' said Veera, waving his fingers. 'I have two astrologers as well on my payroll. Politics in many ways is a lottery.'

'You surround yourself with irregulars,' said Nanban.

Veera looked around the bar towards the young lads who stood in the periphery. They were looking towards him, all the time. They were reading his mood, aware of his gaze and awaiting his gesture.

'You believe they are loyal?' asked Nanban. Veera shrugged his shoulders. 'To me they look selfish, grasping. I would not trust them. Can you predict their behaviour?'

'This election failure has made me look foolish,' said Veera. 'I have lost some good people. Now I have to build again.' He smiled ever so slightly. 'I hope I am transparent only to you,' he said.

'No sir,' said Nanban. 'You have learnt to be transparent to the people around you. It buys you loyalty. They have seen you fail, seen what it has done to you.'

Veera made the smallest of gestures and a special bottle of whisky arrived. A man wearing white from head to toe expertly opened the bottle. He placed two glasses on the table and poured two shots. It was 24-year-old Islay malt.

Veera spoke, 'I know you can do something for me. I am not sure exactly what it is but a man of your education, mishap and fortune should be of use.'

'Don't get involved with politicians,' said Nanban's mother.

That night even Narsimhan tried to dissuade him. 'Politicians are dangerous people,' he said.

Every warning cemented his resolve. 'If I were you I would plan for the next election,' he told Veera. 'The current political movement has run its course. There is a political vacuum. Somebody has to fill that gaping hole.'

'What hole,' said Veerappan?

'The Dravidian parties have no agenda.'

'They are not going to walk away,' said Veera. 'They will fight. In the last elections, they fielded Gounder candidates against ours and beat us hollow.'

'There is a succession problem. The stalwarts are ageing and the next generation has no new ideology. The Dravidian river that was fed by anger and protest now drifts quietly like the Cooum.'

'And why will the voters come to me?' said Veerappan. 'My caste card has failed.'

'The caste card is still powerful,' said Nanban. 'In a multi-party race, the first-past-the-post wins. This system is a caste leader's wet dream.'

'Wet dream?'

'With a 30 per cent vote share, you can win an election,' said Nanban. 'You haven't gone about it the right way.'

'I see,' said Veerappan. 'And why should I believe you? What is your unique qualification?'

'Forget my MBA,' said Nanban. 'I have a track record in disruption, in engineering upheaval. I understand the importance of chaos in this peaceful state. Caste is rife in Tamil Nadu and the lower castes are restless. Dravidian parties are atheist and cannot play the caste card. You have an opportunity.'

'Don't I know,' said Veera.

Nanban hadn't felt this way in a long time. That night, he had pain in his abdomen and it wouldn't go away.

'You are bleeding inside,' the doctor told him. 'A stomach ulcer that is behaving like Mount Vesuvius. From time to time it erupts.'

'I know,' he said.

'How so? Coloured stools?'

'Yes.'

'Tell me, are you an anxious person?'

He felt restless until it hurt. It was a vague feeling that stepped up his metabolism and it interfered with his sleep. It made him throw the covers at night, walk up to a window and stare. He went to a gym where he tried to sweat it out. He tried a yoga studio and he joined a meditation group but the feeling persisted.

'I am not tense. I feel restless. I feel hyper for no reason. It is weird. It is as if parts of me are getting ahead of the others.'

'I see. You might need a different doctor.'

'Please explain ulcers to me, Doc.'

'There is no settled theory on ulcers,' said his doctor. He twirled a pen over his prescription pad. 'So why don't we just treat them?'

'Doc, I don't want a recurrence. This bleeding is scary.'

'Could you please be seated first? Thanks. Do you sleep well?'

'No.' His mind burned calories while his body rested.

'I guessed as much. Do you drink a lot?'

'Sometimes.'

After an uneasy silence, the doctor asked him what he did for a living. 'Stock picking. Why?'

'I have to warn you that you may need to make a lifestyle change. Cut the drinking. And go easy on anything that makes you tense.'

'I cannot,' said Nanban. 'I cannot be restricted by anything. What is the worst that can happen?'

The doctor was blunt. 'You might bloody your own vodka while drinking it. You might bleed till your blood pressure drops to two digits and then it depends on how long an ambulance takes to get you to the Intensive Care Unit.'

Nanban went out of the clinic in a huff. It was hot as bloody hell and the street was ablaze, the sunlight piercing. Two boys were hitting each other aimlessly. Across the street, a huge movie poster showed unshaven men attacking each other with knives, screaming with their mouths wide open. The street sounds were numbing. Horns were loud and insistent, vehicles braked, tires screeched, diesel engines rattled and, in the smoke and dust, people swore and shouted.

Vesuvius stirred again inside his gut and he felt the ooze. A sharp stab followed. He breathed deeply until the pain subsided.

Moving to Chennai was like bailing out and his mother had not forgiven him.

'You were so happy when you made so much money. I wasn't. I warned you but you wouldn't listen. Easy money is a curse.'

'Who told you it was easy?'

'Beta, you were so young when you became rich. Either you were lucky or you were dishonest.'

'Why is it a curse?' he said. 'You like your comforts. I don't see you scrimping on anything.'

She shook her head, looking sad.

'It is not about me. You will drift the rest of your life, which is why I am sad. You need work to give you some discipline.'

He bore up with her constant carping about the real city, that glorious metropolis called Bombay that she had left behind. She felt lonely in Chennai, especially in the evening when all she could do was eat savouries called bhajjis and kill insects they called boochis. Besides his mother, there was a bristly street dog called Mayandi and the three of them stayed in the ground floor of a building in Besant Nagar near Elliots Beach, next to a cultural enclave called Spaces that had sandy earth, fragrant flowers and grand old trees. Outside Spaces, popular culture trawled the beach every evening, dressed in kitsch, armed with Tamil pop, some extra bass and cold beer.

His mother sat in the veranda and the sea view couldn't rescue her. The sky scowled and a stray cloud spat some rain, the temperature eased, yet she glowered.

'Why don't you unpack your personal effects and make this a home?' he said. 'In Mumbai, you were so house-proud.'

'Are we here permanently?'

It was a loaded question. It worried her, that question. Her husband copped out when she was forty. Since then her only companion had been loneliness.

'Why did you choose this city?'

He had been to yet another nasty and fruitless session in the interrogation room. He had called a particular number in Delhi, spoken to a faceless bureaucrat and said yes. He had received orders and without fuss, he had gone to the airport and bought a ticket to a part of the country he wasn't familiar with. The plane descended on a flat landscape and when he emerged, people spoke to him in an alien tongue.

'It is a peaceful state,' he said, 'a place where I can lie low.'

'Lie low then, but the language is so difficult, beta. "Vadi come", they tell me, then, "podi go". I sit all day, eat bananas and sweat from every pore. I will die here. I will drown in my own sweat.'

He went up to her, sat next to her, clasped her hands. Mother and son. An age-old partnership. Drops of sweat fell around them. Finally, she smiled, and Mayandi thumped his tail on the red oxide floor. The sky cleared and they waited for the afternoon breeze.

'The maidservant is breaking all my crockery. I hope you know that.'

'She is? You must be standing next to her. You can be overbearing with the help.'

'I see. It is always about me. Anyway, she says she is used to stainless steel vessels. Those don't break. So, if you are planning on staying here very long, please come with me and we will buy them.'

'Okay, mama.'

She smiled at him and squeezed his hand. 'I knew you would stay here for a while.'

'Mothers know everything.'

'No, really, this is a kind city you know. People here are kind, more than Bombay. And you are a sucker for kindness.'

He did not like this discussion. 'Who is kind out here?'

'The women, who else? Indian kindness comes from women.'

'It is foolish.'

'Kindness is foolish? I agree. Women in this country don't think for themselves.'

'Mother, that's not what I meant.'

His mind would never mend, he knew it, and though Chennai tried to still it and keep it away from activities that caused him trouble, it was a losing battle.

The mind doctor told him that ulcers came from infections. They should be treated like any infection, by a dosage of antibiotic. That's it?

'Keep your mind busy,' said the psychologist, 'and you will be fine.'

He laughed so loudly it hurt. 'A busy mind is no friend of mine,' he said.

Nanban tried teaching in a city college. For a while, he was busy, diligent in his reading and his lectures. Life in Chennai was peaceful but it felt like fiction, a precarious fiction in which he was fooling himself. The longer this lasted, the bigger would be the denouement. The thought kept him hungry. Eating became pleasurable and the local cuisine was varied and inventive; there were many communities and each had its traditional offerings. He moved beyond the simple vegetarian fare in 'Udipi' restaurants and the non-vegetarian commonplace in 'Military' hotels to Chettinad food, Gounder cuisine, seafood from neighbouring Kerala and spicy meat from Andhra. He had trotter soup near the Royapettah Police Station along with the flaky, layered, oil-filled parotta, made by a bare-chested sweaty chef. He flipped for the tamarind curry that had fresh fish fillets. He sampled every biryani in town, revelling in the marriage of fragrant rice and succulent meat.

A few years passed and he was tipping the scales at 95 kilos, his eyes were red and he had a nervous tic that was choosing a possible location. He was still antsy, still on the phone, bothering people.

'I have done nothing bold in Chennai,' he said.

'Let us return to Mumbai,' said his mother. 'Nobody here will miss you.'

The first move he made was innocuous. He met a young man quite by chance. The youngster had the same restlessness that plagued him. He knew more about Nanban than was healthy.

'Your good name?' he asked the youngster.

'Valiban,' he said. It was an alias, a generic name like Nanban. 'Sir, I am from a college where they rusticated me for starting a movement against the teachers and the curriculum. They gave me a degree to get rid of me. I am jobless now.'

'What do you know about me?' said Nanban.

'Everything, sir. You are from Mumbai. I have seen you at the bar called Chinna Tasmac. You are sophisticated.'

'I see,' said Nanban. 'Sophisticated? I have forgotten what that means.'

'Sir, I have seen you sitting in that bar. Your head is so still and you are observing people.'

'That's all?'

'I feel very soon you are going to do something to them,' said Valiban. 'They are powerful people, but you are going to change their lives.'

'Why would I do that?' said Nanban.

The question stumped Valiban for a moment. 'Because you can?' he said.

'Such a beautiful answer,' said his mother. 'Who is this boy?'

'My Tamil teacher,' said Nanban.

It was true; this young lad taught Nanban. Not just the language.

'Sit facing east,' he instructed Nanban. It was 5.00 in the morning. 'Repeat after me. Aaa thee moo kaa.'

'Is that the alphabet?'

'No sir. It stands for ADMK. The ruling political party.'

'I hope he did not teach you swear words,' said his mother. 'It is better not to know them.'

'Brahmins curses are mild, mostly to do with lack of intelligence,' Valiban had said. 'In English, a Brahmin would call you stupid. When very angry perhaps rascal. Youngsters like me use gutter language, mostly to do with private parts.'

'Could you teach me the private parts?' asked Nanban.

Valiban was patient. He spent time explaining the local festivals and customs. He spoke about inauspicious time, dates and months. He showed him a Panchangam, an almanac/calendar that had daily details. In it, time and tide played snakes and ladders.

'Do you have a resume?' Nanban asked Valiban.

'I have gaps in my resume,' said Valiban. He proceeded to fill them.

THE ENFANT

He began his narration at 5.00 am the next day. 'They call me Valiban,' he said. 'After my father's death, I left home to stay with my ailing uncle Govindan. He took early retirement from a steady job and has since developed an acquaintance with a cheap whisky. I steal a peg a day from his bottle and replace it with water. This has kept him alive. I have grown to fear evenings, the time when he drinks, when his neighbours call him Quarter Govindan. Two quarters and he becomes a wise man, what locals call a Karuthu Kandhasamy, offering unwanted advice to passers-by from his balcony.

'Our family is a close one, an affectionate one, full of menfolk who paused at the wine shop on the way to Sanskrit College. We have stood by each other, always. No one in the past generations has been successful, famous or rich. My ancestors broke tradition, had affairs and some even married outcastes, forgot festivals, ate red meat and performed the wrong rituals. They made strange career choices. Because we continue to visit temples, attend aartis, wear a naamam on our foreheads and a poonal thread around our mid-riff, we have remained Brahmins.'

Nanban had some friends from Indian Institute of Technology, Madras who fitted that image.

'Can I smoke?' asked Valiban.'

Nanban nodded and the youngster pulled out a handmade cheroot and lit it. It smelt of evenings at the Mardi Gras, a festival that IIT, Madras used to host.

'You should know where I come from, sir. I come from a restless sensibility that spawns nagars and purams. Put together, it is a Nadu, perched under the country's armpit, washed by the Bay of Bengal. Chennai, our mahanagaram, has grown quietly in the shade of neem and tamarind trees. We are quiet people, sir, but we have a sense of our own importance. Our gods are many; they are colourful and human. Our culture is ancient and unbreakable, like the stainless steel utensils we use. Of late mofussil types from the interiors have swamped the cities. They have peculiar habits.'

'You sound like a literature student,' said Nanban. He was one. He was a BA Pass from a Vaishnav College.

'My city has two legs, sir, that stretch far south to the temple town of Mahabalipuram. The right leg is the Old Mahabalipuram Road and it is a four-lane highway. Money favours the left leg, the East Coast Road, because it hugs the coastline. Its residents have a scenic view of sand and waves. There are three connecting roads between these two and in one such connection, there is a small puram which is my utopia. It has a posh complex called Elysium. Elysium has thirty white villas that promise idyll and incredible happiness. One day I will own a place there. Outside Elysium is a large hoarding. Stalin, son of our leader Karunanidhi, smiles at me from this hoarding. He is wearing a huge rose garland the size of a traffic island. Why was he named Stalin? Only his famous father knows. He is a playwright and a canny politician. I am in love with his oratory and his dark glasses. The glasses are really dark and they have thick black frames. He wears them even at night. It is fashion. Another chief minister, a matinee idol, a veritable bhagwan called M G Ramachandran also wore them. Once MGR wore them, everybody Tamil did so, especially in summer.'

'Because it is so bright?'

'No. Because of Madras eye, the local brand of conjunctivitis. And, sometimes because of STD, perhaps the local brand of syphilis.'

'Enough background,' said Nanban. 'Begin the resume.'

'I am trying, sir,' said Valiban.

THE FIRST CUT

The whole country celebrates the harvest in January. In Tamil Nadu, it is a four-day affair called Pongal. The first day, we decorate homes with sugar cane and plantain trees and we eat rice boiled with milk, jaggery and ghee. The second day, we decorate cows, if we can find them. The third day, farmers burn the harvested fields in the villages in preparation for the next season. In cities, we burn our rubbish. The fourth day, we roam the city like friendly vagabonds and meet up with family and friends.

I caught a three-wheeler on the fourth day. On the left pillar was a blow-up of the driver that said Ramesh, on the right, his dream girl, a glam doll called Sneha.

'Go straight.'

It was early morning. Every street looked like the other. The litter was the same everywhere; three or four puppies with their mama. Many sniffing papas. Next to them, a garbage bin surrounded by garbage and nearby a small bridge over a smelly stream. Ramesh kept looking at me.

'Stop at hundred rupees.'

'Are you testing my meter?' he said.

I was. I hate autorickshaw drivers who tamper with their meters. We came to a halt in Thiruvanmiyur. I offered him a single crisp note.

'Happy?' he asked me. I gave him an additional twenty and asked him to wait.

A man wearing a smock emerged from a clinic opposite. He looked grim. He told me, 'She doesn't want to meet you.'

'Does she know what day it is today?'

The doctor spread his hands helplessly. 'She is not in a good way today. Some days are bad. You still want to come up?'

I said no. He placed a hand on my shoulder briefly and left. This was my attempt to meet my aunt, an estranged relative. Banished by the family for marrying a Muslim. I met her every year on the fourth day of Pongal.

We left for Valasarvakkam where my mother's relatives stayed.

'Quickly.'

We passed roadside deities, colony temples and one multi-storey temple with different gods on different floors. We were speeding, jumping signals, careening down the road. I remember humming songs into the wind.

'Hundred rupees,' said my friend Ramesh.

'Keep going.'

We sped past purams, swaying from side to side, raced through a colony, two dogs yapping at our wheels. Ramesh started singing, every movie poster we rushed past brought up another line from a different song. We reached an old bungalow in Valasarvakkam. My mother was there and she fed me sweet pongal, ribbon murukkus and filter coffee that I shared with Ramesh.

I made my excuses and left. There was work to do. I walked down the road to another large dwelling, a posh one that had security guards. I waited outside the gate while a Dobermann sniffed my pants. I could not move. It was sniffing my v-front. The guards laughed. A snot-nosed young man sprouting pimples walked out, held by two burly men. His name was Rocket. He was unsteady. I could smell alcohol under his breath. We left in the rickshaw.

We halted at the next bus stop. I paid Ramesh the exact fare. He said nothing and asked for nothing extra.

'How come?'

'Auspicious day,' he said.

In no time at all, the bus arrived. Sitting inside was my friend Kari.

'Dai, English minor,' he called out, 'how are you today?'

Kari is my school friend, lungi buddy and fellow no-gooder, lead singer of an aborted music group called Mandaveli Mosquitoes and a beautiful boy. He was wearing a veshti and a half unbuttoned white shirt through which his tummy was peeping. Black hair that gathered on his chest had made a beeline for his navel. He has a curly mop on his head that he brushes by hand, a gold chain around his neck and a single stud in his left ear. We sat next to each other, thighs touching; Rocket stood beside us, stinking and humming off-key.

'Dai,' Kari told him. 'Why the smell?'

Rocket pouted.

'Did you go to the toilet today?'

Rocket nodded. 'Rowdies,' he said, but under his breath, mindful of Kari's size and temper.

The bus went to a distant place called Vandalur. It is a circuitous route well past the airport; a long journey. In the zoo there, a large group from a boys' school was causing a commotion. They were excitable and badly behaved. They got after some langur monkeys, shouting, screaming, making faces, imitating their actions. It affected the langurs. Encouraged, the boys threw stones at the largest langur and he began to slap his own head and growl. The rest of the langurs threw themselves at the wire mesh, gripping it with their small fingers and shaking it vigorously. Some hid behind a tree. Kari couldn't stand it after a while. He slapped two of the boys hard across their faces. Sounded like pistol shots. In the silence that followed, the teachers came into the fray and it began to get ugly. Luckily, a tiger in a nearby enclosure started to roar. It was a primal sound. It stilled the silly fight.

Everybody moved to the tiger enclosure. There he was, magnificent, full-grown and busy examining his paws. The tiger looked up once and in that one look, there was boredom and disdain. A feral smell drifted past us like a stain.

The children left to eat their picnic lunches in the small train parked at a mock station. Rocket headed off. 'To get some grass,' he said. Kari and I looked at each other. We agreed tacitly, it was a good time for the business at hand. Rocket returned having smoked his weed. His eyes were rheumy and he was smiling, looking at his feet as he walked, because they were going in different directions. We took him by the hand to the tiger enclosure and stood at the edge of the moat that separated us from the big cat. Rocket was lost in a world of his own. He was shaking, his weight shifting from one leg to the other. I stalked the tiger with my eyes. I continued to stand and stare and finally, the big cat walked towards us, intrigued. His padded feet made no sound. We nudged Rocket towards the edge. We waited. Another few seconds and he would have toppled over on his own but a family of four joined us to stand and take pictures. The family refused to leave and in the heat, Rocket started sweating; the sweat stung and he opened his eyes. He looked startled when he caught sight of the tiger. He reared back as if he had been stung.

'No,' he shouted. 'No.'

'Do it,' Kari told him, in his ear.

He shook his head.

'Bloody suicide case,' urged Kari. 'Jump da.'

'Please,' I added, I don't know why I was pleading.

Rocket had drunk poison twice and failed. What were his demons? Only he knew. We did not care about them. We inched him again to the edge and he teetered but stepped back just in time. The family was watching us closely, suspicious by now. I tried to shush Rocket who had begun to babble.

'Total fail,' said Kari. 'Let's go.' We were both breathing audibly by now.

It was late afternoon and the return bus was half-empty. The three of us flopped at the rear and fell asleep. Halfway through the journey, the bus conductor woke us up. We bought tickets for Kotturpuram. We got off near the Adyar Bridge and began walking, holding Rocket between us. The Adyar River flowed below. Some rocks jutted out of the water under the bridge. Traffic was thin and nobody was around. We stood in the middle and looked down. This was one of the two bridges in Chennai where jilted lovers and desperate debtors jumped.

'Dai suicide case!' said Kari. 'Are you awake?'

Rocket nodded. He was still in a daze. We tried not to look at him as we stood there. He was holding on to our hands. His fingers slipped as he toppled forward. He teetered at the edge, holding on to our shirtsleeves. A few seconds passed and I couldn't handle it.

'Push him,' I whispered. 'Be done with it.'

'No,' said Kari.

Nothing happened. We returned to the bus stop feeling a little sheepish. We looked around as we walked away. The city ignored us. We caught a bus.

'You are supposed to meet a relative today,' I told Kari.

He shrugged his broad shoulders. 'Not so important,' he said.

The truth was he wasn't sure where he was from and who his parents were. His actual name was unusual. Karim Bai. I heard it as Currimbhoy. In Chennai, there is a family by that name with a long history. I had seen the store called Currimbhoys, a retail establishment that sold crockery, cutlery, kitchen appliances and such things.

'We are from Gujarat,' Kari had told me once. 'Like the Jamals of Poppat Jamal. My forefathers had a small store in the Evening Bazar.'

'Your forefathers?'

I wondered how he felt being someone's shame. He was the only school pass-out without a birth certificate.

'Muslim?' I asked him.

He shrugged. He cupped his hand to my ear. 'I discovered that in my teens.'

'You went to a home?'

'Yes, brought up in an orphanage. No need to get choked up, minor.'

We hopped off the moving bus at Besant Nagar opposite the shop we came looking for. Kari crossed the road to meet a potential relative. I watched him hesitate and then step through the open door of a small store right next to Currimbhoys. The board said Karim Bai.

It seems there was an old man at the counter and the shop was chock-full of cigarettes, beedis, matchboxes, chewing gum, talcum powder and newspapers. 'Does your family have a history, a family tree?' Kari asked. The old man inside said, 'No tree.'

'Is there anybody in your family who went missing?'

'Nobody missing,' said the old man, a little irritated. 'You want to buy something?' Kari persisted. 'Was there any baby in your family that was said to have died at birth about twenty-five years ago?' He asked that question casually. He behaved as if the answer did not matter to him.

'There was one,' replied the old man.

Kari returned, a spring in his step, looking happy. He gave me a warm hug. We walked for a while, aimlessly. Our thoughts returned to the zoo, to that bridge and to what should have happened. We looked at our companion. Rocket emitted a muffled cry. Poor guy. He had inherited some expensive property that his relatives wanted to wrest from him. This Kaanum Pongal was his day of reckoning.

We spent that evening at Elliots Beach in Besant Nagar. It was overcrowded because all of Chennai was outdoors. It was the same with Marina Beach, where hordes had gathered. This was a festival day when all of Chennai went out, compulsorily, roamed about, some got lost, others found friends, fed birds and met a relative or two. In the evening, you found your way to the eastern waters that lapped at your feet, teasing your toes till you decided to step in and the waves then waded into your shorts, tickled your balls and sprayed your face. The wind blew your hair from your face. You stood there with your feet embedded in the sand, rooted in your little utopia. You tasted salt and you healed.

Then, it happened.

My hair still stands when I visualise that scene. Rocket began walking into the water. Foam gathered around his ankles, the tide was like a swing, it came back and claimed his knees and he kept walking, dragging his feet in the sand, the next wave found him hip deep. Kari looked towards me, I shrugged my shoulders, and we stood and stared, mouths open, as Rocket walked on swinging now from side to side, half-floating, using his hands to make way. The water reached for his head. We heard him coughing above the sound of the waves. A cry stayed stuck in my throat as he disappeared. The next wave came and the next till our eyes tired. A few minutes later, a piece of cloth.

Nanban had his mouth open by then. In his mind was a question he was finding difficult to ask. The matter-of-fact narration of the death and its instigation disturbed him. Finally, 'Ermm, so there is a designated day in the year when you just roam around and try to get lost?'

Valiban nodded. 'And the whole city lands up at the beach in the evening.'

'The city has its quirks,' said Nanban.

'Forget the city, sir,' said Valiban. 'The day describes our life. We are Velai Illa Pattadharis. The Unemployed. For us, every day is like Kaanum Pongal.'

'A day spent at random in search of a prayer?'

'A day that is a spinal tap for the orderly. For a few hours, we find our surrogate selves, we wander away from our life as we know it.'

Nanban marvelled at the young lad's language.

'That bit about Rocket. That is a story, right?'

'It is a true story, sir.'

'I see.'

'We were supposed to escort him to places where suicides happen. It was an assignment. We had to keep doing that until he succumbed.'

Nanban stared at Valiban. 'What is the backstory?' he asked.

'Sir, Kari stays in a fishing village where the local don is Pasupathy. Pasupathy asked him to handle Rocket, to get rid of him because clients who were after Rocket's property were paying good money for it. Kari had no choice in the matter. Other than the method. We found a humane way to do it.'

'I see.'

Valiban's face stayed expressionless.

'So, these are the gaps in your resume?'

'Yes, sir.'

'So, what happens now?'

'I am no longer a Brahmin,' said Valiban. 'I cannot be, not anymore.'

'You wish to atone for Rocket?'

'No sir, for all that my predecessors have done.'

A few days later, he performed a ritual exorcism. Up until then, he bore the marks of a South Indian

Brahmin. It was a Friday. After the morning puja, he erased the caste mark from his forehead.

'What, kanna?' asked his unsuspecting mother.

He held his cute little ponytail taut and snipped it with a large pair of scissors. It fell and rolled on the ground, like the detached tail of a gecko. 'Kanna!' shouted his horrified mother. He held up his poonal thread, which hung around him like a seat belt, and snipped that as well. He made a neat pile of all his white veshtis. 'Amma,' he said, 'donate this to a home for the aged.'

She consulted all the elders in the family, the family priest and, finally, Nanban sir. Valiban had grown a moustache by then. When summoned to meet Nanban sir, he appeared before them and his mother gasped because for the first time in many years trousers parted his legs. Tucked into them was a shirt that had buttons and a collar.

'A bloodless coup,' he announced. 'I am now a Dravida.'

'Help me,' said his mother. 'My son has become a communist.'

'He is trying to make up for something,' said Nanban. He turned to Valiban. 'Technically, you cannot become a Dravida. But, you can join the Dravidian movement.'

'I am no longer a Brahmin,' said Valiban. 'And from today, I will sleep with my feet facing north because that's where Hindi people come from.'

His mother looked for something handy to throw at Valiban. 'Badwa rascal,' she shouted. 'You think you are a politician?'

'I am the "resistance",' said Valiban, ducking. 'Today, I will invade Connemara.'

'Moodevi,' she shouted at him as he left with Nanban.

They went to the Connemara Library and he sat pillion on Nanban's Enfield Bullet, a boom box of a motorcycle that thudded its way over the Cooum River and down Pantheon Road. Under Nanban sir's tutelage and direct gaze, he read biographies of kings, philosophers and thieves. The library had a curious smell that came from musty books and middle-aged farts. In quiet moments, the bookshelves groaned; in the reading area, the newspapers rustled.

'Your English is extraordinary,' said Nanban. 'Better than my Tamil slang. Why do you mix the two?'

'Sir, we are all brown bastards of Queen's English. The vellaikarans left their language behind, they are usurpers, sir, they took Tamil from our tongues.'

Nanban looked at the five feet four inch pocket edition of the resistance. He was a little fond by now of this complicated youngster. Valiban wasn't done yet.

'I will be the colloquial king, sir, adding words every year to their lexicon. Not like the others, happy being the spice in their curry, the melagu in their tawny.'

'Melagu?'

'Black pepper, sir.'

'Tawny?'

'My colour as the whites see it.' He hated explaining his language excursion. 'And mulligatawny you must have heard of, a bastard soup.'

Later that evening, Valiban watched Nanban drink his whisky and, after a few too many, behave unlike himself. Those around him could see how unpredictable Nanban was. Yet he was riveting. He had stories to tell that opened a window to the world he had left behind. He was eating nethli, a small fish that was crunchy and consumed whole, and a bunch of them peered at him from a bowl. He locked eyes with them in that dim lighting holding them up one by one before he ate them.

THE BAR

The state government controlled the liquor trade in Tamil Nadu under an umbrella organisation called TASMAC. The outlets had 'Wine Shop' name boards, a euphemism for hard liquor sold without finesse. In R A Puram the locals called their outlet Chinna Tasmac. It looked like a hole in the wall. The decrepit building smelt of piss on the sides and had nothing to commend it other than a hair-cutting salon upstairs that used a good shampoo and yet paid the rent. In the small attached bar, Nanban had his following – a small group of regulars who came in upright and left as if they had been shot in the knees. They worked 9.00 to 7.00, and before they found their way home they had a quarter or two. Local brandy or dark rum. Water in a plastic sachet. Half-cut lime and salt served as sorbet. Fingers stood for pegs. Mere nods sufficed for regulars and that was to be treasured, the easy familiarity in a shop where you had to merely show up to be served the usual and this happened only after you had earned your stripes among men.

'Wotha dai,' was a term of endearment in Chinna Tasmac. So was 'koodi' and 'mayiru' and 'manam ketta nai' was used when things were really heated up and affectionate.

Nanban took some time to belong to this motley crew. They called him 'English' because of his diction, his command over the foreign language and his ability to look upon them occasionally with benign contempt. His voice was rich, a baritone, and he could roll his consonants at will, stretch vowels as if they had been blessed and make words dance in the dark. They were open-mouthed when he spoke and they understood very little when it was poetry, especially when it did not audibly rhyme. For a while, he was admitted into their fold as a curiosity. When English started humming the latest Tamil film songs, discussed early tunes of the maestro Ilayaraaja and then drummed 'dappan koothu', the local rhythm, on the table with authority, they took to him and he was promoted above the reigning raconteur, a 'kuruvi' called Tamil Selvan. Kuruvis were on-board couriers who travelled to free-trade airports like Singapore, Kuala Lumpur and Dubai carrying spices; they brought back electronic items and anything else that bore high local taxes. Tamil Selvan was a senior kuruvi who travelled 'business class' because then he was eligible for a higher baggage allowance. He wore the latest watches and designer glasses, bright shoes and heavy perfumes and he had tales to tell about customs officers, cheap deals and 'Chinese' girls who worked on your privates with their nimble fingers and made you cry. The first time English met Tamil, he told him that he too brought with him an item for which they all had paid the highest duty.

'What item?' asked Selvan.

'The English language,' he replied.

It might sound strange but Nanban treasured this awkward place despite its rough and ready manners, its dim lighting that hid its small creatures, its stains, the leftover smells and the fact that there was only curd rice as a main course. He preferred this place to other posh protectorates in star hotels. This was the last wilderness in Chennai, a lair for the local wolf. Men could scratch, burp, even mewl; they could curse, argue, fight and occasionally come to blows. In this realm of the ugly unaware, you could be your uncouth self. There were those who were not welcome here, principally those who came like tourists so they could tell others.

There was membership in Chinna Tasmac for the 9.00 pm gang. Those who were allowed to stay after 9.00 pm were members, which meant that the owner Thangabalu had approved of them.

Thangabalu was stout, he had a black bushy moustache, a hard stare and, if you can believe it, a heart. He was married to a former nursery school teacher. They had a child, the child grew up, his wife took to dogs, they had six of them in different shapes and sizes, his smoking increased and that kept the dogs away. His family was affluent and his father was brilliant in his real estate dealings. Thangabalu diminished the family fortune, lacking luck, making mistakes, in the end renting what remained. He retired, set up a booze shop where the counter was busy, but at the rear was his dominion where he chose his company. Evenings, this dark place was a refuge; at nights, it was a closed club. He eyed the juice, saw what it did to people and kept his hands to himself. He liked the fellowship but he passed on the communion.

At the rear, a certain kind of clientele formed on its own, comprising people who were interesting, who had a backlist of misdemeanours. Politicos, film financiers, fixers, finders and their keepers – privy to all secrets worth knowing. Like money problems, sex lives, strange proclivities and silly tendencies. The current members had among them a businessman called Raman, a history-sheeter from Madurai, a retired revenue officer, a Sindhi financier, the politician Veerappan, the journalist and filmmaker called Narsimhan who stuck to a corner, the raconteur English and some young hangers-on that included the latter's protégé. The role of these youngsters was to look up to these seniors, hold their phones, take calls when told, manage their cigarettes and bring out their private stash of imported alcohol from the large white SUVs parked outside.

Each member at this table was waiting for the 'big move'. At the head of the table was Veerappan Gounder.

Chinna Tasmac was secure. Skeletons stayed in its cupboards, dirty linen within its four walls. The consequences of parting with secrets were public and brutal. The police chose not to investigate these incidents.

'Today is the anniversary of something,' Nanban told his mother.

'It always is,' she said.

He resigned from his college assignment. When his mother demurred, he told her, 'I am tired of hiding. I have found an arena that deserves my attention.'

'Another lethal scheme?'

'I have found something big enough. I have found someone whom I will convert to my way of thinking.'

His mother shuddered. Her son was addicted to making a difference. He had an inflated sense of the impact he wished to have. It was frightening.

He brought Valiban home and introduced him to his mother. He had no idea why he did that. They seemed to get along and Valiban promised he would teach her some stock Tamil phrases. She gave him some cake she had baked and sent him away.

'Do you know he is gay?'

'What? Mama, sometimes you surprise me. I have seen him staring at girls.'

She was sure. 'Trust me,' she said. 'I can see he is gay. Not that I mind. But you should be aware since you are mentoring him.'

'I am not mentoring him.' It got him thinking, the fact that he missed these cues and his mother, of all people, caught on to them.

'By the way, we are having maidservant trouble.'

'Now what?'

'It is quite silly. While coming here, a crow flew over her and plucked at her hair. She is scared because it is a bad omen. She says her time has come. She stood outside speaking Tamil, refusing to come in. She shook her fist at the sky and shouted "Paavi".'

'She will be back, you wait and see.'

'I hope she doesn't do something silly. On TV, I saw these people walking barefoot on hot coals and piercing their cheeks with small spears.'

Nanban needed to know more about the young man he was recruiting. He called Valiban for a meeting. They met at Raiyar's café in Mylapore. It was a fabled hole in the wall in an obscure lane. They sat on a bench with some regulars.

'How many of you are there in your group?' Nanban asked.

'Four. Kari, me, Antony and Thambi. All unemployed, which is why we hang around Chinna Tasmac. We do odd jobs.'

Nanban aerated his coffee expertly and took the first sip. It was very good.

'Education?'

'Two school pass, two college pass.'

'VIPs?'

'Yes, sir. Unemployed.'

'And you move as a group?'

'Yes, always together. You can find us at bus stops, beaches and outside women's colleges looking busy.'

'And why are you still VIPs?'

'Because every job application mocked us. Even after we filled them, there were many blanks so we did not submit them. We did odd jobs for a year but we got into fights and they blamed us saying we had an "attitude" problem. We became delivery boys, cleaners in restaurants until immigrants came and you know they are cheaper and they work without complaining. Now we just steal what we can get our hands on.'

'Petty crime has no future,' said Nanban. 'Join politics instead. I am advising a political party. You have seen Mr. Veerappan Gounder at the bar. Right? He heads the Kongu Lions Party. We need people like you.'

'For what, sir?' asked Valiban. 'It does not sound like an office job.'

Nanban smiled. 'There is no pension either. You are street-smart and a survivor. You will do well in politics.'

'Sir,' said Valiban, 'I always wanted to ask you. What were you doing in Mumbai? Why did you run away?'

'I was drag racing,' said Nanban, after some thought. 'All of Mumbai drag races. We fight the city and we fight each other. After a while, we fight the fight, every day, until our insides burn out. Lifelong chutiyas skidding headlong from goalpost to goalpost. I made so much money and I made it early. But I was still drag racing.'

'And why…?'

'I don't know,' said Nanban. 'There is no good reason.'

NANBAN

Waking up early is inevitable in this city because of the harsh sunlight. The fragrance of filter coffee, the tintinnabulation from puja rooms and temples, the plaintive call of street vendors, the cawing of crows, the thud of *The Hindu* – routine has begun to rule my mornings. People here do not question. Hordes swipe ID cards at offices and factories and disappear. Waking hours elapse, modest accomplishments form small piles, the evening bugle blows and the ant-like behaviour continues – people scramble through unlit roads and narrow streets to their quiet abodes to bring up children. In a million middle-class homes, street dogs settle at the doorsteps while old folk slap mosquitos in the small verandas.

My Chinna Tasmac circle is restless, bothered to death by time passing while we wait for the big move. As each day palls, we become fearful of having to endure our tepid evenings and vapid nights. We arrive for the antidote at this bar every weekday without fail. The evening at this bar is a shared addiction. The group is tight-knit, addicted to numbered pegs, to seated apathy in earmarked chairs, to languid hours spent in Thangabalu's cave, comfortably numb.

I could not imagine walking home cold sober, toeing a straight line. I could not imagine confronting the night clear-headed. I could not imagine visiting Sharada without the rakish mentality that comes to me with a few stiff ones inside. It is a High Income Group building in Besant Nagar, a locality with a number of old people who can barely walk without assistance; it has salary earners and pensioners, each with a home-grown penis.

I am at my best now as I ring her bell, three sharp rings, leaning against the wall in my pointed shoes, my opening gambit ready, the first few words composed and the expression deadpan because she loves deadpan.

Sharada has dark tresses that taper at her hips. At night, her eyes are pools that absorb light. She wears handwoven saris that she drapes with a certain carelessness that sets my pulse racing. The glimpse of a hip, the cheeky cut of the blouse, the swish of air as she moves; a sari is where eternity hides. Sharada is my muse when time hangs heavy on weekends, resting as I do on the windowsill in her apartment. I stay indoors, look at her, busying herself, aware of my attention. She has big lips. We kiss. When I kiss her, I am willing to damn the world and damn the lesser men in it.

She spends her time reading books that promise her a holistic life. A weekend with her goes by; blinds drawn, lights low. I give up on revolution, happy in this garden of domestic bliss. Otherwise, I am a proponent of overthrow. I seriously think that upheaval is the only way change can be brought about, especially when her neighbour sings loudly and his son plays the harmonium. This interrupts lovemaking. Making love to Sharada needs a little cranking. She is slow to get going but the effort is worth it because once she gets going there is no one in Besant Nagar that can stop her. At the peak when she is astride, she is voluble, but to begin with, she wants me to recite poetry and I have to oblige even if I forget some lines when I am sweating. I am nervous in bed. I am nervous about that one thing that men are famous for and that worrisome thought has burnt itself into my head. I try diversionary tactics but no, they do not help. I have tried chanting a mantra to stay in the saddle. One day while we were at it, 'What are you mumbling?' she asked me. 'Nothing,' I said. A little later, she said, 'Stop that sound.' 'First, you stop,' I said. She couldn't stop her oohs and aahs, and fuck it, that sound was killing me. I began chanting again. 'Are you trying to say something?' I shook my head, doubled my efforts, chanting away. 'Hold it.' I could not. I flopped to the side, hopeless and spent. She groaned, then laughed. 'Look at you,' she said. 'Look where?' I said. 'Early bird,' she said. 'Look at your worm.'

Despite this, on some days she was happier, my efforts notwithstanding. It was a puzzle. I watched her closely. Her eyes were shut and she was lost somewhere in a private world. 'Hey, where are you?' 'You don't want to know,' she said. 'Were you dreaming?' She opened her eyes and stroked my cheeks. 'I just died,' she said.

We are a truly mad couple and we know it. Together, we lose our reason and it is such a relief to be careless about time, about day and night, and about who rang the doorbell thrice and then banged on the door.

Sharada is not coy about her body as some women are; nor does she treat it as an asset to be put away for safekeeping. She is 'bold' in her community. She visits the parlour, gets herself waxed and comes back grumbling, asking me to try it one day. She takes a jar of cold cream and runs her hands over herself, looking at me from the corner of her eye, occasionally smiling. She does not need a plus-size store and I think she has to thank her high metabolic rate for it. She has a loud and hearty laugh. She eats well, tucks into seafood and shares with me a love for crustaceans. She spells correctly. We actually write letters to each other. She has an earthy sense of humour that often takes aim at my performance in bed and she describes our lovemaking as though she is writing a short story. Luckily, she writes those stories in Malayalam. 'Do they have happy endings?' I asked her. She laughed loudly, slapping me on the back.

How did this thing happen?

I was sober that day, a natural disadvantage. But there was chemistry. In my life, there are two phases. If my life is proceeding at an even pace and nothing is happening, know that this is my 90 per cent. The other 10 per cent is when things happen to me and not to others. At times like these, I believe there is a greater being, a benevolent sutradhar, and I can even distance myself and watch as Sharada and I are in a Nilgiris Store and we arrive at the same carrel and reach out for the last measly packet of Kellogg's muesli.

'Take it,' I said.

'No, it is fine,' she said. 'You take it.'

'Actually, it is not healthy, is it?'

'I am so glad you said that,' she said.

We both left it. We discussed healthy food and healthy options and she took me to the first floor of a building nearby, to a place called 'Eco-food' where there were coarse grain breads, ragi biscuits, natural honey, sesame laddoos and some other mouldy looking organic savouries. She took me next to a small house that ran a modest eatery that specialised in millets. We sat and had some snacks and drank a pungent coffee called 'sukku' that was made from dried ginger. By this time, she was sitting close to me, closer than was good for my health and I was noticing things in her, normal things that ordinary males saw. I was hoping she would not notice my irregular heartbeat and my complete lack of interest in millets even as I polished off what was on my plate.

The next weekend we were both in Nilgiris, we met of course and we walked to the beach. There were youngsters there, more than I had seen all week. They seem to hide somewhere for five days and then show up on bikes on the weekend. They had girls with them who had wrapped their dupattas around their heads and their hands around their men. I was busy that evening trying to get ahead with her. For every move I made, there was a mistake waiting to happen. Very soon, I realised that she was in control.

We got drunk on Saturday evenings. It was a ritual and an important one. We would start at eight and in a couple of hours, we would be expansive, soaring above the rooftops, expressive, quoting verse and humming songs we both knew. Inevitably, the high would wear off, she would look despondent and I would struggle to stay awake. Some Saturdays, she would shed a few tears before we slept. I would dream then of my past life in Mumbai, wake up at odd hours, slip out quietly, walk to the beach and tire myself out.

On Sundays mornings, I would look like a curfew victim – bloodshot eyes and fearful. And the inevitable would happen even as I tried to fight it. My thoughts would travel back to my time in Mumbai. Mumbai, my muse, and Muskaan, my singular love.

It was dark and I stumbled. I stumbled because a stair was broken. I knew which stair was broken yet I stumbled. I rang the bell and she opened the door. I rang the bell because I had forgotten to take the key. She opened the door on my first ring. Because she was waiting. She was waiting to say something. She smelt my breath and her nose wrinkled. She took a deep breath to calm herself and the smell needled her some more. I could smell my breath. It reeked of a fishpond, the corner of a dark alley, the chimney of a tannery. She spoke before I did.

'Listen to me,' she said.

'I am listening.'

'You can pee later.'

'Okay.'

'Look at me.'

'Oh come on.' I tried to brush past her but she held me. We walked together into the living room. I kept walking because I could not stop.

'Somebody has to tell you. Who will tell you?'

'Tell me what, that I drink too much? You are there for that. Say it.'

'You drink too much,' she said. She never said it all the years in Mumbai, not once, not even when others brought me home. I waited at my bedroom door.

'Go back to Mumbai once. You have not been back for so long. Three years? Why? Has Muskaan hurt you so badly?'

God, this was an awful time for this discussion. I could barely stand straight.

'I need some water.'

She bustled into the kitchen and brought me a jug. I held onto the wall with one hand, leant back and drank, spilling some down my shirt.

'Steady,' she said.

I hated this moment, drunk with my mother watching.

'Can't a man recoup in peace?'

She stared at me. 'I know what you are thinking. Why doesn't this old woman disappear?'

The next morning she made tea, infusing it with ginger, honey and mint. I almost puked. I had to hold my head because someone was inside it holding a drill, boring holes through my temples.

She was relentless. 'Go back today. Don't think too much. Just do it baba. Go meet her.'

I needed time to recover. I bought a ticket for the next day. I looked at the printout. It said Mumbai in capital letters. I called her. I told her I was coming. 'On business,' I said. 'Are you in town, are you free, in case you are…'

'I will pick you up at the airport,' she said.

My mother was happy. I was too.

I got drunk again that evening at Chinna Tasmac. For some reason, a screen had been set up in a corner of an adjunct room and a projector faced it. Veerappan was there, so was the kuruvi Tamil Selvan and he was sitting with Raman, his biggest client. Raman was fond of the fine things in life as I was. I loved art and Raman liked antique sculpture, crafts, old jewellery, old Chettinad paintings and coins minted by old kingdoms. Tamil Selvan had brought him a pashmina shawl and a shatoosh shawl and he claimed both were antique. 'Made in China,' said Raman. Tamil sputtered and protested angrily. They got into an extended negotiation. Tamil pulled out an 'ancient' Persian carpet. 'Made to look old?' said Raman. 'Still, I will buy it. But give me some time for payment.'

Veerappan and I sat a little away from them. 'Look at them,' said Veera. 'Tamil Selvan has prospered. He has set up an outlet called Badshah Fancy Store, a smuggler's den that sells jhak mak and jalra items. And look at Raman. The idiot borrows from the market paying high interest rates. Will he be able to sell any of the antiques he is buying?'

'Only some,' I said. I looked at the projector. 'Are we seeing something today?'

Veerappan nodded and a young man came up to the projector and switched it on. 'This is the film that Narsimhan made; a documentary that was supposed to help me in the previous election.'

I hadn't found time to see what Narsimhan had given me. 'My childhood and upbringing,' said Veerappan as the film began. I tried hard to focus on the screen. It took some effort because I was more interested in the unmade sequel, which could have been titled, 'My electoral debut and disaster'.

The camera traverses the rural countryside. It is early morning and the sun rises behind some tall trees. A dog runs across the picture frame, nose to the ground. A couple of hens scatter.

'I was the third born,' says Veera on the voiceover.

A small settlement comes into view. The roads are mud pathways marked by cart tracks.

'My father worked very hard, walked, it seems, to three temples that had some peculiar power, ate some tasteless leaves and drank some bitter juices, and when he felt he was ready he went up to my mother.'

An old woman walks down the pathway holding a large vessel.

'My mother was like a sieve,' says Veera. 'They tried. Nothing happened for a couple of months.'

The camera zooms into the woman's face. She stares for a few seconds.

'How do you get a man child?' she asks.

'Our ancestors had a simple caveman solution,' says Veera. 'Kill till you get one.'

The woman walks on, a bent mannequin, her bony frame holding up a sari.

'Today you go to a diagnostic laboratory and find out,' says Veera. 'It is a more humane process, they tell me.'

Another woman emerges from a hut; she is younger.

'My mother,' says Veera.

'You know what they did each time?' she says. The camera moves back in time. A rural clinic. On a narrow bed lies Veera's mother. Her legs are lifted and spread wide, placed in what looks like stirrups.

'What are you doing?' she says.

'Just scraping,' says the doctor.

'Why?' she asks.

'After two daughters, your family is taking no chances,' says the doctor. 'Dilation,' he tells the nurse. 'Curettage.'

There is a funereal air to the scene. After a short while, Veera's mother leaves the clinic. She has come alone. Nobody has accompanied her for this procedure. She looks into the camera.

'I was suffering by then from a strange feeling. The lower half of my body wasn't in my control anymore. My in-laws had taken it over.'

She returns to her hut, walking awkwardly, turns around and brushes her hair from her face. Tears that she had perhaps held back form and fall. She stands in the doorway and looks at the harvested fields. The earth is brown, bare, with portions singed black, burnt in preparation.

'A bi-annual cycle,' she says. 'Year after year the land yields to the plough.' She looks up at the sky. 'There was a time when the first rains were special and the swaying lush green paddy made my heart sing.'

She turns back and stares expressionlessly. 'Now I see it differently. I am the farrow. I hate it that every year I have to yield.'

'The procedure happened twice, I was told,' says Veera.

A man walks into the picture frame.

'My father,' says Veera.

The man looks a little tired and his dark skin bears dust and sweat in equal measure.

'Each time the procedure happened, my father went away on a short trip, ostensibly on work, and he returned head-bowed, shame-faced, like an elephant from Munnar that had lost tusks in a battle.'

Veera's father washes his hands using a pot of water. Then, he washes his face and uses the towel that hangs on his shoulder.

'The firstborn was a girl, natural birth, brought by the midwife with half a smile, uncertain step and a slight shrug. The second-born also turned out to be a girl.'

Veera's father walks into the village enclave where relatives have gathered. It is evening.

'The family was reasonably happy because the second child was cute and made them smile. Even the die-hard embittered veterans who broke their backs in the fields managed a snicker.'

One of the elders stares into the camera.

'There is absolutely no allowance for a third daughter,' he says.

A small boy comes into the enclave rolling a shaped nongu shell attached to a stick.

'I have a feeling that half-way through, even up to the third trimester, I was a girl. And then something happened.'

'He looked like a girl,' says Veera's mother. She stands at the edge of the enclave. 'He lay on a towel, teeny weeny, with a small important speck between his legs.'

The enclave is masculine. Here are the bare-chested, veshti-clad men who stand in clusters and scratch fearlessly. Deep bellows of laughter come from heads with black uncombed hair. Armpits that house human salt, and red-flecked eyes. They come together as a brotherhood and welcome Veera, tossing him around; one plants a smack on his cheek before he gives him away to Veera's mother.

The camera follows a child into a hut.

'I was raised in low light under bamboo and thatch.'

It is raining.

'I grew up with water that made a tick-tock sound as it fell from crack and crevice. I could crawl through puddles at an early age. I could make bubbles and I could spit a fountain that rose in a curve before it fell back into my mouth. I crawled longer than I should have. The mud packed floor was soft and it was hard to let go of that feeling, that comfort that earth gave.'

The child lies on his back, at peace on the mud floor.

'Earth held me long after I could straighten.'

An older child gets up from a corner and runs out unsteadily into the rain. Veera crawls on all fours behind him.

'My cousin was born a week after me. Look at him.'

The cousin is out in the open, walking without control, flailing his arms, unable to stop for fear of falling over. Veera crawls into the rain gurgling with delight.

Back in the enclave, the elders gather as a medicine man comes. Veera's father is in pain.

'They put my father on a slab to straighten him out. He looked crooked when he stood.'

Facing him, you can see the curved hairline to his navel, a sure presentation of muscular spasm.

'From behind, his back looked like a tree that had grown its way out of a veranda.'

Veera walks up, stands on his toes and sees his father grimace as he lies down. He curses for a while. When his back straightens, it makes twig-like sounds. The medicine man clambers onto Veera's father and walks on his back. The sound that follows is primal.

'It is good that he screamed. Bottling up that pain would have killed him.'

'Where is she?' asks Veera's father.

'He remembered her, finally, my old man, when it hurt so badly that he thought he might be dying. He was not asking about her. He was not asking how she was or what she felt. Just as well. She might have said something that he wouldn't have been able to handle.'

A bus arrives at the village and a visibly pregnant woman barely manages to clamber onto it.

'Once again she left for her mother's place with a swollen belly.'

The inside of the bus is quiet and then the ranting starts. Veera's mother is slumped in her seat, holding her swollen belly. The conductor looks hesitant. Should he even approach her? 'Go away,' she says when he moves to help. She lets go. She rails, rants, weeps and sobs through the short journey. She is helped out of the bus by passengers. Her mother stands outside flapping her hands. She looks at her daughter helplessly.

'Stop being a drama queen,' says Veera's mother. They hold each other and weep.

Seasons flash past and Veera marks a calendar a few years later. He is in his teens.

'We made some money after a few years and soon we had an Ambassador car.'

It is thunder grey in colour.

'It was a member of the family.'

His father wanders around with a cloth, polishing it.

The map of Tamil Nadu shows up with routes snaking up hills to Ooty and Kodaikanal. In a ghat section, the car stands at the side of a winding road, its bonnet open. Veera's mother has packed sandwiches and filled up coffee in a thermos. She looks harried but happy. Veera and his sisters and brother fill up the cavernous car. The chatter is chaotic.

'We went through towns, hill stations and beaches. We spent very little time in these places. Driving was a form of escape for my father. Travel was tension for my mother, who had to pack and unpack every two days and handle the rigour of road journeys where toilet meant a bush and water was scarce.'

Veera sits in the driver's seat on a cushion and peers over the steering wheel. He fiddles with the gears; the car lurches forward and then stops abruptly.

'All these travels and tours were an education for a young boy and my parents weren't aware of the good they were doing. At fourteen, I was driving the car.'

They arrive at the village and turn towards the small track that leads them home.

'At sixteen, I was handling the farm. At eighteen, I learnt English. I gained some polish but my rustic voice gave me away. Under stress so did my grammar.'

A young man looks into the camera.

'Yet I was confident.'

He moves around wearing western wear. A tight shirt, brown belt, bell-bottoms. He looks self-assured.

'If you heard me speak, you would have said this boy has grown up, for what is left that he has not discovered yet?'

A rising sound outside his house. A temple chariot dragged by two lines of young men trundles past urged on by two bare-chested men. A bunch of others beat sticks on large drums. The small idol on the chariot is black and surrounded by a flower arrangement.

'Deep inside, I am still a village boy. The idea of ritual was ingrained in my village and it took hold of me. Where I grew up, there was no English calendar.'

The procession recedes into the distance. In the ensuing silence, the young man turns around one last time and courts the camera, looking a little self-conscious.

Someone asks him a question, an inaudible one.

'Yes, stories. There were so many. But none like the old women told me.'

The film continues in this vein, showing old women seated in a distant courtyard, their singsong retelling of folklore begins, tales like the classic *Annanmar Kathai*. When the moon rises, they pray to Periyakandi Amman, extolling the valour of the brothers Ponnar and Shankar. Finally, they relate stories of Dheeran Chinnamalai and Kattabomman.

'Dheeran captured my imagination,' says Veera. A still shot of Dheeran comes into view. He looks like a veeran, a warrior astride a horse with the standard of a lion.

'Imagine, he was the first South Indian to oppose the British and he won battles against them in 1801, 1802 and 1804, battles that pre-dated the Sepoy Mutiny. I was so proud that he fought these Polygar Wars, the first significant attempts at rebellion against the British rule.'

The segment ends with a village scene showing a film screening in the village, in a tent strung up a distance away. The entire village and some people from neighbouring villages have gathered.

The lights came on and everybody looked towards me. I had to react. I was trying hard to hold back my initial response, which was – what the fuck was this intimate narrative supposed to achieve? It was a well-made film and Narsimhan had great potential but it would have done nothing to boost Veerappan's electoral prospects. The documentary would have been received well in a festival as a study of patriarchy. In the election, it would have helped Veerappan lose his electoral deposit.

In tune with the day's lunacy, Veerappan asked me to visit a sculptor in Mumbai. He wanted to buy a dinner table and chairs. Yes, that is what he said. Even if I was sloshed, I could hear very well.

I was happy I was heading back to Mumbai. I missed the carefree air of modern Mumbaikars, their half-baked expressions, their brusqueness, their khaali-pilli fights and the temporary truce they called jaane de. In Chennai, I had been waylaid by parkalaam, a noncommittal let-us-see that had me climbing walls. The city practised a tyrannical yes-no nod that was hard to divine. I had slowed down to keep pace with Chennai's thoughtful demands on my time. My time stood apart, it borrowed from the city I was in. In Mumbai, time was a bachelor, in Chennai, a widower and, in Delhi, it was forever a prickly adolescent.

The thought of a day in Mumbai suddenly gathered its own importance and I could hardly sleep.

MUMBAI FALSETTO

The alarm went off at 4.30 am and I got ready in a daze. I wasted two minutes buttoning my shirt. The voltage was low, the air-conditioner had tripped and I had spent the night sweating. The taxi arrived just as I had begun to worry.

'I am on my way,' I said, calling her needlessly.

'What on earth is the time?' said Muskaan.

It was a quiet ride to the Chennai airport chasing a mosquito in the backseat, slapping myself in the process. I had forgotten something. The more I tried to remember the more I felt like killing something. At the check-in counter, they wouldn't give me a window seat. I had to sit between two individuals I instantly disliked because their elbows intruded. One tried to open and fold a newspaper, the other dropped off to sleep and snored. My intestines rumbled. No, I spoke up, now is not a good time. I ate breakfast, chewing slowly and fell asleep while eating. I awoke as we descended through nimbus clouds, the plane shuddered and I gripped the armrests. We swayed as we lost speed and landed with a thud. I was still woozy. My black bag inched towards me on a crawling centipede.

'Are you here?' I said. 'Have you come?'

'I am circling the car park.'

I was nervous because Muskaan would be there. I had rehearsed my lines. I had imagined meeting her, cool, nonchalant. When I saw her outside, standing, looking out for me, I felt a pang and the old helpless feeling returned. We hugged a little awkwardly. I was careful. 'Will you drive?' she asked. She knew I liked to drive her car. It was a low-slung Audi and it had a serious engine that begged to be revved. Exiting the airport, I let loose those horses that strained under the sleek bonnet and I opened the throttle until the red line growled. Fuck. We had many near misses as I drove quickly through the Western Express Highway. I saw gaps and closed them; I saw others trying to compete like they always did in this big bad city but I truly did not care. I always won these road races because others were afraid of death. We arrived at a petrol bunk where the red vision next to me got out and made payment. I saw her designer jeans, the gap between her legs, her tall Gucci shoes with buckles and one end of a Diesel belt that hung near her knees. Her jeans were low, lower than her navel, and her navel had an inward whorl.

'Why don't you continue driving?' she offered.

Now fully awake, I shifted the seat forward and adjusted the mirrors. The car lurched and I settled into a slower rhythm. My ears had blocked when the flight had descended and they hurt badly. Music was playing, and she was switching channels and chattering cheerfully. I swallowed a few times, yawned deliberately and said something, and suddenly my ears popped and the hurt almost blinded me. I could hear and, strangely, I could see clearly as well.

'Take a right off the highway. We are on Andheri-Kurla road. Keep to the right lane, yes, that's it, now we have to be patient.'

She smiled, crossed her legs and looked out of the window. Her hands were on her lap. She was well-groomed and she smelt of Black Opium or maybe Black Orchid. The sinking feeling returned and I could have wept. It was a sense of hopelessness that returned every time I was in Mumbai. The case that had ruined my life would not go away, what with the government pronouncing me guilty without a trial.

I had met her father and he had advised me to give up the money I had made. He said he would broker a deal. I had refused. It was money that I had earned I told him. That was closure. Suddenly his daughter had no wish to see me. What hold did he have on her? I looked out of the window on my left and then looked up.

The rain had fallen, a few clouds remained looking forlorn and without purpose. Water bodies lay on the road and traffic had slowed down as if in mourning. Thank God, she was with me; otherwise, I would have been depressed. This was a professional visit. She and I had a tryst in the suburbs with a man who tilted at windmills. He was always nattily dressed, we were told, outwardly calm and a glutton for hard work. I had heard other things about him. 'He is a Dalit,' someone had whispered as if that was a badge. Okay, fine, I will carry that nugget, be on the lookout for a man who had a 'fire burning inside him' like Namdeo Dhasal. I had never met a 'Dalit' by name, I was not meaning to. The term meant so much sometimes and then so little.

We parked outside an ATM. I withdrew fifty thousand rupees. The notes felt cool and fresh. She took one wad, rustled it and smelt it.

'Heavenly,' she said.

We ran to the car and ducked in. She removed her scarf from her head and wrapped it around her neck. Her arm fell onto mine.

'Illicit money?' she said.

'I have no idea,' I said. It was not my money.

We were stuck behind a bus and it started to rain again. Soon it was pelting down on shanties and shelters that flanked the road. In the car, we were snug but the roads were filling up and the pace stayed funereal.

'When you moved to Chennai, you called me every day. Now you don't speak to me.'

I was tongue-tied because I had to ask her one question.

'What drama a cloud makes,' she said, peering out of her window. She looked up at a malevolent black one that hung heavy and grumbled now and then. I saw rainwater glisten in her hair, saw a drop trickle down her neck and disappear.

'Insolent fellow,' I said. 'Pissing wherever he wants.'

Minutes added up as we crawled. We watched the windscreen wiper keep pace with the intensity of the rain.

'Have I lost you somewhere?' she said suddenly.

I realised I was smiling, thinking of how I was back in this city in just the manner I had left it – under a cloud. She was canny, observing even from the corners of her eyes. Ever since she picked me up from the airport, I was aware of her gaze. The windscreen began to fog at the corners and we were helpless and given soon to peering.

'How did you know?'

'I just know,' she said.

'Isn't life inferior when you are merely viewing?' I asked her.

I knew what she was all about. She did things for a lark because she was bored, because money sat in her bank account and pickled. Her old man was very old and a tonne of money awaited his demise to be set free, dispensed with. It was currently in a holding account and managed by a wealth management firm.

I sneaked a look. She had a deep throat that dived into her chest making a perfect V. She was wearing a black bra. She caught me looking and looked down herself past the scarf at the soft creamy curves that peeped out, and she did nothing to cover them.

'You have a girlfriend now?' she asked, holding the edge of the scarf and playing with it.

'Yes. Not a girl,' I replied, thinking of Sharada, suddenly aware of her in Chennai, perhaps waiting for me to return. 'She is a little older.'

'A fling then?' she asked. 'I knew it. I cannot imagine someone like you being idle in such matters.'

We had so much time in the car and I could not help flirting.

'You have a mole near your lips,' I said.

She smiled. 'It wasn't there in the morning.'

I turned the rear-view mirror towards her. 'Look.' She looked at herself leaning forward. There was a black speck near her upper lip. She had highlighted her lips and given them a slight gloss.

I remembered kissing them. She knew how to kiss, for sure she knew so much more. I just looked at her seated, casual, aware and very real, not some goddess that I remembered ever so often in Chennai. She smoothed her jeans and examined her hands, adjusted her hair and sneaked a look at me. I should have retreated. It was not that Sharada and I were into anything serious, but still.

'You still watch porn?' I asked.

'What about you? Dirty old man.'

'Do you?'

'Maybe, now and then,' she said.

'Is that a real scar?' she asked. She held my left hand, the first touch, and she turned it over to see how far the scar travelled. The knife had started below my wrist and sliced right across it, deeper than necessary. The scar was ugly, highlighted by crude stitches that a nurse had hurriedly carried out. Everybody had panicked after seeing how much I had bled. She took longer to let go of my arm because she had questions. I made a desultory attempt to clean the windscreen. I was fighting the bile that was rising in my belly. The bile was acidic and it burnt as it came up my windpipe. I could smell the flight kitchen breakfast and very soon, I would retch. I clenched the steering with both hands, waves of nausea hit me and I had to shut my eyes.

'You said something?'

I fought to look out of the car and urged myself not to do what I would in the normal course, which is to hurt myself. I looked out and I was sure my eyes were red. For the next half an hour, she kept chattering whilst I lapsed into a sullen daze.

'Are you still into your medication?' she asked.

I nodded. I had a strip of low-dosage antidepressants that I carried with me all the time. I could do with a tablet right now. She did not ask me to explain the scar. Did that mean she did not care?

'They have been pouring concrete over the Andheri-Kurla road in Mumbai,' she said. 'This road is a lifeline for transporters and daily commuters,' she said. Really? 'You think this is traffic? You should see it on festival days or on days when there are processions. You should see it when some truck breaks down.'

'It is a long stretch of road,' I said, to keep the conversation going.

It was bearing the brunt of heavy vehicles and cars, a long harsh summer and then a prodigious monsoon. There were potholes and craters and vehicles were thudding into them splashing water onto two-wheelers and pedestrians.

'Concrete is the new verb in town,' she said. 'And flyover is the new noun.'

I laughed, relieved she could be light-hearted.

'There is a bottle of bourbon in the rear seat. Could you get it?'

She hesitated.

'Please?'

She leant back, turning around halfway, brushing my side. Her perfume swept over me. Come on, I told myself, hold it together.

'You like bourbon before sunset?'

I loved Tennessee bourbon. In Mumbai, I could have nothing else. It is a dark whisky, a little sweet, a drink with no pretence, unlike Scottish Malt, which comes with an essay attached.

I opened the screw cap and she leant forward, opened the glove compartment and pulled out a couple of plastic tumblers. She looked around, looked out. The evening was getting away from her. It was darkening. I poured a slug and offered it to her. She said no. I poured it down my throat, straight, without hesitation. The spirit spat inside me, my cheeks reddened, the warmth spread. The stop-start traffic was getting to me by now. I poured another shot into the glass and shut the bottle. Between Saki Naka and Marol Naka, we were at a standstill.

'Could you stop blowing the horn? It doesn't help.'

I cursed. 'Bloody suburbs,' I said.

'Just because the traffic is rude you don't have to be as well.'

We got off the main road into an asphalted one. We drove into a narrow side street, also clogged. From the side street, we turned into what looked like a long mud pit. The smell hit us before we saw the corporation dustbin. It had overflowed.

'A refuse pit that belies its name,' she said.

'Ha ha.'

Crows hopped about picking and choosing and there was a cow as well. A water tanker shook dangerously as it crossed us and some water escaped its hatch and strewed itself on our windscreen. The shed was right there under an arc of black cloud, framed in the evening light. There were other sheds but this one seemed right. Wires, thick and thin, snaked into it. We heard the clang of metal and the hiss of welding. There was a low door in a corner that was half-open. A chokra stood outside, next to a pile of gas cylinders, smoking a cigarette, if you please.

I opened the car door and stretched my arms and legs. The car was a mess to look at. It needed a thorough cleaning. I stepped carefully past puddles of water to the half-open door, peeped in and gaped. A full-sized truck had taken root inside. It was brand new and shiny. Thirty labourers made of metal stood in it and watched us wordlessly. Welders were applying finishing touches to them and two workers were assembling a wheel. Sparks flew around us and the glare was dazzling. Beads of sweat formed and fell. Outside, the rain had started again. It had taken us two hours to come here. The ride back would be a journey.

A young man with a beard and dark eyes walked up to us. He was wearing jeans, a white shirt, a check scarf and a jaunty cap. He smiled warmly.

'Please come in.'

He took us around. The truck and the thirty migrant labourers inside it were made of small steel disks. A tonne and a half of steel, two years of hard work with no possible buyer; this was financial lunacy.

'It is rare for a young artist to take such risks,' said Muskaan. 'He feels he has to highlight the plight of migrant labourers, the kind who are making this thing.'

I saw in it a representation of an ageless classic. Astride a shaky steed with a blunt weapon, this was Don Quixote daring the earth.

'Are you Valay Shende?'

He nodded. 'You have come from so far,' he murmured.

'Yes,' I replied. 'I have come looking.' For what I didn't say. I wasn't expecting heroism.

We moved to a smaller space that had what I had come looking for.

'Why would you ask a sculptor to make you a dining table set?' said Muskaan. 'What were you thinking?'

It looked like a set from a furniture store, albeit a store that had a clientele which preferred the showy and ornate. The chairs were coloured silver, the edges carved and they looked like royal heirlooms. The table was a large one and could seat eight; one imagined it hosted feasts. It was bare and the salt and pepper shakers placed in its centre accentuated the feeling. They were small, shapely, glass bottles.

'Are you telling me that what the two contain are ashes of a farmer who committed suicide?'

She nodded. 'From a Maharashtrian village in Vidarbha,' she said. 'One has the ashes of Narsinglu Rukmawar and the other has the soil that he cultivated. A farmer and his accustomed earth.'

This was art; the kind that robbed you of your appetite. Exactly what you would get if you asked an artist to be a carpenter.

'What if I wanted just the furniture, you know, without the salt and pepper shakers?'

She thought for a while. 'No problem, you can take this set and we will get another made. It will be much cheaper and of course, the artist will be disappointed.'

'It is that simple?' I said. 'The only difference between sculpture and furniture is two ounces of ash and ten grams of soil?'

'And a backstory,' she said. 'Don't forget the backstory. This is the region Valay comes from, a place where farmer suicides happen often, like this one.'

She was expressionless. She raised an eyebrow, looking at me closely. 'Who is your client?'

'A man called Veerappan Gounder. He is a politician.'

'What kind of a name is Gounder?'

'His caste name is Gounder,' I said. 'It is a large population in Tamil Nadu.'

She was puzzled because something did not add up. 'You have come so far and spent so much money to get him some chairs and a table?'

'No,' I replied. 'I lied. Veerappan wants the sculpture. He wants the chairs, the table, the ash, the soil and the backstory.'

She was genuinely surprised. 'Why?'

'Because he is in love with the backstory. Veerappan comes from a farming background and though he is a prosperous farmer, he knows how hard it can be for the small tiller. Veerappan doesn't know much about art but he wants other works like this.'

'Which are?'

'I don't know because he hasn't told me. I know politicians do not normally buy art but it is a political piece, isn't it?'

She was not convinced. 'It would make for good conversation at his dinner table,' she said.

I paid the advance and discussed the balance and we left promising to stay in touch. The place had a curious effect on me. It was unreal – the sculpture, the shed, this ambitious artistic enterprise helmed by this modest individual – all of it was unreal.

As we walked out and sat in the car, I took a while to get going. We had some time before my return journey, enough for me to ask her some questions.

'Are you still in touch with that artist you shacked up with in some wilderness?' There. I had asked her the prepared question.

'No,' she said. I was relieved to hear that. 'And I hope you will not use the term "shacked up" again.'

'Does he still mean anything to you?'

'Not as much as he means to you,' she said.

'Why don't you drive?'

We exchanged seats. She adjusted the mirrors and the seat and started the car. 'Are you done with your questions?'

'Your turn now,' I said.

'Are you just a messenger boy for Mr. Gounder?'

'No. Hell, no.'

'Then why are you behaving like one?'

Was I?

'And why do you hate yourself?' she said, looking at the cut on my wrist.

She drove the car to the airport. She was an expert driver and in my books that counted for something. She was conscious of my gaze and my barely hidden curiosity but it did not affect her and I was disappointed that it did not. Sitting idle, I looked out occasionally and I saw slums. There was a bustle in there as well. A crummy landscape reduced me to taking photographs.

'Why are you a lowly art consultant?' I asked. 'You have so much money you could buy all that you peddle and it wouldn't even dent your fortune.'

We were at a signal.

'How much do you know about my father?'

'You are a Piramal and that is a big name in Mumbai and in business circles all over India, but you are not from that branch of the family. In fact, your father is far removed from the known Piramal clan, the one that has corporate governance in its breakfast menu.'

She nodded. 'My money is ugly,' she said.

We drove some more in silence. 'Why so?'

'Well, it came mostly at night.'

'Was it ill-gotten?'

'Must be. It was badly stashed.'

'Shouldn't it be treated with respect?'

'You tell me. I know it was spent in a profligate manner.'

That was ugly money? I had seen stapled notes, bundles in sacks, new wads stacked from floor to ceiling in a room, a remarkable sight, a different smell. Black money was raw purchasing power that bought influence, cut deals and made mice of men. It was skittish, had wheels and velocity, especially during elections, a time when politicians gave rise to the term, 'cash is king'.

'Currency notes are like kites,' Veerappan told me. I had refused cash compensation and he was making a case for it. 'They cut deals and then fly away.' As a favour, he offered me used notes. 'Fresh wads with consecutive numbers can be easily traced,' he said.

'What colour is Veerappan's money?' asked Muskaan. 'What colour is yours?'

I shrugged. 'I don't know about him,' I said. 'I have not seen my money for a few years now.'

Veera was in a halfway house right now. He was an almost politico. Soon, he would be in that fairyland where he could choose to erase his past or give it shape. History would be his to write, a part of his political inheritance.

'Should I bother about any of this?' I said.

'Why does he buy art?' she asked. 'Is it because he needs to park his cash? It must be an investment vehicle for him, a haven for his undeclared money?'

'What if it is? He is not buying shit. Not if I can help it.'

She laughed. 'You are getting defensive. So if he is buying good art then it is fine, the fact that it is hot money shouldn't matter?'

Did I care? Deep down did it really matter to me if hot money bought art? What was holy about art that it needed money with provenance and buyers with a pedigree?

'Through the centuries, hasn't art pleasured patrons?' I said.

'Art has always been fair game for market men,' she said.

'And carpetbaggers? Tell me, does art really care?'

She shrugged. 'Art cares a fuck. Art is money's consort. I get it.'

'Exactly. The rest is foolish socialism. That is what I have learnt in my previous life.'

'So Mr. Veerappan has an eye?' She was still sceptical.

'He could be a collector,' I said.

I truly believed in what I just said but my tone was light. She laughed. Then, I told her the truth.

'Have you heard of the Shadow of Tipu Sultan?'

'No, but I have heard about the Sword of Tipu Sultan,' she said.

'There is history to this,' I said. 'I had Veerappan study the history of monarchs and their patronage of the arts. He is now acutely aware of how Tipu, the Sultan of Mysore, overshadowed all his contemporaries. One of them was Veerappan's ancestor, Dheeran Chinnamalai. Besides being a fearless warrior and wily politician, Tipu built a remarkable collection of art and art objects, palaces, swords, daggers, guns, garments and coins. He lies buried in a beautiful monument called the Gol Gumbaz. The place of his death is a tourist attraction. Dheeran Chinnamalai left nothing behind. He was colourless in comparison and hence easily forgotten.'

'And so?'

'Veerappan does not want to make the same mistake. Gounders have no recall on the national stage. Even in Tamil Nadu, they have no bite. Veerappan wants to stride on to the national stage. How does he do it? He picks on high art. No one expects him to, so he does it. The surprise is everything. Imagine Veerappan wearing a veshti and chappals with a towel slung on his shoulder walking into a private art gallery in Bombay.'

'Perhaps Veerappan in a Christie's auction room bidding for a million dollar Raza?'

'Never will he do that,' I said. 'No, that's not him.'

'I am glad,' she said.

'He might set up a sculpture museum and possibly sponsor a film festival. Think of the impact. There is a vacuum in high art patronage today. Businesspersons and politicians are culturally deprived. It is a great opportunity for someone like him, a visible farmer from interior Tamil Nadu, to capture the national imagination.'

'That sounds plausible,' she said. 'And you are advising him?'

I nodded but the truth was I was not an expert and luckily, Veerappan had a mind of his own.

'Will we meet again?' she asked as she drew up at the airport. I had my luggage airborne and it fell. I would love to meet her again. She had no idea.

I had a flight to catch and yet…

'So that's it, you are off?'

The car door was half-open, one leg was out and she had that look. This was what Mumbai did to you, I remembered, just as you were leaving, it foregrounded reasons for you to stay.

I sat back inside. She made a sound that I took to be a triumphant laugh. As we pulled out of the airport, a flight took off, roared over us and headed out over the ocean. I saw it bank to the left and rise into the clouds.

Veerappan called me and the ring was urgent. 'Namaskaram,' he said. I spoke in Tamil and he responded warmly to the news of the acquisition. 'I am glad,' he said. 'I hope Mr. Shende is happy.' Was he? I had not asked him or noticed. 'Veera, I am staying over in Mumbai for a couple of days,' I told him. 'Good' he said. 'Don't forget to visit the Siddhivinayak Temple in Prabha Devi.'

I clicked the phone shut, took a deep breath and turned towards her. 'What is your backstory?' I said.

She sat on a designer chair that descended from the ceiling in the style of cloth hammocks that swung infants to sleep. An elaborate lamp leant over the chair. It looked like the branch of a tree and each bulb was a pod with two leaves. She lit the lamp and sat on the chair. It was a set piece and she belonged. Legs crossed, one leg touching the floor. She was wearing shorts.

'Let me show you a work that I love,' she said.

I followed her from her living room through a long corridor that had windows on one side and each opening showed a leafy vista. At the end of the corridor, the wall was painted ochre and the door was a bright yellow.

She walked ahead, looking back at me as we progressed. Moonlight filtered through each window, casting shadows. She paused at the bedroom door, framed.

'You said something,' she said.

'I don't trust myself,' I said.

She opened the door. 'You are not a romantic, are you?'

I entered behind her and the door shut itself with a hiss and a click. I turned her around gently, she got onto her toes and I kissed her. She let me. I stroked her back as I kissed her again. She closed her eyes. When I kissed her neck and then her breast, she moaned. Her hands stayed by her side.

'When will you return to Bombay?'

I eased her shirt off her shoulders. There were pale lines beneath her bra straps. I followed them to her naked breast. She had small pert breasts and large nipples. I kissed them and she moaned again. Her hands came up my back to my neck, she turned my face down and kissed me, and her tongue slipped in through my mouth. My breath quickened and I said something. She slipped her hands inside my shirt and tugged me closer and then we moved towards her bed.

We made love. She was talkative after and I was happy watching her, nuzzling her, taking in the room, looking incidentally for the artwork she loved.

'Did you answer my question?'

We sat on the bed and watched a movie. I forget which one. Halfway through it, we made love again. She had a small wine chiller in her room. We opened a bottle of red wine. I did not check the label or note the vintage and I spilt some on the bed as we tumbled to the floor onto a soft rug that protected my knees.

Where was that work of art? I looked around carefully. I found it beneath the bed; a granite plaque by the artist Harsha that said 'Art is elsewhere'. I burst out laughing. 'Life is beautiful,' I said as we held each other under the bed. Art was our magical mystery tour, the only religion we knew. It pursued us. Without it, we would be like the rest – mammals in a swamp, plain needy and perennially hungry.

I was brushing my teeth, looking at myself, making faces. I felt guilty. I barely managed to wear my clothes and as I left, she saw me with one eye half-open and she smiled. She looked like what she was – ten years younger and vulnerable.

The next day, we met again in South Mumbai, in Colaba in a restaurant that served craft beer. It was a warm day and it was lunchtime. She sat facing the window and kept looking out at passers-by. She turned towards me and I was staring. I looked away, pretended to be busy rearranging the cutlery. When I looked back at her, she smiled.

'Your turn,' she said.

What could I tell her about Chennai and Tamilians? Everything was so different. The culture, the cuisine, the resistance. It is hard to describe a place and a culture that you have not grown up in, without sounding like a tourist.

My neighbour is an elderly man; I drop in often at his small place, make him coffee. In return, I receive an earful. Everyone calls him Thatha. Age eighty-five, full name Thathachari. A widower, Thathachari stays by himself. Asleep or awake, he lies supine on a low-slung chair, his forgotten specs on his nose, his teeth in a tumbler full of water. His lower jaw moves, all the time, like a cow. He is hard of hearing and he shouts assuming we are as well. He speaks using his tongue, making hissing sounds.

'Tamil has been alive for centuries but are Tamils a people?' he shouted when I met him last. 'You think that is a foolish question?'

I said, no.

'I grew up when the word prejudice wasn't invented. Segregation was rampant and unquestioned. If people of the lower caste were dark, it was because they were unclean. Do you know I bathe twice every day?'

'We Brahmins have rules and we follow them,' he said. 'Our houses are spare, spic and span, the entrance is swept and decorated with attractive rice patterns. We leave our footwear outside.'

'I have done pujas for other communities,' he shouted. 'I had no problem conducting them. But I noticed things. The Chettiars and the Mudaliars are carnivores. They even eat the liver, brain and hooves. Is it legal to eat all that?'

I nodded. 'It is also nutritious.'

He snorted. 'The homes of the merchant baniyas were full of cheap glitter,' he said. 'Shiny saris, shiny furniture, showy chandeliers and shiny gods. They even had a new coinage, a gold coin, minted by the Temple Trust for special blessings.'

He paused to consider this modern blasphemy. Then, he switched tracks.

'Have you heard of the two tumbler policy? I still practise it in my house.'

I held a different shaped glass, I noticed.

'The Supreme Court has banned serving tea, coffee and water in different tumblers to different castes. They are idiots. Have they seen how people drink from tumblers? The Brahmin holds the glass aloft and pours. The others, they are spitters; they sink their dirty fingers in the glass and drink with their mouth on it.'

'You have been listening to me?' he asked, every now and then.

'Of course, Thatha, when old people speak, I listen.'

'You are a Bombay person,' he told me. 'Such a lovely city, so modern, so liberal and such nice people those Parsis, always this wala or that wala. Bombay thinks it is the centre of gravity but in this silly country, it is a remote place. You should go to small towns and villages. They are the caste capitals. You should stay in a Brahmin agraharam, if you can find one. We did not allow anybody inside, not even their shadows.'

His memories distracted him. I gave him his bowl of soup that his maid had prepared. He spooned it into his mouth in a regular rhythm. Some trickled down the sides.

'Any medicines for the night?' I asked him.

'No medicines,' he said proudly. 'Brahmin's body has a ninety-year warranty.'

He was beginning to ramble as I had seen old people do.

'First cinema invaded politics,' he shouted. 'Now life imitates bad cinema.'

'They want caste to be done away with,' I said.

'I never knew there were so many castes. They all surface for the freebies and quotas. A big queue. Thevars, Gounders, Vanniyars – hundreds of sub-castes. Never a single kingdom in this country. Even in the old days, we had Pandavas, Cheras, Cholas, Chalukyas; all in this small land parcel.'

'Do you still give maths tuition, Thatha?' I asked. I was about to leave.

'Yes,' he said. 'For free. Boys and girls both, caste no bar. Five children of domestic servants also come.' His eyes twinkled. I heard he had thrown out students who turned up with body odour, who picked their noses before him and came with colds and coughs and no handkerchiefs.

'Could you please lock the door when you leave?' he said. 'And leave the key in the flower pot where others can find it.'

'Lock the door from outside?' I asked.

'Yes, please,' said the old man. 'I don't go out anymore.'

Finally, we were driving to the airport. The city was awakening slowly on a Sunday morning. It was a bad time for tourists. Whole families slept on pavements wrapped up, head to toe, in sheets. Used packets, empty bottles, cartons and newspapers littered the roads. We drove through the outskirts of Dharavi. I had received a call from Sharada and I had advanced my ticket. It seemed a sudden and rude end to the visit. Muskaan looked at me sideways as she drove expertly through the traffic.

'What?' I said.

'You are still the same smug, supercilious sonofabitch,' she said.

'I am?'

'I remember every line of yours when we first met,' she said. Her nose curled, perhaps from the smells through which we were driving.

'They weren't rehearsed,' I said.

'How could they be?' she said. 'Only you could come up with – you need me – on a first date.'

We laughed.

'I love you,' I said.

One hand came off the steering wheel and adjusted the rear-view mirror. She sneaked a look at herself. 'You do?'

'More than this city,' I said. 'But it is a close-run thing.'

She waited. A roadside signal blinked.

'I would give anything to stay back,' I said.

'No,' she said. 'That's not true.'

'Chennai is an incarceration for someone like me,' I said.

She laughed, perhaps at the irony.

'You don't fool me, mister,' she said. 'Why do you even try?'

She glanced at me.

'Look what you have become,' she said. 'You are up to something. I can sense it. What shall I call you? Malicious malware? Or a Trojan in Chennai?'

QUARTER CUTTING

They cut chai to save money. In the land of 'full thanni', they shared booze by the drop. They called it quarter cutting. They shouted 'goinda goinda' when their money ran out.

'No money, no cigarettes,' said Nadar the shopkeeper.

'No credit, no dhool,' wept Thambi.

'Month-end has come,' wailed Antony.

'Talk of the devil,' said Kari.

They sat in a row like prisoners and ate rice kanji. There was a tin drum for water, a tin roof for the ceiling. A tapped line served free power. For this foursome, the word municipality had no meaning. They were used to the smell of litter and the sound of scrounging. People trusted their luck in kuppams, sifting through bins. In the coastal police station, constables wrote assiduously into their history sheets. It was a list of minor infringements. The biggest crime, the worst form of domestic violence, went unrecorded. Because nobody had enacted a law against scrimping.

There was snark on the streets of Foreshore Estate where they lived. Cursing was social currency. Names were used that described personal places. Poolu the dick, come meet Koodi the cunt. Machan, meet Mayiru.

'Poda, mayiru.'

'Neveru,' said Valiban. 'We won't give an inch.'

'We have dil, we have fight,' said Antony.

'We will sing,' said Thambi. A threat.

Their songs were gaana pattu. The women, they called figaru. They sang gaana to a dappan beat. On the open terrace in the midst of pipes and clotheslines, it was full galatta. They leapt, they sprang and the hip thrust was jalsa. In their mind was drunken goodal. And there was hurt, hurt that came from love. This love was unfulfilled puppy lust, an unbearable yearning.

They surprised themselves by their success in stealing. They had few principles and in their upbringing, there was no risk manual. If you saw the four of them ride motorcycles, as they often did in Besant Nagar, you would dismiss them as local rowdies. They drove recklessly, in and out of traffic, ogled girls as obviously as they could and sometimes passed comments. They were forever looking at their reflections, adjusting their hair and dark glasses, and they would swagger to every pan-beedi shop to buy cigarettes, one at a time. Cigarette-buying was a ritual, smoking a mere aftermath. They were non-vegetarians and watching them eat was torture for families. They kept bones in their mouth, sucking loudly, cracked and chewed the chicken joints, and left the debris on the table around their plates. Each meal looked like a vulture's feast.

Ponnuswamy, Muniyandi, Thalappakatti – these restaurant names appealed to them. They sounded like a frontal assault on Brahmins – those pussies ate vegetables and curd rice in placid places called Bhavans. They liked very few Brahmins because the community was small-minded. How much money others made bothered them. High caste did not invite people home. High caste plucked flowers from neighbour's houses. In the perimeter of their existence, high caste knew where the last naya paisa was.

'Why are you sucking up to this Nanban character?' Kari asked. 'Firstly, he calls himself Nanban. The name is not right.'

'He is nobody's friend,' said Valiban.

'Is he rich?'

Valiban laughed aloud. 'What a stupid question? What I want to know is why he is lying low here, pretending to be nobody.'

'He is a Hindi and he speaks Tamil. He must be a central spy like those shady fellows in the Hindi Prachaar Sabha who roam around Dakshin Bharat in plain clothes.'

'He behaves like a spy. He has a figure in Besant Nagar, a woman called Sharada. They are intimate.'

'Aaargh.'

'I want to have Brahmin sex,' said Undony. 'Milk and fruit on the side table, rose petals on my bed and one plump jolly.'

'I want to star in a saami padam,' said Thambi. A saami padam was an x-rated film that began with devotional songs just to fool the cops. Once they left the cinema hall, the sex scenes started.

'Minor,' said Kari, 'are you a genuine high caste?'

'Only by birth,' said Valiban. 'And Thambi is a Gounder, a middle caste.'

'That makes sense,' said Kari. 'Thambi is closer to a monkey than you are.'

Thambi tried to say something.

'What about Undony and me?' said Kari.

'Without religion and caste, you are nobody,' said Valiban. 'You cannot even fill a form.'

'Which caste should we steal from?' said Kari.

Brahmins were the easiest to steal from. They chose elderly couples in the suburbs, doddering fools with silly habits that kept them poor. They kept gold sovereigns at home and money bundles inside a flimsy almirah. To prove their intelligence, they wrote clever letters to newspaper editors. Robbing from an old Brahmin was easy. All they did was protest loudly. When threatened, they pleaded, mortally afraid of being touched by low-caste ruffians.

The gang began as minor hoods; soon they were serial thieves. Kari did it for the 'kick'. The only time he smiled was when they were stealing. The rest were busy picking up money and trinkets. They hit suburbs at random and in each case, they left an imprint. It did not need a clever cop to figure out who was pillaging elderly Brahmins. Staring at the police at every site was a signature. At some point, Thambi asked, 'Why? Why are you doing this?' Valiban was at the entrance door sketching a naamam, the mark the Brahmin used on the forehead. It resembled a Y. They also ate at every place they burgled. Kari was perennially hungry and he would raid the fridge and finish most of what was cooked.

Inspector Murthy, the crime specialist at the Kotturpuram Station, had a puzzle on his hands. The new series of burglaries had occurred in three different suburbs.

In one case, the burglar/s had disabled an electronic security system.

In another case, the burglar/s had used a wine opener successfully.

In a third, the burglar/s had consumed a full meal by using dishes from the refrigerator, heating them in a microwave and serving them out on dinner plates with serviettes. The family was away for a night show and was to return for a midnight repast.

Murthy had seen many petty thieves. They were small-made, wore only shorts, they oiled their bodies so they could not be held if caught, they could climb very well and they were usually barefoot because footwear made noise. They carried a knife or similar sharp implement and a half or quarter of hard liquor which gave them strength. Straggly hair and red eyes, no friends of barbers or tailors, these men were skittish cowards. At the first sign of discovery, they turned tail and fled.

Inspector Murthy made a surprise visit to Kari's room, hoping to find clues. He was convinced these four rowdies were the ones. He had years of experience and he came in like a sniffer dog.

'I can smell infection here,' he said. 'Stale underwear infection.'

Kari's room looked like a weapons store. There was a long iron rod called a kadapparai that leaned in a corner, used to break ground. Next to it with a mud clump still stuck on it was a digging implement called a mumti. Two aruvaals lay together on a shelf above them. These scythes could cut through anything. A bent saw with its teeth intact lay next to them. There was a pair of gardening shears, six knives of different sizes and a pair of green dumbbells that were badly dented.

The inspector surveyed the domestic arsenal and he asked just one question. 'You have all the implements but where is your garden?'

There was no garden nearby. Kari looked at Valiban and for once he had no answer. They stood silently until the inspector left. He left them feeling a little unsettled. The foursome felt small.

'Uncertain times,' said Valiban. 'Let's face it.'

'Why minor?' said Kari.

'Nobody respects us, not even this Murthy. We are minor hoods. We need to announce ourselves.'

The Timur episode happened soon after this and it was a game changer.

THE SECOND CUT

Timur was a territorial bully in Kari's kuppam, a small player with a mere hamlet at his command. He had a singular quality called thimiru. Thimiru is a Tamil noun that takes equally from aggression, arrogance and pride. Thimiru can consume you. When it did, you could see it and the one so consumed was called a 'thimiru pudichavan'. Timur was one and so was Kari. People in the kuppam looked at them from distance and did so discreetly. 'Look at the face first,' warned those who knew better. 'Not its features but its expression. Hear how Timur speaks, feel his stare. The stare demeans you, dares you to look back at him. If you do…'

'Morakriya dai!'

'Do not stare back. That could hurt you. Do not lock eyes. That could kill you.'

Timur was slippery, a don in the making. The kuppam watched his false modesty in front of the elders in the hamlet. He had a knife with a serrated edge. He had taken apart a rival using a Poclain machine, then lugged the remains to a slow fire.

'Right now, he has the upper hand,' said an elder, 'because he has tested himself. He knows that he can kill.'

'Watch out Kari,' warned his gang members, 'watch out for this Timur.'

'Too late,' said the elder. 'He will be your nemesis.'

'Stepping-stone,' said the Kari gang.

Timur came from the slum near the Buckingham Canal, where it yielded to an overhead rail track; there was a small bridge that crossed it and there was government housing made long ago, which was full of middle-class wimps who paid him money for peace and good health. Cutting Timur would make Kari an established hood, an upgrade from a common criminal. Timur had status and he had access to smack. Good smack that he could retail after mixing but he was in love with it.

They saw him often seated on the floor, his nose running, his hair unkempt, his sleeve torn, his left hand holding apart his toes, his right hand holding a 5 ml syringe and off he went climbing, his head exploding and he looked up when he surfaced and he smiled. At that moment, he could pleasure them. That Timur was without thimiru – with smack inside him he was unbound for a while from his private hell.

'Fying' was an English adjunct to a Tamil verb. What was he doing? Samalchifying – which meant making up. If he was glad-eyeing girls, he was sight adchifying. If he was drinking kallu arrack, he was kudichifying. Hell was when Timur was doing what he was good at. He could knife them with his right hand, he could knife them with his left and there was no ready term for that ambidextrous killichifying. Getting rid of Timur would be big because his writ was deep, ingrained in a fishing village. The meen kuppam was next to government housing that was literally falling apart because the concrete had melted under the groaning weight of the shit of the grandfathers and grandmothers, the aged gentry who refused to die when they should have. Kids kept getting born and all that was happening was there were more mouths to feed than there were fish in the ocean. Timur went twice into the waves every day and each time he came back, there was a catch in his boat, salt in his mouth and redness in his eyes, and he headed to the arrack shop where he sat till they pleaded he go away. Fuck the catch, he said, when someone told him it was rotting. He was then ready for the night shift and his brokers came to him with small business, with stories of hurt and injustice, and this was grist to the slippery don's mill. Transactions happened which were never recorded. When he was asked to do something heavy, he would change as though he was slipping into a storm's eye, all calm, a neatly pressed demeanour and his hands would be sure, his gait would be straight and his eyes would be holes. He was not to be crossed then; other hoods who knew there was still some life to be lived would avoid him.

'Timur has heard of us,' said Valiban. 'He feels threatened by you, Kari.'

Word was out that Timur did not like Kari. Why? Because Kari was also a 'thimiru pudichavan'. He knew, Timur did, before others, when someone had to be put away. It was he or Kari and things were on the boil. For two days, Kari and Valiban sat in their little fort, fortified themselves with booze; and the crude implements they had, looked more and more inadequate.

'Should I get a gun?' asked Valiban.

'No,' said Kari.

'Should I go to Nanban sir for help?'

Kari laughed at the suggestion. He wasn't saying much and Valiban could sense something build up inside him.

Finally, he asked Valiban to send word. 'I am ready,' he said.

Valiban knew Kari, knew what he was capable of, so he had word sent to Timur's boss, Pasupathy, that Kari was available. The contract was put out on Kari. The whole kuppam knew when that happened so they could stay away. Nobody stayed away, in fact, they gathered. Timur came where Kari was meant to be and there was an audience on the sidelines. Timur carried something for Kari and he had every right to deliver it because he had taken money for it, money from Pasupathy whose word was law. Kari was a goner for all purposes. Only Valiban knew better. Valiban knew Kari's left hand worked better than his right hand did, so as Timur came up with his knife, Kari had his right free to defend and it held a mere stick that got cleaved easily, but it held momentarily, and that was enough for his left that held a broken bottle that found Timur's eyes. Whoever said they were hollow had lied, and Timur was still seeing in a strange kind of way through that gash before he fell. They all came up to see him as he lay and they spat beside him and cursed him before the cop van came.

'Dhandasoru,' said a grandfather, he who was a salary earner.

'Not true,' said Valiban, 'he was a fisherman, an honest one, and he kept a family going, let us not take that away from him.'

'So you are dialogue adichifying for him now?' asked the old man. 'For this street dog?'

Valiban said, 'Maybe.' There was always a 'maybe' when he wanted no argument and he had to get away too, take the cash from Timur's pockets back to Pasupathy, each bloody note save one that he would be allowed to keep.

'Pick one,' said Pasupathy, a fat, swarthy goon used to smarmy underlings. He smiled at his new henchman, his beady eyes seeking out familiar weaknesses.

Valiban picked one. 'Henchman I am not,' he said, 'neither is Kari. Not for you or anybody else, and no disrespect to you, sir.'

His life hung in there by a thread, prey to what went on in Pasupathy's head but he was prepared for whatever was decided. Pasupathy was angry, furious that Valiban said this in front of his men. He let him be. 'Dhandasoru,' said Pasupathy. 'I am deeply disappointed. But Kari and you are like my sons.' That way he saved his face and Valiban and Kari lived.

Kari came to Valiban fresh from the incident. He came at him, this big burly man. Valiban loved him and he knew it. He held him. Kari was shivering. He cried, sobbing loudly. His big shoulders shook, he heaved and he brought up his insides. He wasn't weak but he needed somebody to leach the chill the first kill brings.

'Did you not see what happened?' he asked. 'How are you so calm, minor?'

'You did what you had to do,' said Valiban.

Kari recovered slowly. 'Was I good, minor?' he asked.

'Of course.'

Valiban kneaded his shoulders that had bunched into knots. Kari moved away to the window, stretched his arms above him and twisted his neck, making cracking noises.

'Did you see the look on Timur's face?'

'I did. Timur wasn't expecting it. He looked surprised even if he couldn't see by then.'

Valiban had to help Kari out of his shirt. It was blood-soaked. He could not help running his hands up and down Kari's broad back. Kari was exultant by now. Valiban stroked his shoulders again. Kari hit him. Valiban took it standing. He loved him more than he did anything else. Kari hit him again. Valiban sat where he fell. Kari towered over him, looking every inch a big bad 'thimiru pudichavan'.

Kari became famous after this incident. Soon, he did not have to pay for the air he was breathing, that air belonged to a flat he did not own. He merely occupied it. Whose was it? No idea, said the owner who had been warned about Kari. He had no wish to be famous.

Nanban was oblique when it suited him. He heard Valiban relate the story and all through it, he remained expressionless. 'Moving,' he said finally. His protégé looked surprised and disappointed. 'When did you first experience violence?' said Nanban.

'This was the first time,' Valiban replied.

Nanban smiled. 'Poverty is your neighbour and unemployment your friend and you still need a knife to get hurt?'

Kari was nervous for a few days after this incident. He expected police action. He did not know that cops wasted little time on gang killings. He looked gloomier and gloomier, day by day, looking like he had not evacuated his bowels. The amount he ate, he needed to clear inventory and if that did not happen, his sweat began to smell of garlic and onions.

Inspector Murthy called Kari to his station for a chat.

'You are the next Timur?'

'No, sir.'

'Will the burglaries stop now?'

The gang members were open-mouthed. 'He asked you that?'

Kari shifted his bums and leaned to a side. 'Murthy followed us one day when we went around on bikes in Nanganallur, looking into Brahmin homes. I was testing the window grills, it seems. Thambi was looking up and down the street and Antony was making faces at the old men.'

'I told you we were being followed,' said Valiban.

'Murthy said we are amateurs and catching goindas like us is beneath him. According to him, I am a weak leader.'

'What did you tell him?' asked Valiban.

'I told him I will soon be a politician. He laughed. I told him he deserved a posting in the Dockyard Station where real crime happened. He agreed. He said Kotturpuram is too genteel. The morons here actually stop at red lights.'

NANBAN

The traffic is heavy despite the late hour. At day's end, courtesy is missing. It takes a year's internship on city roads to drive badly. Two cars screech to a halt ahead of me making way for an old woman who crosses the road, shaking her head in disbelief. An act of civility gets magnified into kindness.

My country is a fit case for Chaos Theory. The theory states that an earthquake happens in your backyard because a butterfly flapped its wings in another continent. This makes perfect sense in India because cause and effect do not form a logic chain out here. So much happens around us without our say that negotiating our way through daily life, we throw up our hands and entrust our karma to a greater being.

A week at this cinema will confuse the finest. Nothing will surprise them after a while. The first casualty is deep thinking and the second is precedent. Soon, like the locals, visitors begin to believe that in order to succeed all they have to do is try. The wheel of karma will turn their way. Frighteningly, it does. Even for people who don't deserve it. Especially politicians. It is unnerving to watch them rise above their station.

Can I express this philosophy to a disparate group seated at the high table in a TASMAC Bar? They are sharp, shrewd and extremely practical.

I am sure Chaos Theory will not impress them. I cannot tell Veerappan that you will win seats in the next election because, hey, shit happens in India. Serendipity cannot be the winning strategy even if the political landscape is chaotic. What I will tell him is, 'We will create our own chaos. We will move the tectonic plates of Tamil Nadu by placing ourselves on its fault lines and flapping our wings.'

What Veerappan expects from me is a market research project on the Gounder community followed by an advertising campaign. This is the business school approach. He thinks this is what I am capable of doing. He is wrong. I am capable of a lot more.

'Cheers,' said Raman as I walked in. Narsimhan was there in his corner. He was down a few, his eyes were droopy and his shirt stuck to him like a wet towel.

'Cheers brother,' said the Sindhi financier.

'Look who has come.'

'Thangabalu, give him a drink.'

We met every other day yet we clinked glasses like long-lost brothers. My Sindhi brother turned towards Narsimhan. 'Director Sir was telling us about his last film. I did not realise he is a filmmaker.'

'Every TV reporter thinks he is a filmmaker,' said Narsimhan. 'I am no exception.' He was holding onto the table to stay seated. When his elbows slipped, he collapsed.

A second glass of whisky came my way. The first I grasped, the second I held. I nodded at Veerappan who was observing everything with a slight smile.

'Say something,' he said. 'I know you want to tell us something today.'

'I do.' I took a swig of whisky and waited for it to burn its way down my throat. 'I have realised one thing Veera, market research and advertising are not enough for a fledgling political party.'

Veerappan turned towards the others for the umpteenth time and said, 'He is an MBA from the Indian Institute of Management in Ahmedabad. The Harvard of India.' I tried to hide my embarrassment. I need not have bothered.

'I hate MBAs,' said Raman, the small-scale industrialist. 'They question everything, that's all they do.'

'One young MBA told me I charge too much interest,' said the Sindhi financier. 'On declining balance, you are charging 36 per cent, he said. I said thanks but how much are they paying you to tell me that?'

Raman laughed loudly.

'MBAs can be predictable,' I said. 'If I was to ask an MBA to help Veera, he would come up with this.'

I removed two files from my attaché and placed them ceremoniously on the table.

'Each file contains a report from a study conducted on behalf of a national party. They paid a lot of money for them. The first report is *Segmentation and the Art of Reaping the Caste Dividend*. The second is *Multivariate Analysis of a Caste and its use in Targeted Politics*. If you hire a team of MBAs, this is what you will get.'

'And what is wrong with that approach?' said Veera. 'It sounds scientific. Can you give me a copy?'

'Mr. Veerappan, do not succumb to this language. This is the language of the clever. It is as sure as it is seductive. Your party is young. It needs doubt and revolution.'

'I see,' said Veera. 'Now you don't sound like an MBA.'

'I get restless when what I planned happens, when what I predicted fructifies. Such easy outcomes give me no pleasure. Take the hard road, learn the hard lesson, join the real men who are risking enough.'

'You may be a rash gambler and you may have succeeded,' said Veera, 'that by itself is not reason enough for me.'

It was hard to explain the nature of a political enterprise in India to a politician.

'Sir,' I said, 'in politics, safe bets are what losers take.'

Veera looked confused. 'Are you telling me I am a…?'

'Sir, your idea of risk is not in sync with our political environment. The people are wilful. Our civil society is disobedient. There is no scope for safe behaviour. We need to forego our middle-class upbringing. We need to cut the Tamil population loose, disrupt their lives and make them uncertain.'

'I am not convinced we need to start a disobedience movement, if that is what you are suggesting,' said Veera.

'Sir, the two parties in Tamil Nadu are well-entrenched. It is a duopoly, a worse situation than a monopoly. They take turns to rule. It is very hard to break these two silos, but we have to. How? Safe methods? A waste of time. We need interventions that will plunge the state into uncertainty, which will fracture the mandate.'

'What kind of interventions?'

'Large-scale interventions. Look at the political history of this Nadu. Fifty years ago, religion and caste were the entrenched silos. The Dravidian parties shattered them. They polarised resentment. They told people – you are not just Tamil, you are Dravidian. Your time has come. A Dravidian will not accept Hindi imposition. A Dravidian will cut the Brahmin's noose. A Dravidian will break the yoke of religion. They embraced atheism. This was radical thought in a peaceful state that had more temples than pharmacies.'

'It worked very well,' said Veerappan.

'Yes. The change agent was Periyar. He kickstarted the anti-Brahmin and anti-religion movement. He and his followers walked down the central arterial called Mount Road, carrying framed photographs of Hindu gods, each garlanded with chappals, sandals and shoes. Just imagine. The power of that public action blew people's minds. Then came the occupation. Nobody has written about the occupation but just try and remember how the Dravidian parties took over Mount Road and Marina Beach, the two public spaces that matter. Cortège after cortège passed down Mount Road. First the leader Annadurai, then M G Ramachandran. Each time a sea of humanity that dwarfed the Bay of Bengal that day. And they buried them. Yes sir, no funeral pyre but a burial. On the iconic Marina Beach. They erected huge memorials. The act was one of occupation.'

'Let us say we postpone my funeral,' said Veera. Everybody laughed.

'Uncertain conditions will produce a confused mandate,' I said. 'Once voting patterns get fuzzy, we have a chance. In the first-past-the-post system, we need just 30 per cent of the popular vote. That is our magic number.'

'Gounders are a large enough population?' asked Veera.

'Yes, but we have to polarise them,' I said. 'Gounders have to realise that history favours only those that write their own.'

'And how will this work?'

'Sir, the scale of our movement has to be large. We have to swamp the state and gain mindshare. Meaning newspaper columns, television and social media. Periyar was the butterfly in the Dravidian backyard. He caused a shift. We will have to come up with something similar.'

I had in mind the bogey of a separate state for Gounders. At some point, Veera would have to raise it. Right now was too early.

'I see,' said Veerappan.

'I will finish my preamble with a quote. *"As far as the laws of mathematics refer to reality, they are not certain, and as far as they are certain, they do not refer to reality".*'

'Who said that?' said Veera.

'A man called Einstein,' I said.

I had not won them over. I was convinced that elections had taught voters more than candidates. They had developed a resistance against familiar entreaties, hoary incentives and cheap strategies. Most of all, the voters in Tamil Nadu hated having to choose between the same two parties, who had informally formed a mutual benefit society. An inefficient duopoly had seen the emergence of a visible inept feudal political class.

'We will set up gangs,' I said, 'like your ancestors did. Gounder history speaks about gangs they called kootams. We will mobilise young men, hundreds of them, wherever Gounders have a presence. These youngsters will build your future.'

'You mean graduates?' said Veera. 'Educated, intelligent youngsters?'

'No,' I said. 'The unemployed, the hungry and the street-smart. The less successful. Those who have faced rejection, experienced deprivation, suffered isolation. An example is this quartet that hangs around here. People like Valiban and Kari and the two others called Antony and Thambi. You will have hundreds of such examples.'

'Raw material,' said Veera, emphasising raw.

'But potent,' I said. 'Anxiety, shame and fear drive them. We can do wonders with this energy.'

'And what will these gangs do?'

'They will disrupt. They will misbehave. They will scare the shit out of the status quo. Their behaviour will be unpredictable. Imagine hundreds of these uncontrolled elements in a civil society that can be easily affected.'

'I see,' said Veerappan, staring into his glass.

'You need a private army, Veera, a Gounder force filled with youngsters straining at the leash. People will notice them and begin to fear them. The key to fear is unpredictability. There will be unrest and, most importantly, the press will come after you. Your image will change.'

'What will happen on the ground?'

'Political rallies, diktats, protests, bandhs and other forms of disobedience. Dheeran Chinnamali fought the British; you will fight the Dravidas.'

'That's it?'

'We will make a film,' I said. 'We will make a film starring Dheeran Chinnamalai. We will make an icon out of Dheeran. He will be able to stand next to Tipu Sultan and not fade.'

That got his attention.

'We will make a movie that will capture people's imagination. We will do for Dheeran what Shivaji Ganesan did for Veerapandia Kattabomman.'

'And I will be in it?'

I counted until three and took the plunge. 'No, you will not be in it.'

'And why is that?'

Now was the time. 'Because you need to win an election first. Once you are in power, you may treat the whole state as your fiefdom, plastering your face in every street corner, even on state-subsidised products. Right now, this film cannot be a vanity project.'

Inside, he must have smarted but all Veera said after a pause was, 'And when will you learn?'

'Learn what?'

'Learn how to mince these big words that you use?'

Everybody in the room breathed again and some even laughed in relief.

'And he will be the director?'

We all looked at Narsimhan. His right hand came up, the small finger extended. Nobody was paying him attention.

'You need a capital city, Veera,' I said. 'Chennai won't do. You need to go back to your ancestral place Odanilai that the British razed to the ground, to Sankagiri Fort where they hanged Dheeran. This is the historic centre you need to resurrect and make your own.'

The next day Veerappan came home for dinner. My mother cooked for him. I told her who he was, the leader of one of the biggest caste groups in Tamil Nadu, a successful farmer, a budding politician and a friend. She slaved over the meal and she was an inspired cook when she was in the mood. Veerappan came in his traditional finery – crisp cotton, some gold jewellery and slick combed black hair – and he arrived in his Prado with an escort vehicle. He removed his footwear, washed his hands, touched my mother's feet and sat on the floor. He was served mutton in pumpkin gravy, prawns with ladies' fingers, mutton sukka and crisp dosai. He ate heartily and carried out a detailed conversation with my mother on ingredients and he promised to send her some produce from his farm. After that, we retired to the living room, lit up and smoked, and I poured us some cognac. When we settled down, he had questions but my mother joined us and despite my frowning at her, she stayed.

'You don't have a daughter-in-law to help you?' asked Veera. The bastard was setting me up.

'He is in love,' said my mother.

'The girl is in Mumbai?' asked Veera.

'Of course, where else? She left him to be with a painter, a famous painter who is on Page 3 every week. There is a waiting list for portraits painted by him. What she saw in him, I don't know.'

'Is that painter as famous as M F Husain was?' asked Veera.

'Unfortunately, he is,' said my mother.

Veera looked towards me. 'I need a portrait painter,' he said. 'We need a portrait not just of Dheeran; we need a series of paintings on the legends in our folklore epic *Annanmar Kathai*, like the brothers Ponnar and Shankar. I will build a museum in Odinalai around the series. Could you meet him and convince him?'

'Of course, he can get it done for you,' said my mother.

After Veera left and we had cleaned up, we sat for a while and my mother waited patiently for my question.

'What do you think of him?'

She pretended she was thinking for a while. Finally, she brushed her grey hair off her face. 'I couldn't help comparing him with you.'

'Ohh.'

'It is natural, all mothers do that. I have to say he is interesting. I didn't realise South Indians could dress so elegantly. He touched my feet and that says a lot about him, not me. And he is observant, far more observant than you.'

'That's it?'

'He is used to leading from the front, he is very sure of himself, he trusts you; what more do you want me to say?'

'Nothing. I don't want you to say anything.'

She smiled as if she understood me, as if she knew me more than I did even if I had grown up outside her gaze.

'I cannot say anything negative,' she said. 'Sorry. I don't know what politicians do in their work, but there must be something there I would not like. But one thing you should do for sure.'

'What?' I said.

'To understand him, you need to visit his native place. See where he comes from. Meet people close to him and see how they behave.'

GOUNDER LAND

The toilet was outside the traditional dwelling. It was so quiet, bowel sounds carried to the neighbouring village or so I imagined.

'I need to have a bath after the journey,' I said.

An elderly retainer of the family took me to the washroom, which was also outside the house. It had a rough cement floor, brass taps and a steel bucket with its adjunct lota, which they called 'chembu'. Hot water came in another bucket and was poured into the one inside. The old man gave me a bar of green soap called Chandrika. There were no hooks inside so I flung my trousers over the wooden door. I whistled as I bathed, sat on a stool and poured hot water down my sore back. As I soaped myself, suds flew and I could hear giggles outside. I stopped my whistling, opened the door, just a peek, and thrust out my hand. I received a thin knitted towel. I dried myself vigorously and then poked my hand out again. I received my jatti, an XL from Marks and Spencers. I emerged refreshed, hair still a little wet. There was nobody outside.

It had darkened by now. Out in the open, the countryside stretched into the horizon, a vast flat land that dwarfed fully formed trees. The sound of bells came from returning cattle and carts. Lights flickered and winked in houses and streets. There was a temporary hush. Strange shadows loomed on walls and a light wind blew, rustling leaves. I thought I heard voices. It was eerie. I walked the short distance to the house and someone switched on a bright lamp as I walked past. I stood under it for a while. 'Hello,' I said. I heard clothes rustle and the sound of anklets.

They left me for a day, to be on my own. The village ambience wasn't as I had imagined it. There was caked mud on my leather shoes, the smell of dung clung to my socks, insects found their way through my clothing, small ones crawled into my ears and my nose; this idea of personally experiencing the land where most votes came from was a form of punishment. I tried yoga in the open till a bevy of flirtatious frogs croaked nearby. Again, I could sense someone standing nearby. 'Hello,' I said. 'Hellooo.'

My mother tried to call me but the connection was poor. Muskaan sent an urgent message that arrived late. Late at night, I received a call from a Delhi number on my second phone, an old model Nokia.

'Are you on vacation?'

'No,' I said, 'I am on a school excursion.'

'Funny,' said the caller. 'Veerappan has an unmarried sister. I thought you should know.'

What the fuck was that supposed to mean? Was it a warning or was it an invitation?

'Does she wear anklets?' I asked.

'They all do,' he said. 'If they make you wear a veshti then you better watch out.'

'Why?'

'The chieftain likes you more than is reasonable,' said the caller.

Veerappan arrived on the second day and I greeted him like a long-lost friend. Veera had a very basic bar for visitors in his country dwelling. I poured myself an Indian scotch. Big mistake. After tasting it, I poured half of it into a flowerpot. It was in Veerappan's farm that I realised the Gounder leader wasn't married and never was. He had five sisters of whom four he had helped settle and, in the years that took, the family forgot he was single.

I surveyed Veerappan's farms. I noticed he had mechanised his farming using semi-automatic machinery, rather than fully automated options. This minimised retrenchment. The operators were his former labourers and they came from a lower caste. He had them trained and he gave them uniforms.

'Stay for a month,' said Veerappan. 'Look at small farms and see what labour does to the labourer.'

'No dignity in labour?' I asked.

'No. Only a slow death,' said Veerappan. 'Look at their legs, their toes especially, see how they have deformed. Look at their cut lips and the gaps between their teeth. And look at the scabs.'

The labourer had begun to resemble the land.

'English is being taught in every local school,' he said. Veerappan had funded this initiative. He was very uncomfortable when workers bowed before him, sometimes with folded hands. He shouted at them but old habits would not go away easily. Veerappan acted from instinct; he wasn't a deliberate social reformer. Nevertheless, I could see the political potential. His inclusive approach would help broaden the vote share. I noticed the caste divide was deep-rooted. There was a pecking order everywhere; in the markets, in the daily routine, in common gestures, in temples and though prosperity cut across some caste lines, the old order still prevailed.

What was my takeaway from the trip? I had a useful slogan, a powerful slogan that could get Veerappan national attention because it debunked an age-old cliché.

'There is no dignity in labour, only a slow death.'

'Tie a veshti before you leave,' said Veerappan. I demurred. By now, the sound of anklets was hounding me. Veera insisted. 'Did you meet my sister?' he asked. 'She was here on the first day.'

I got a new veshti, the colour of cream with a thin gold border. I wore it around my waist and stepped out gingerly. A line of people stood in the veranda and watched me approach. They folded their hands as I passed and I felt like a feudal lord. The veshti was made of crisp cloth, it rustled in the evening silence and dogs raised their ears and their heads off the ground. When I reached the main entrance, Veerappan and his closest kin arose, straightened their own veshtis, and came up to me. We walked into the inner courtyard together, a grand patriarchy, sweeping the ground. An elaborate family dinner followed.

'My sister made a special sweet pongal before she left,' said Veera. 'She is wilful and headstrong, like you. She has refused to get married, till now.'

I almost choked on the pongal. 'She used extra sugar,' said Veera. 'I don't know why.' The ghee showed up in every spoonful.

'Did you speak to your mother today?' asked Veera.

I shook my head.

'I did,' said Veerappan. 'She is a fine lady. Next time, you should bring her here. Then maybe she won't ask you to leave Chennai.'

Veerappan and I began the drive back to Chennai, stopping at shrines en route. Open shrines on the outskirts of villages had deities called Kula Deivams. Some temples had large fierce guardian deities called Kaaval Deivams. Temples with female deities were smaller and were called Ammankoils. We stopped at a shrine that featured the female characters from the epics, Kunti and Draupadi.

I brought back holy ash, some for my Amman and some for my Devi, Sharada. On festival days, Sharada smears ash on her forehead and wears a Kerala sari and those days affect me deeply, when there is a fragrance in her house of a freshly brewed puja.

Our drive back was through the interiors of Tamil Nadu, through state highways, through country roads and cart tracks. A couple of turns took us through villages. We paused where culverts had broken, where village functions had taken over the road, and where the vista was arresting. We chatted about our childhood on the way. When we stumbled upon people, Veerappan spoke to them in their language. It was dark. We received some mangoes and directions. Nobody was in a hurry to leave.

After the visit to the farm, there was a bond between us. I had respect for where Veerappan came from. There was good-natured banter on the single status we shared. I had learnt never to get too close to people but with Veera, some barriers had broken down.

'I am beginning to trust you,' said Veera as we reached the outskirts of Chennai.

'I will never be a part of your family,' I told him at the next red light.

'We are all one big family,' said Veera. 'It is time you met up with Perumal. He is our trustee. The trustee handles our finances.'

'Why should I meet him?'

'Because you are a finance expert.'

The trustee controlled the treasury, monitored property transactions and ensured no information leaked. Each political party had a common pool of funds, officially large, unofficially huge. Donations and contributions to parties were often unaccounted. The trustee was hardly visible in Chennai circles.

Perumal came home and met my mother. He came bearing gifts. There was a nine-yard sari with a thick ornate gold border that ran its length and it flared up and flowered into the pallu. There were four silver tumblers and one coffee filter made of brass.

'Is there a wedding in the family?' she asked him.

Perumal laughed and winked at me and I stared woodenly back.

'What should I do?' she asked me. She looked at Perumal, 'We cannot just accept this,' she said. 'Unless there is a function.'

'Just take it for now,' I said.

'From today he is like family,' said Perumal.

I was being co-opted into the inner workings of the party. I spent a few days with Perumal. At times, I was uncomfortable especially with the way money was handled and the trust implicit in the system.

I was aghast at the size of the 'unofficial' banking channel, at the velocity with which cash moved in and out. From time to time, cash was converted into property. The property documents were in the names of trusts, charitable or otherwise. These trusts set up schools, engineering colleges and medical colleges. Money was very occasionally lent to business. All the information, the documentation and the records, was stored in an obscure office on TTK Road behind a vegetable shop.

'Unbelievable what you can get away with,' I said after a walk-through. It punctured the look of pride on Perumal's face.

'The previous trustee was indiscreet,' said Perumal.

'Where is he now?'

Perumal spat into a dustbin. We got into a Scorpio and headed for his farmhouse. We sat in the open under a large neem tree that was quite old and must have come with the land when it changed hands. Cool coconut water was served. Perumal was beaming by now as he watched me look around.

'All hard work, sir. I have come here every week for five years. This farm is very profitable now.' He winked at me. 'On paper,' he said.

'You are a lucky man," I said. 'Agricultural income is tax-free.'

'All thanks to the Tirupati temple,' said Perumal.

Perumal visited the Tirupati temple every year taking with him a small bag full of gold sovereigns. The donation seemed to be working for him.

'See my wife,' said Perumal. 'Look at her. She doesn't pray and she doesn't visit temples. She makes pickles, jams and chutneys but very little money.'

'Why?' I asked. 'Because she pays taxes?'

Perumal had stopped responding to my needling. It seemed he did a lot for his community, hosting a number of young men on his properties. Some of them were utter failures.

'We are a minor sub-caste. Just three villages and no political power. One day, we will have a town, a proper bus stop and a railway station. I will then divert a highway so it passes nearby. Once we have a nearby highway we will be fine. Then we will put out full-page ads and sell farmhouses to rich people.'

Perumal had earned so much money, he set up an engineering college on the road to Thirunelveli. The buildings were ready and all sanctions were in place. What the place really lacked were teachers and students. But it was good for him, the image of an education philanthropist and the approbation of elders in his village near the college. He had a white SUV with a party flag and a bad driver and they honked their way down the city roads and ran amok on the highways. He wore white all the time, had a phone stuck in his right ear and he sat in front of his car next to the driver because that showed he was a man of the people and his followers could clearly see he was democratic.

'My driver has been with me for twenty years,' he said proudly. 'I pay him a fortune. You have to trust them. They know where all you go, what all you say and what all you carry inside the car. I will get you a good driver.'

I learnt later that he kept upgrading his car just to keep his driver happy. By now, I was having giddy spells. I was unravelling.

'People look up to me now,' droned Perumal. 'I can feel their expectations. I call them every now and then. They talk and I listen. People need someone who listens to them.'

'Very true,' I said, wishing I could flee from this diatribe.

Perumal's phone rang. It was a small outdated black phone with upraised buttons and no touch screen. He was scared of new devices that revealed the location and usage patterns.

Before I left, I couldn't help looking at the neem tree once more. It was a magnificent specimen, gnarled and noble.

'From my father's time,' said Perumal, standing under its shade.

'A gentler time,' I said.

'A time when there was only one kind of money,' said Perumal. 'There was only cash those days and life were so simple.'

I reached home and by now, I was finding it hard to breathe. The meeting with Perumal had affected me badly. The irony, I told myself, the fucking irony.

'Where were you? What happened?' said my mother. I pushed out a hand and stalled her.

'Nothing is wrong,' I said, 'just some pain.'

'Are you sure?' she said. 'You look ill.'

'Just leave me alone.'

I slammed the door shut behind me and held onto a table while my head swirled. My heart was thudding against my ribcage. I knew my eyes would be red. I staggered towards the washroom mirror and pulled out the Nokia 5110 phone that was in the medicine cabinet. It was black and clunky, and in terms of features, quite dumb. There was only one use for it and only one number in the contact list – the Delhi number. I dialled it. He picked up on the third ring.

'What's wrong?' he said. 'Why have you called me in the middle of the night?'

'You fuckers,' I said.

'What?'

I could hear him breathing.

'I have spent the last few months with a politico,' I said. 'I can handle that. I have just met their bagman, their loot handler.'

'You mean the treasurer? Good, you are gaining their confidence. That's a good sign.'

'Damn your signs,' I shouted. 'Everything I have heard is true. These people are running a laundry. Money is flowing through it. This man is blithe. He behaves like the Income Tax Act doesn't exist.'

'I see.'

'Can you? Are you bothered at all? These people should be in a court of law. They are not. The Economic Offences Wing should be knocking their doors down. No, sir. Not happening. Instead, where are these miscreants headed?'

'To the State Legislative Assembly?'

'Exactly. And who will get them there?'

'I guess, you.'

'Right,' I said. I had to sit down and calm myself. My voice dropped. I was suddenly tired of it all. 'Spare a moment for me. Who am I, sir? Let me introduce myself. I am the prime target of the Economic Offences Wing. I bent a rule; I broke no law. Look at me. I am hiding. I cannot spend a penny from the money I made. And the best years of my life are being whiled away in a TASMAC Bar.'

'You are feeling sorry for yourself? What did I tell you? No Mohammed Rafi songs.'

'Can you see what you are putting me through?'

'We all have work to do, Nanban,' said my cohort, his voice soft.

'Fuck you, Raghavan.'

Raghavan clucked. 'You are hurting,' he said. 'I can see that. Be patient. Cuts hurt, but mark my words, your wounds will heal.'

'I love your homilies,' I said, stroking my wrists. 'Will you do me a favour?'

'Let me guess,' said Raghavan. 'You want some of your money?'

MUSKAAN

I called Muskaan and told her why I wanted to meet her. She was surprised I had decided so quickly on which artist would paint the portraits.

'Normally my clients ask for a portfolio and high-resolution images before they decide.'

'Veera was very clear,' I said. 'It wasn't my choice.'

She said that personally, she had no wish to meet 'that' artist again but 'professionally', she would organise it for me. She sounded distant.

'Could I come, like soon? I need to see you.'

'You could,' she said.

The next morning, I was on my way. I arrived in Mumbai with a strange anticipation and we met again at the airport. She gave me a quick hug and a kiss on the cheek. It felt like the consolation prize at a fair concession. We walked towards the car park.

'Don't be so businesslike,' I said.

'Sweets, you are in Mumbai,' she said. 'We are like that only.'

She had come in a small car, a new MINI Cooper in an electric metallic blue colour. It looked edible. I walked around it a couple of times, admiring its retro look and its brilliant detailing. Her money wasn't ugly anymore.

'Nobody drives all the way to the airport to pick up somebody,' I said.

She tossed her hair and jangled the keys in her hand. 'Do you wish to drive this thing?' I said yes but she wouldn't let me. This was a first. I loved the feel of the car and the ease with which she piloted it. For a few minutes, we drove in eloquent silence. The new car smelt new and occasionally the engine roared as she switched lanes and overtook some young pups in their Audis hot-rodding their way to some steel-glass tower. I was very near happiness by now, in my city, sitting next to this fellow traveller. Call us privileged. We shared a wavelength that had a narrow band flanked by art and hedonism. Both were islands that set us free. Nevertheless, there was a bone in the dal, Azmi, whom I had to tackle.

'Back to business,' she said. 'Have you seen his work; actually seen it?'

I had seen only reproductions and, personally, I thought Azmi with his palette knife and impasto had a style that harked back to the Progressives.

'Would you like to see a portrait that he has painted?' she said.

'Good idea,' I said. 'I don't trust reproductions.'

She mentioned there was one portrait the painter had done of her. It was in a museum.

'You sat for a portrait?'

'I posed. But he painted from memory.' That did not make sense. She sounded off-key. I had to be careful though, asking questions.

'Erm, is there a backstory? Of your portrait, I mean?'

'There is. I would rather not tell some things to your face. Here, read this while I drive.'

She thrust some papers into my hand. I began reading and quickly realised this was more about her than about my search for a portrait painter. It was seemingly an attempt to write the biography of a painting – her portrait. I found it very moving. What did she see in Azmi? Why did she love him? I had partial answers.

'I spent two years with him in the middle of nowhere,' she said. 'We were in a valley and there were no roads, not even a pathway. In that time, he painted a portrait of mine. I was his, till it got done.' She sneaked a look at me. 'Then, one day, it was all over. I had to leave. The shared experience was precious but it was meant to be fleeting. How was I to know? How was I to know that like the others before me, I would have to leave too? He painted a singular portrait of mine but in the end, I was no different from the others. That hurt.'

We were stuck on a flyover. I had lost count of the many we had crossed. I coughed and cleared my throat. I did not know what to say.

'Err, two years to paint a portrait,' I said.

'Yes. In that time, I got pregnant,' she said. 'The child came later, after we parted. It made no difference to him. He was on to the next portrait anyway.'

I tried to lean across the small divide inside the compact car but she turned away.

'Am I like him?'

She smiled. Then, she nodded.

'No,' I said.

She shrugged. We kept our silence, the seatbelt chafed and I shifted in my seat.

Muskaan rarely liked people but when she did, she fell in love. She wasn't choosing well.

We were in Byculla by then and as we rounded a driveway, we could see the museum. We arrived at this beautiful building and we walked inside. She led me to her portrait. It was a nude, it was life-size and a slight swell in the stomach region was noticeable. Where the fuck was the child, I wondered.

I could not take my eyes off that beautiful work. She was glowing, so different. Azmi had captured her. She was looking at him while he painted and I couldn't bear to see the expression in her eyes. So much must have happened between them, so much more than I had imagined. I stood there, rooted, an interloper, between the painter and his muse. The thought depressed me beyond words. Muskaan hugged me from behind, spontaneously. I turned awkwardly. She ran her fingers on my face as if she was reading my expression. Her smile was warm, her touch was comforting.

'Where do we go from here?' she said.

'Odd places,' I said. She had a child. That simple fact was killing me.

'It is an odd time,' she said. It was early evening.

'I want to meet your kid,' I said.

Her face fell. Tears formed quickly and she averted her face.

'Sorry,' I said. 'Did I say something…?'

She shook her head and wiped her eyes. 'A boy,' she said. 'He was stillborn, with his cord around his neck.'

I took her to a place on Malabar Hill where the wind blew caps off heads. It was a modest café and the tea was bearable. We left, strolled to the Hanging Gardens and on a park bench, we held hands as we used to. She did not say much and I was quiet as well yet we filled in the gaps that the years had caused.

'Are you up to something in Chennai?'

I needed that question.

'Politics,' I said. 'It is unreal. And politicians more so. Just look at who they are and how they change lives.'

She sensed I wanted to chat so we left for her place. I removed my shoes in the foyer of her house, standing on one leg at a time. In the shoe cupboard, there were two pairs of men shoes. What were they doing there? One was a well-used pair, handmade, unbranded. The other was a very expensive, exclusive creation. They belonged to different men. She saw me looking.

'Don't you spoil this evening,' she said. 'Notice the new sculpture?'

I could not miss it. It was a large work by L N Tallur – a plump seated impossibly grinning Buddhist (?) monk, his head crushed by the weight of a giant (Bodhi?) tree trunk that had fallen on it. Moksha at the moment of death?

I needed a drink. I picked a wine from her chiller, opened it expertly and served it as I used to, taking care to get everything right. She played her part, sniffing, swirling and slurping, and finally collapsing in a heap, laughing at the look on my face. We kissed like old times and snuggled up in her bed. She found a mole behind my ear while I chatted and soon I was wishing that this could be my life.

'So, what else is happening in your southern paradise?'

'Crime,' I said, 'being committed even as we speak. The culprits admit to it freely. It is unnerving.'

'You are a witness?' She filled our glasses.

'Yes. Does that make me guilty?'

'Are you just a bystander?' she said. 'I find that hard to visualise. I can see you as an instigator.'

'Thanks. I really needed that.' I turned away. 'There is so much shit happening, you have no idea. And it is so brazen. They might as well make political immunity official, like diplomatic immunity.' I got off the bed. 'Next will be bureaucratic immunity. Then, the citizens will be put to sleep in pods.'

'How delightfully dystopian.'

I looked at myself in her full-length mirror and sucked in my stomach.

'Who are you manipulating these days?'

'Everybody is doing a number on everybody else,' I said. 'Politics is so refreshing.'

'Someone has your number?' She sounded pleased.

I couldn't help slipping a hand into my pocket where my second phone nestled.

'I am trying to trigger a movement. There are these four boys assigned to me. I am supposed to give them orders and I am finding it hard to get directly involved in the shit that I am perpetrating.'

'Why don't you get them jobs?'

I twirled my glass and watched long legs descend. 'I plan to, but only as a distraction.' I held the glass against the light. 'Sangiovese?'

'It is,' she said. 'Come back here.' I sat next to her. 'Tell me, as a language, does Tamil need Sanskrit? Or is it the other way around?'

'What? I don't think so. No.'

She smiled. 'Do Dravidians have monks?' she asked.

Was she serious? 'The Dravidian movement believes there is no God,' I said. 'But they worship cine actors and cine actors turned politicians.'

'Back to your boys then,' she said. 'Tell me, what are they like?'

'Loose cannon. Capable of anything. I have kept them in Chennai, close to the seat of power. All I need to do is create agency. Then, we will wait for the tipping point.' I lay down again and balanced the glass on my stomach.

'How abstract that sounds. You think four random young men will trigger your wholesale movement?'

'Yes. To start a forest fire a ray of sunlight has to find a piece of glass. You don't need TNT. We will create a combustible situation in the state. In the mix will be these volatile youngsters. Call it conflagration or epiphany. It will happen. Without their volition.'

'Fascinating,' she said, sounding like she meant it.

'You think I should do a TED talk?' I asked, jokingly, knowing she was addicted to them.

'No,' she said. 'The questions that I raised deserve a TED talk. The questions that you are raising? I don't know what they deserve.'

She dipped two fingers into her wine glass and took a few drops into her mouth watching me look at her all the while.

'How is that for sacrilege?' she said. 'Bring out the Bad Boy, will you?'

Bad Boy was French, a Bordeaux wine, a lusty Merlot with a hint of Cabernet Franc. I unveiled it. A few glasses later, I massaged her feet starting with her toes. Done well this has an aural ending. A symphony that she conducts when her nerve ends sing.

I had taken Valiban with me on this trip because Veera had bought an art installation and there was some cash to be handed over. I wasn't handling the cash. Valiban, who had been to Mumbai, was the bagman. He made the delivery and we shared a taxi for a ride around the city before heading for the airport.

Valiban found me observing him and he smiled.

On this second trip to Mumbai, he witnessed a kind of life that he had seen in old Hindi films. Large art-deco apartments ringed a bay. Old money resided in them, gentrified. I took him on a taxi tour through Malabar Hill, Carmichael Road, Carter Road, Worli Seaface and Pali Hill, names that, like art-deco, had an American zing.

'Can *you* afford this, sir?' he asked.

I nodded. He was mystified. I think Mumbai tickled his curiosity in many different ways. He scratched his head. 'I wonder what life is like in Mumbai.'

'Very busy,' I said.

'It doesn't hurt them,' he said.

He looked out of the window all the way to the airport and his expression kept changing. I remembered then how young he was and how impressionable.

VALIBAN

The Mumbai trip affected Valiban. The world seemed a smaller place in Chennai. When he walked into Kari's room at the kuppam, the others were in their usual places. Nothing had changed. Nobody had moved an inch.

'Kootalis, we need to do something,' he said. Nobody responded.

'There is a big world out there,' he said, 'that created Nanban. I have seen it.'

'Your mother called,' said Kari. 'Your phone was switched off.'

'What did she want?'

'She sounded worried. She said Aadi month has started.'

His mother had an unexplained fear that surfaced in July every year. Last year, somebody drew a red-bordered kolam outside her house. It was a sign, she felt. On Aadi piraparam, first day, middle of July, a dead crow was at her doorstep. Crows did not fall out of the sky without reason. Nobody needed to tell her that was a bad sign. July was a lean month. Shopkeepers sat in their shops and swatted flies. Everything was 'For Sale' and yet unsold produce rotted in the heat.

He met her as soon as he could. He took her for a walk to prove nothing unusual was happening. It was a hot day. She looked up at the skies, at the sun. It was burning a hole in her head. She washed her hair to cool herself and then stood at the doorstep with a towel around her head. The land breeze turned turtle and blew in from the south and her saree swirled.

'Kanna, don't do anything this month,' she shouted. 'Wait till Aadi maasam is over.'

Nanban called and asked the four of them to report to him immediately. They hurried and reached Chinna Tasmac where he was waiting. He stood before them and gave them a briefing.

'You know who the Gounders are, right?'

They looked at Thambi, the resident Gounder; he wasn't the best example for anything.

'From today, you are part of a kootam, a gang. I will be giving you orders. You have seen Mr. Veerappan at the bar. He is going to stand again for election, leading his Gounder Party, and he needs youngsters like you to build its future.'

Was he finally offering them jobs?

'You will get assignments from time to time. Periodically, you will be paid. You have to be available at all times. Things could get rough. I will never take no for an answer from you. Other than today.'

He looked to see if any of them wanted to drop out. He wasn't asking if they had any questions.

'You need to be fully committed. I repeat, you need to be available, no questions asked.'

And, finally, 'If things go wrong, there will be nobody else to blame.'

It was clear they would be indentured labour. With nothing in writing. My mother was right, thought Valiban. This kind of offer was in keeping with Aadi month.

The others looked to Valiban. He was a firebrand in his imagination, a rebel in his dreams, but on the first step of this ladder, he would be a ready accomplice. This assignment was so unpredictable, it had chosen him, he felt. He had to say yes.

And so, the Kari Kootam was formed. Historically, Gounder Kootams had warriors and their caste appellation was Kongu Vellalar. They had small fiefdoms and the fragmentation worked against them when they had to defend themselves against the British and their feisty neighbour, Tipu Sultan. History was in danger of repeating itself in the twentieth century. Nanban was out to change that.

The list of Gounder Kootams ran into many pages. Each kootam was identified with a village, a temple and a deity – graamam, kovil and kuladeivam. Interestingly, while Tipu Sultan adopted the tiger as his symbol, the Kongus thought of themselves as lions.

The four assembled in Kari's room, a small part of an unfinished building. There was a terrace in the building where they spent the night, drinking, smoking and singing, using up most of the cash advance they were given. The next morning, they did something for the first time; they all had a bath. They emerged into the city and like young men of Tamil Nadu, they hung around stag, a small herd, shoulder to shoulder, arms slung casually over one another, looking for a 'figure' – a girl or a young woman. Thin or fat, tall or short, it did not matter because the closest they would get to one wouldn't be close enough.

'Drop the sir when you address me,' said Nanban. They would have rather dropped the Nanban.

They took him to Shastri Nagar for a meal. They stood in front of a building whose façade was marred by hoardings, each in a different colour, size and font, and they had to choose between four eateries. The unspoken writ in the group was non-vegetarian and the principal flesh was chicken. Previously, they had visited a protein shop where they stocked up for dinner. The shopkeeper separated three white hens from a bunch hanging from a cycle. Undony lifted their feathers and chose one. The bird went in and emerged vastly reduced in a plastic packet wrapped in newsprint. Next, they had gone to a departmental store for more chicken. Kari liked good portions that he could hold and so they bought a packet full of thighs.

It was a choice between Thalapakatti and the new chain, endearingly called Junior Kuppanna. Nanban chose the latter simply because it was Kongu-style cooking. They had lunch. Nanban hadn't seen appetites like the four of them had for rice and chicken. There were gravies in shades of brown and red and they were delicious. One had a coconut base, one had a tamarind flavour and the third was a smorgasbord of spices that had the effect of an aphrodisiac.

There was still cash left to burn and the next morning was a good time. They filled gas in the two bikes they had and posed casually, two to a bike, with the latest gana song playing in their heads. The beat belonged to the street. They drummed with their fingers, tapped with their feet, each plugged in, as they watched a girl cross the road. 'Figaru,' said Thambi, the lookout. She was wearing a white salwar kameez and a blue silk dupatta kept blowing into her face, highlighting her features. She clutched a bunch of files to her chest as she looked left past them. A motorcycle arrived driven by a helmeted office warrior who lifted his visor, wiped his eyes and smiled at her. He said something and she aimed a slap at him and missed. She swung a leg over the black steed and held him by the hips. The visor dropped and with a muffled roar, they left.

'Escape,' said Undony.

The bike became a speck as it climbed up the flyover and disappeared. Kari said nothing but he, the only one among them, had noted the make and the registration number. A habit that befitted police officers and thieves.

They revved their bikes and set off in chase, their cut silencers making a road-splitting sound. They raced each other up the flyover, weaving their way through cars. The wind picked up as they crested the slope and their balls contracted as they swooshed down towards Sardar Patel Road. A few screeches followed in their wake and some curses too. They spotted the bike ahead reaching the OMR signal. The bike halted, the visor went up, her arms came off and the couple chatted. The next thing they knew, two bikes arrived behind them and braked, turning from left to right at speed, black smoke spewed and the smell of burning rubber rose from the tarmac as the bikes careened. It was a slow-motion u-turn, four heads turning, looking at her, before they sped away, back to where they came from. It was over in a few heady seconds.

'Escape!' Undony screamed.

'I saw her face,' shouted Thambi. 'She looked at me.'

They powered their bikes towards the beach, whooping along the way. They parked parallel, removed their helmets and shook their hair like Formula drivers. They looked at each other and a sand gust whirled by, propelled by the sea breeze.

'Koothu,' shouted Kari, wiggling his hips.

'Soothu,' shouted Thambi, pointing to Valiban's arse that jutted more than most.

They straightened, brushed their hair, drew up their dark glasses and swaggered up and down the road looking at their shadows. A figure walked by with a shopping bag. She hurried past them looking down, using her dupatta to cover her chest.

A couple of bystanders who overheard their comments were horrified. 'Pigs,' said one of them. A car drove past blaring the latest Tamil film tune. 'I am single and I'm young,' it trilled. They sang the chorus, 'Tamil is my mother tongue'.

They caught a bus that headed towards Abhirampuram. It was eleven in the morning, the school and college rush was over and the office crowd had thinned. They alighted at Lloyds Road and walked up to a small garage. It bore a blue painted board that said Easwari Lending Library. Inside, there was just enough standing room and the dank smell of books printed many years ago. Most of the books were popular and dog-eared and had been bound by the owner using local board and rice paste. Kari stood in front of a carrel that said *Westerns* and took a deep breath. His fingers caressed a J T Edson and a Zane Grey and then settled on a Louis L'Amour. Thambi gathered courage as he stood in a corner waiting to catch the owner's attention so he could get a red-hot porn novel that lay hidden below the cash counter. Undony looked out of place because he did not know English. He peered at some covers.

Outside a land breeze, warm and occasionally gusty, made a mess of the garbage bins. The old folk looked uncomfortable. The rhythm was all wrong. Underneath the tar, a slight tremor was building. The dogs could sense it and they chased each other up and down the streets, and then stood with their pink tongues out, gasping. A few bent around their bodies and gripped their own tails with their teeth, trying to bite insects that troubled them. The roadside vendor looked into his muddy curry when someone complained. What had he added that he should not have? He retrieved a packet of masala that had fallen into it, unopened. Used plastic bags flew past the food cart, swirled in the air and entangled in a tree's branches. Finally, an old man stood up and tried to walk away; he stumbled and fell. 'What happened thatha?' someone asked.

'Blood is gathering,' he said, 'in temple.'

Valiban imagined it as a day when lovers quarrelled, when families rewrote wills, gangs pulled out knives and temple priests were summoned for unscheduled pujas.

Heads went swirling like wooden tops when the ground shifted quietly at 2.30 in the afternoon. The old man who had fallen had struggled back to his feet but this time, he went down in a heap. A dog bit into its tail drawing blood and set off down the street, yelping, and the rest joined in and howled and the barking echoed up and down the colony as people rushed out of their homes holding their hands to their heads and some rushed back inside to fetch their children. The Adyar River took a turn and tumbled quietly into the sea.

The four rushed to the beach, like others, looking for a safe open space. The fishing boats were coming in, with the tide.

'What a high tide,' said a fisherman, reeling in the nets. He looked nervously at the north-west, for the ill wind came from there, the wind that turned his boat over once, spilling his lunch and bursting his lungs. There was no wind. 'Severe,' he said, holding his head. People, including his family, were milling around. The muddy water rose and fell, splashing the sand.

Everyone had felt an earthquake after a very long time. They watched the buildings from a distance, wondering vicariously if one would fall. Some hands in the crowd felt heavy. In the library, many books had spilled from the carrels and the four had squirrelled away a couple each.

'Month of Aadi,' mumbled Valiban. The month their kootam took birth, the very month when the British defeated and then hanged Dheeran Chinnamalai, the Gounder icon.

'I sensed some reluctance,' said Nanban. 'Any misgivings?'

'None, sir,' said Valiban.

Nanban had called him to show there was more to his efforts than creating a goonda force that would merely misbehave. He had a small office, hidden away, where he spent time establishing Veerappan's online presence. He had hired two sociologists, post-graduates in behavioural science, to handle social media.

'Hurt has no ration online,' he said, 'and anger is easily aroused. We understand that. We use images, documentary-type postings, comments and motivated accounts to spread the word and shake things up. Most of it is in Tamil.'

Valiban was fascinated. He could not still grasp all that this office was up to.

'And there is trolling as well,' said Nanban. 'Even goondaism now has an online cousin.'

Valiban read some posts on Veerappan. He also read the comments, some of which were caustic.

'Politicians are very conscious of legacy,' said Nanban. 'They want to be remembered well.'

'You are managing that as well, sir?'

He shook his head. 'It is not entirely in my hands. If he loses this election, he will be remembered as a rowdy. No wonder these days his veshti is in a twist.'

Valiban returned to Kari's cave and sat amongst his kootam, and they looked like what they were.

'More than one monkey has been lost to mankind,' said Kari as if he divined Valiban's thoughts. He looked at Undony first and then Thambi as if one was a mere progression on the other. Kari was tall, fair and, hence, fully evolved in Tamil Utopia. He had a chiselled nose, a good head of hair and square shoulders. He moved with a slight wiggle of the hips. He spoke rarely which was just as well. His language was street, his lingo was rogue. On the street, his animal spirit found admirers. Unbounded energy possessed him, its centrifugal force wrested the others from their moorings. Valiban was frequently aroused in his vicinity.

Maria Antony, whom they called Undony, was a convert from Perambur, a beneficiary of a Catholic quota. He received convent education in a Tamil medium school run by fathers and brothers who bumped up his marks in moments of grace. In such Christian institutions, discipline was enforced, punctuality prized, Christian rituals were de rigueur and in the playgrounds, the song 'Please believe me' played on loop.

Thambi sat, the other two ran with Valiban, the groaning bus was slow; they hung onto the footboards as they crossed Stella Maris College, a girls-only college that had, according to Kari, only virgins, unlike the Madras Christian College in Tambaram, a co-ed college where girls were experienced. This description got Undony hot under the collar. He stood outside Rosary Matric School for a week and roiled. Why Rosary Matric? He wouldn't say. There were dark-skinned girls there who were less prosperous, unlike Church Park and Good Shepherd where girls were fair and affluent. Undony felt nervous next to those types, he felt inadequate. He was impossibly dark himself and scratching at his skin did not help him.

Kari took him, and Valiban, to Church Park and they stood in the car park, looking. Big cars came and girl upon girl emerged, spic and span, hair combed and knotted, drivers helping them with their heavy school bags.

'Undony, what is happening?' asked Kari.

Undony looked guilty. So many nubile figures together; it was all a bit too much for him. He toyed with the sand using his foot to describe a circle. His oiled hair curled at the edges, his specs were thick and a little dusty and his manner was that of a choirboy caught peeking at vestal virgins.

'Can you smell anything?' asked Kari.

There was a smell about the place.

'Lowe,' said Undony, looking like a bashful Romeo.

'Myrandi,' said Kari. 'This is the famous Church Park smell. It is a mixture of Lux soap, Nivea cream and Cuticura powder.'

There they stood, the three of them, bursting their balls, with nothing profound in their heads; the camera panned away from them, zoomed out until they were specks on the ground and the city blinked a few times and disappeared above the clouds where the evening sky was Dravidian, the gods were atheists and Tamil Utopia a black hole.

'Can you feel anything?' asked Kari. Undony was horny and Valiban was bored.

Undony hung around Kari like hangers-on did around politicians and wannabes around Tamil actors. Kari was his steed, his only chance was to hitch a ride. Kari knew it, so did Valiban. They treated him badly and, while he bore up with it, Valiban felt an undercurrent that said, 'my time will come'.

Undony ate mounds of puffed up rice that gave him a round belly. It looked out of place, plonked on spindly legs. He had childhood pox marks, hair with matted curls and a posture that was gawky. He had reason to look at a mirror and dream. Strangers treated him badly. People clicked fingers at him in a restaurant where he worked some evenings, cleaning tables. People did not introduce themselves to him or ask his name before they spoke to him. 'Dai,' they said. All this added to his reservoir of hate.

He believed he would have been treated better if he looked half-decent. A crisp shirt would have saved him or say perfect teeth. He had a borrowed wallet that he swore he would return. It had alien family pictures inside that burned him. He used up the currency buying fragrant toiletries. He ran his fingers on the plush leather when it emptied.

'What I really need is rebirth,' said Undony.

'Why take the risk, Maria?' said Valiban. 'You could be born a woman. Then?'

Undony shuddered at the thought. Who would give up male privilege? The uncommon pleasure of a communal piss, bonding against a boundary wall, spraying patterns with strangers, watching mosquitoes flirt with your glans. A few shouts in the dark. Women protesting, just a few, most of them a silent majority. Men may be cads, bums, nose-pickers and arrack-swillers and yet they were apples of their mothers' eyes, Indian mothers who would swear to the high heavens their son could do no wrong.

'Be glad you were born a Hindu, Maria. Nobody keeps track of you, tells you what to do or worries if you enter a convent.'

'I want to escape,' said Undony. 'I want to run away from here.'

'Where will you escape to, you runt?' said Kari. 'To your illegitimate family in the kuppam? They will feed you to the fish.'

'I am not illegitimate,' said Undony.

Undony sat on his stool looking away from the others. They were drinking and it was past nine in the night.

'You are not a proper Christian, you runt.'

'Because real Christians are recorded in Church records,' said Valiban. 'They record each and every birth.'

'Unlike our temples that record nothing,' said Thambi. 'Temples cannot even keep a record of their deities.'

'Poor thambis show up at Missions as lost,' said Kari, 'and turn into Antonys.'

'How do you know I wasn't born a Christian?' said the resident Antony.

'Your old man told me,' said Thambi.

The old man was not Undony's father but a fellow in the kuppam who made a living from sorting garbage and finding things of value. He carried a sack on his shoulder; his beard was unkempt, veshti at half-mast, barefoot, clear-eyed until 6.00 pm, guttural and pathetically kind-hearted, so much so, that street dogs followed him to distraction. Even cats, that never followed anybody, sometimes trailed him briefly.

'Maybe the old man is really your old man?'

Undony laughed; it was a harsh sound. 'Old man cannot poke anybody,' he said. 'In the nights, he is half-naked and I have seen. His samaan is missing. A scorpion bit him there and they cut both his swollen kottais.'

Undony was hurting. He showed no sign and looked stoic but Valiban knew.

'Mother Mary will come for you one day, da,' said Thambi, 'for sure she will come, to this drunken hole, and take you home.'

'She will come one day,' said Undony, 'in a posh car with Boost and Complan, Viva and Horlicks.'

They laughed.

'She must be a lady, a high-class lady. That's why she had to desert you.'

'Must be an actress, a proper figure,' said Thambi. 'They are man-eaters.'

'There must be a family resemblance somewhere,' said Kari.

'They told me I was actually high caste,' said Undony.

'Of course, you are high caste,' said Kari. 'If you have a bath, they might even worship you.'

The night ended without further mayhem. As always, the alcohol wore off leaving them supine, sad and helpless. Nothing changed in that couple of hours every night but looking at the ceiling, life seemed unfair.

'Where is my inheritance?' Undony asked around midnight. 'The priest said Mother Mary will help me find it.'

'Truth is your father was a cheat, a 420,' said Kari, 'and your mother was a website aunty.'

Undony reddened, his right hand searched for something, anything he could use as a weapon. Valiban got up quickly, put a hand around his shoulder. Undony was breathing heavily and his eyes were bloody.

Kari watched, cool as ever, waiting for a move that never came.

'We can't live like this,' said Undony, through clenched teeth, staring at Kari.

The next day all was forgotten. Undony sat on a stool, in a corner, his legs drumming the floor, his knees parting and closing. Kari stood outside, flexing his muscles. His exercise routine lasted just fifteen minutes punctuated by the sound of bone joints expelling air. After watching

TV, he attempted slow-motion taichi moves. Thambi and Valiban started laughing. It was comic. But Undony observed every move, expressionless, said nothing and did nothing. The moment Kari looked at him, he jumped, ready to do his bidding.

Sucking up to the leader was ingrained in Tamil politics with politicians often prostrating on a public stage in front of the 'leader', and then rolling over, temple style, with hands folded over their heads. Valiban could imagine Undony roll over, just as they did. This did not make him harmless; it was a sign that the day he did something for himself, it would be toxic. He had venom inside gathering strength every day because he hated the life he was living, those he was stuck with, and Kari because he frightened him. Above all, he hated himself.

Kari was depressed by his setting. Setting referred to a locale that could be manufactured. It changed frequently in the movies but in Kari's home, it stayed helpless. A slum next door housed people who shat on the roads in the morning, a daily occurrence he never got used to. The sight, the sound and the smell – from people he knew by name. His room had a door that sagged, a small door. He had to bend to enter and occasionally, he forgot. Inside his abode was a bachelor's minimum. To date, nobody had filed a civil complaint. He roamed around bare-chested at home because Brahmins did so. Most of these Brahmins were old, their skin had folds and their flesh had drooped. Kari's impressive shoulder width narrowed slightly at his hips, his ribcage presented itself, taut and springy.

A boy ran his errands, an effeminate fellow with a high-pitched voice who everybody called Pavadai because pavadai was a petticoat worn by women. The boy organised Kari's mornings ensuring essential supplies were in place. Cigarettes, coffee, raw garlic pieces, herbal toothpaste. A neem stick as standby because Kari often chewed his toothbrush to shreds. A dog came to the doorstep, unfailingly, and was fed bread and milk. Kari would sit next to the dog and read the Tamil papers. The dog's name was Porikki. Porikki would finish breakfast in two minutes most of which was spent licking the pan clean. Kari liked how dogs ate without complication, wagging their tails and then, licking their whiskers and coming as close to smiling as they could.

Help was always at hand. There were many girls in the neighbourhood who offered to spruce up things for him. Middle-aged women would drop in now and then to borrow this and that. It was all in good humour, which was a cover for a deeper intent. Undony looked on darkly. He knew the women wanted to wrestle Kari to the ground, open his veshti and check on his vazhapazham because it was rumoured that in there was an imported-sized banana.

Kari wasn't very intelligent but he was self-aware and worldly-wise. He had spent his early teenage years chasing don'ts. In school, he knew how to deal with padres. He was suspicious of bachelors who abstained so he had a few simple rules. Try not to be alone with them in the evening. If the padre says bend over, do not. Extend your palm and take the caning. Do not sing well. Keep clear of carols and choirs. Refuse invitations to attend the evening service. Avoid treats.

'Dai Thambi!' Kari shouted. 'What are you reading?'

'English,' said Thambi.

Thambi breathed Tamil, had read Tamil literature, could quote Tamil poetry verbatim. He had a voice fit for recitation and a dopey look that some girls liked. Dear Thambi had promised to pass the English exam because he was under the spell of a girl who had a Master's in English Literature, who wore spectacles and quoted somebody called Barthes. The first time Thambi spouted some Tamil poetry she quoted something by Barthes. Thambi lost his footing. Every time he saw her, he came up with stanza and verse and she quoted Barthes in return.

It happened after college when all of them were sitting at a coffee place; they had nursed their coffees to the last drop. This girl liked Thambi more than was reasonable; after all, Thambi was an ordinary fellow. She set her mug down and looked at Thambi as if she wanted to do something to him – something the rest could feel inside themselves, a nice warm and wet feeling – and this dolt sat there not getting it.

'Language is my skin,' she said. 'I rub my language.'

'What?' Thambi said, looking around at the others for help.

'I have words instead of fingers,' she said.

'Really,' said Kari.

'Fingers at the tip of my tongue,' she said.

'What?' said Thambi.

'My language trembles with desire,' she said.

Those who heard it were scalded for life. They could see that Barthes was a true lover boy. Which girl could speak like this? Thambi looked towards the other three. He knew he had to rise to the occasion. The time for poetry was over.

'Language experiences orgasm upon touching itself,' said the girl.

That did it. Kari rose abruptly, pushing his chair back so hard that it toppled over and fell. It clanged and bounced off the floor and hit a boy carrying a hot coffee who spilled that… and so on and so forth till Thambi had to lean over and clean up with a paper napkin what the girl had spilled on her lap. That took a while. Other than Kari who had left for the entrance to breathe freely, the rest were witness to this travesty caused by Barthes that true love comes to those who do not deserve it, not for a moment.

An amorous embrace followed, right there in that coffee place in full view of three remaining croissants. The three of them were jealous men, who suffered because it was plain as day that love was banal. Love in the coffee house was merely two cupcakes and cold coffee, and yet the way to such confectionery was barred.

It was hard to describe Thambi without trampling on clichés. He looked local, an under-class low-income kid, a street-side universal thambi. No silver spoon and no sliver of sunshine peeping out of dark clouds. He too was gawky and his manner was awkward. Most days he was sleepy or stoned. He too had his share of hate. He hated alcohol especially when he was drinking it. He gulped it down, daring it and daring others. When he was high, he could lull you with his talk. To hear him speak Tamil was special, especially the old Tamil that few understood. Poets wept when he recited their poetry. He could imitate Kalaignar Karunanidhi and deliver a stirring speech in his signature style.

Thambi was tired with his situation. 'Why can't something happen?' he kept saying.

'Like what?' said Valiban.

'Look at me. I am like stagnant water,' he said. 'I am leftover rain.'

'You are a poet,' said Valiban. 'You should teach Tamil poetry.'

He laughed.

They were standing before a building made of steel and glass. Thambi reached out and touched his reflection. 'I want to be proud,' he said.

Valiban had never met his parents. Thambi never discussed his family with anyone. 'I want to stay with some happy people,' he said.

Clearly, life was at a discount. He stood there, small of stature, looking like the world rested on his shoulders.

'Pretend,' said Valiban. 'Actually, let's go for a film.'

It was often the only solution, to be cossetted for three hours in a dark hall watching underdogs fight the odds. Cinema heroes fought the system, grappled with injustice, cruel fate and a few villains. In the end, for the ticket price, there was redemption.

None of the four was special, each was past their teens, creating a fiction that helped them survive. Things were getting desperate as days left them behind. They had been to college, Valiban excelled, Thambi barely graduated, the other two dropped out. Without further education, Valiban felt their stupidity would soon be palpable. He dragged the herd to libraries, tried to make them read biographies of people who had lived extraordinary lives.

Life tugged at their heartstrings every now and then, mostly when they were alone, most of all when nobody reciprocated.

'That girl used the word proclivity,' said Valiban.

Kari was combing his hair, an important activity. A weak spot in Kari's armoury was his fetish for orderly hair. He viewed it as a farmer would, holding a plough before marking his furrows. You could hear him comb his hair and you could see some of it standing like crop, electrified by static.

'What does it mean?'

'Proclivity? I have it, you have it, but mostly Thambi and that girl have it.'

'Disease?' asked the combing sultan inspecting his field.

'No,' said Valiban, flipping through his Oxford. 'It means tendency, a predisposed condition.'

It did seem to Valiban that in their different ways they were not what the Maker set out to do. Whichever factory they came from, whatever the mould used, it was clear that they had gone rogue. They were careless children, conceived when musth ruled over reason. The guilt coursed through their makers once the spasms subsided. The hurt belonged to them.

'We are bastards,' he said. 'We are furtive children.'

Kari looked at his comb and pulled out some hair. 'I told you not to use big words,' he said.

SCRIPTING ISSUES

There were many discussions that Veerappan and Nanban had with Narsimhan. After he had studied the history of the Polygar period that saw local leaders like Tipu Sultan, Kattabomman and Dheeran Chinnamalai fight the British, Narsimhan asked Nanban, 'You want a docudrama or historical fiction?'

'Both are possible?'

'There is a problem with the docudrama option,' said Narsimhan. 'Veerappan's political career is not interesting enough and there is no distance from it in terms of time. You understand?'

'Yes,' said Nanban.

There were few dramatic moments.

'It will be a short film,' said Narsimhan. 'Unless we do historical fiction.'

He wanted an actor right away. He said it helped him visualise. They decided on an agency and screen tests began. Narsimhan rejected everyone who showed up. They gave the agency some more time. 'I will travel the state in the meanwhile,' he said.

He spent two weeks travelling through small towns and villages in south and west Tamil Nadu, carrying with him a DSLR camera. Why a still camera? 'Because stills are dots on a page,' he said. 'Then the moving hand will write.'

He read whatever material he could get his hands on and he found much more on Tipu Sultan than on his muse Dheeran Chinnamalai. There were no British records on Dheeran and it seemed whatever existed locally had been destroyed. Even the fort at Odinalai, where Dheeran stayed, had been razed to the ground.

'Tipu Sultan's life and reign are extensively documented. He spawns multiple narratives. Simply said, Tipu has conquered written history as well.'

'So what do we do?' Nanban asked.

Narsimhan decided to use the material available on Tipu Sultan to set the atmosphere for that period.

'Why do you like Tipu so much?' Nanban asked him.

He thought about it. 'He was an intelligent marauder. He knew the difference between pillage and plunder.'

'You mean he knew what to keep?'

'Yes. And he got to the marrow of things.'

'Don't end up making a film on Tipu,' said Nanban.

'No need,' said Narsimhan. 'You will always meet Tipu in other people's stories.'

'Sir,' said Nanban, after a pause. 'Continue with your research. I hope you find something interesting.'

After a couple of weeks' absence, Narsimhan was back at the bar. Nanban buttonholed him and popped the question.

'Found anything interesting, sir?'

'No.'

'So what can we expect from you Mr. Narsimhan?' he asked.

'My answer is – a compelling fiction. You need a stone that will break the silence of the Gounders, right? I will give you a bullet that will start a battle.'

'I hope you mean a documentary-style feature,' said Nanban.

'Yes,' said Narsimhan. 'It will feel real. The Gounders will experience a sense of discovery that will lead them to your holy grail – Kongu Nadu. What more can I give you?'

Nanban patted him on the shoulder. 'And you don't see a problem, sir?'

'I don't have a contemporary protagonist,' he said. 'Without that, the script will not work. You have to find me a young actor with a personal narrative.'

THE THIRD CUT

The induction into the Gounder Kootam brought some respite from petty crime and poverty. The orders came thick and fast. 'Stop thieving'. 'Don't dress like rowdies'. 'And please grow up'. Kari bristled, Valiban was anxious. They got the shit jobs. They earned small change for serving Veerappan and his cronies at the bar and elsewhere. Some strange errands paid better.

'When will things improve?' asked Valiban.

The other kootams were busy and soon newspapers began reporting their activities. There were incidents in different parts of the state every day. Some kootam members became famous, their names found mention in the media, they appeared on television. The Kari Kootam sat in Chinna Tasmac near the seat of power doing nothing. Perhaps the proximity was an issue. Perhaps Nanban was unable personally to execute the mischief he was propagating.

They were getting paid but they wanted more. Nanban suggested alternative vocations for each of them. He promised Valiban a job in a picture shop. Thambi and Undony could become security guards. 'Thieving is a good résumé for that job,' he said. There was a good market for guards because there was an acute shortage in the city. Old people, even infirm people, were being recruited and they sat outside urban villas and buildings hoping to have the effect that scarecrows had in a paddy field.

Valiban was having trouble with his phone. His mother's posh neighbour Kalyanraman caught him darting up and down the street holding it up like an Olympic flame. 'What are you catching?' he asked.

'Signal,' replied Valiban. He held up the phone to the vast and vacant sky.

Kalayanraman was an affluent Brahmin. He went to the office in a Mercedes. He had a mansion and Valiban's mother stayed next door. Valiban called him Maama. Maama was supercilious, arrogant and used to looking down at people from the balcony of his palatial house. Usually, Valiban was in his line of vision.

'I believe you have left your mother and shifted to a rundown place?' he said.

Valiban nodded, searching his phone for precious bars.

'Your mother is worried, you know?'

'I know, Maama.'

'Who are you working for?'

For whom was he working? He was working for a political party. Was that a legitimate occupation?

'Be careful,' said Maama.

What Valiban did not tell Maama was that Undony had joined a security agency and they had assigned him to Maama's place as a security guard. It would be a short tenure knowing Undony's inborn hatred for the likes of Maama. It lasted just one week.

One evening, as Valiban was watering his garden, Maama told him the whole story. In retrospect, this episode set the tone for what Undony would do later, something that would change all their lives.

'For many months, I was harbouring a fear of getting burgled. I was also harbouring an old man who was nourishing this fear. I would wake up in the middle of the night and a thousand thoughts would bother me. I would lie half-awake. I would throw off my bedding cover, wear my slippers and walk down the stairs in the dark, counting the eleven steps to the landing, then a turn, and then seven more to the ground floor.

'My heart would be thudding and my hand would be out just in case some stranger was there. If I were lucky, I would reach the front door without knocking my knees. The front door has two latches, two door locks and a safety chain. It would take me two minutes to unlock them and then, I would look out slowly. "Periaswamy?" I would call, softly.

'Usually, there would be nobody. My eyes would adjust to the dark and all I would see was the rusty metal chair near the gate. Some days, I would lock up and return upstairs. Some days, I would step out despite the worms that would be crawling outside, stinky worms or the furry, rash-causing kamli boochi. He would be there. Would you believe it?

'The fellow would be awake, standing on the road outside, his back to me, smoking a beedi. I would retreat noiselessly, climb the stairs, gulp some water and place my head on the pillow. I would keep thinking until sunrise.'

Valiban had seen these watchmen. The security company that contracted Periaswamy sent old men to work. Each was a retiree and none of them had ever watched over anything in their life. They became watchmen when they had poor eyesight, poor hearing and sagging muscles. They were happy. They came with their dinner in a small box, a cloth to wrap around themselves and they sat on a chair through the night. Late at night and early in the morning, they rattled a stick against the window grills and knocked on the cement floor to comfort the house owners. They would light coils to ward off mosquitoes and they would walk across to neighbouring buildings to chat with kindred elders. That was the extent of their capabilities.

Maama continued his story.

'If a thief comes by, what will he do?' asked my wife. Every time I saw Periaswamy that question arose in my mind. I worried and I lost sleep with the thought of marauders at my door stepping over this old man on their way to work in my house.

'We lost a tap today morning,' Maama said. 'Our beloved watchman was asleep. We lost a lot of water as well. The family stood around and gaped. Everybody was shaken. They looked towards me. I was supposed to do something, perhaps lose my temper.

'Later someone asked me, "Why is he still here?"

'Periaswamy was hanging around even though his duty hours were over. There was guilt written on his face.

'"Seriously, why is he still here?" my wife asked. "Did you not ask him to go away?"

'I enquired with the agency if they had a replacement. They promised to send someone else in a couple of days. Do you have somebody young, somebody fit and with experience in combat? They sent someone called Maria Antony. Antony was young so we breathed easy, but he had serious challenges. He spoke with a time-lapse. Every question took time to register. He wasn't hard of hearing. The family did not like him.

'"He smiles for no reason," someone said.

'"He keeps staring at us. When we look back, he smiles."

'Antony was told by his bosses to adopt a martial air. Whenever he saw me, he threw a salute, literally. His hand threw his palm away and he retrieved it just in time near his forehead.

'"What is wrong with this fellow?"

'There was something wrong. He was a puzzle and that was the last thing I needed. After a couple of days, there was an altercation with my wife. She came up to me to complain.

'"This boy is a rebel," she said. "He sounds like a communist. I did the usual thing and gave him his own water bottle and tumbler; you know that aluminium tumbler we keep for servants? I caught him drinking from one of our tumblers. I came down this morning and he was holding a stainless steel glass and sipping from it."

'I took a deep breath and asked her to just explain things to him. "Explain?" She looked ready for a fight. "He told me it was illegal." Illegal? What is illegal? "He says two tumbler policy is illegal and we should drink from the same tumbler. He also told me aluminium utensils were for beggars and for lepers."

'I called Antony and took him to a side. I thought I would reason with him. Look boy, I said, I don't want to lose my temper like my wife. Look at me as I drink. I held my tumbler not by the rim but by the middle, opened my mouth, leant back and poured water down my throat, taking care not to touch it with my lips. Can you do that, I asked him? Can you do that every time and not forget and do what you usually do, which is to wrap your fingers around the rim as they do in Udipi hotels and then slurp from it?

'"Sir," he said, gritting his teeth, "you are a Brahmin. I know that. It is written on your forehead so everyone can see it. I… I should just leave. I will ask my boss to let me go. I told him not to send me here."

'Okay, fine, I said. Will you ask Periaswamy to come back? Could you speak to your bosses and send him here? He shook his head, grinning. "That old Brahmin will not come back," he said. Why? "I took care of him, that's why."

'It sounded sinister and I thought I should probe further but I hesitated. Suddenly I wanted that boy to go away quickly so I paid him some extra money. He grinned again; I hated that grin by now. He looked insolent. "You have given me small notes," he said.

"Why?" Why what? "You think I deserve only small notes?"

'You want a big note I can give you one, I said. "You think I cannot spend a big note?" he asked again. He threw me a parting salute, looking cocky, waving the currency notes like a fan. "I forgive you," he said before he went away.

'The wife watched him open-mouthed. "Is it illegal to give him a separate tumbler?" It was horrifying but true. Yes, I said. The Supreme Court has said two tumbler policy is illegal. I am not joking. If Antony complained, you could be arrested.'

Maama looked at Valiban as he finished. 'Brahmins are so easily accepting,' he said. 'We have lost our voice and we do not care. These servants have usurped us.'

He expected Valiban to support him, say something appropriate. He had no clue what Valiban had been up to.

Later that evening, six stainless steel tumblers appeared on the pantry shelf in Kari's place. They stood in a row and near the rim was etched their owner's name. S. Kalyanraman. Undony saw the rest looking at them and he laughed. He looked wild and Kari held him by the collar, took him out and asked him to calm down. 'What else did you take?' he asked him. Undony pulled out a gold chain from his pocket. It was the gold thali, the Kalyanraman wedding chain, stolen from a cupboard.

Valiban had to concoct a story and return the thali to Kalyan Maama. They kept the tumblers.

One disaster followed another. They caught Thambi in the act the next day. Kari, Undony and Valiban returned from an evening near the beach, a productive evening, spent looking down at rich boys and girls in their cars and fancy bikes. They heard some noises as they opened the door. It was a rhythmic noise punctuated by muffled shouts. They entered and then bumped into each other because Kari had stalled in his tracks. Thambi had a girl under him; he had tied her to a chair, bound her hands and stuffed a towel in her mouth. He was forcing himself on her. By the sound he was making, he seemed about to come. Kari caught hold of Thambi with both hands and pulled him up. It was a strange scene. Thambi was still wearing his pants and they were wet. He looked at them with glazed eyes. The girl looked at them wild-eyed. She was the literature student.

They tried to manage the situation. They were embarrassed and a little scared, at least Valiban was. This was terrible. Kari could have killed Thambi, going by the look on his face. He was very gentle with the girl though. He kept averting his eyes and saying sorry as he untied her. Undony and Valiban escorted her to a rickshaw stand where they chose an old driver. They paid him the fare in advance.

When they returned, there was a deathly silence. Kari and Thambi were both drinking and Kari's right hand was around Thambi's bony shoulders. 'Drink,' said Kari. They sat away from them and drank up. Something was sure to happen. What would Kari do? That was what everybody was thinking. He began massaging Thambi's shoulders, making soothing sounds. It was eerie because Thambi was cringing and trying to wriggle away. He made a choking sound and then blurted something.

'Speak loudly,' said Kari.

'Anna, please,' he said.

The massaging spread to his neck and his scalp.

'Don't, Anna,' said Thambi.

'Get me a knife,' said Kari.

Valiban got him a large kitchen knife, one that they had never used. It was shiny and the metal felt cold; it had a pointed tip so small that even dust could not rest on it. Valiban was tempted to feel its edge. Kari held it by the wooden handle and scraped the metal edge on the floor. There was a screeching sound causing their hair to stand, yet he continued to scrape the knife. He held Thambi's finger and drew it along its edge. 'Did you feel it?'

Thambi shook his head.

'It won't hurt,' said Kari. The finger bled along a straight line. A few red drops appeared and fell. 'I thought your blood will be dark,' said Kari.

He gripped Thambi and turned him around with one arm and with the other, he lowered the knife to Thambi's crotch and snipped his pant buttons, one by one. 'Take it off,' he said.

The terror-stricken Thambi's legs were shaking as he stood. He removed his pants. He was wearing striped undies that were old and a little loose.

'Kneel,' said Kari and as the boy did so he wiped the blood on Thambi's shirtsleeve, lowered his undies and let the edge of the knife lift some skin in his abdomen. Thambi screamed. Valiban would never forget that scream, ever. It was loud and in that small room, it bounced off the walls.

'Don't,' pleaded Thambi. 'Don't cut me,' he said. He was on his knees holding his hands together as Kari held his hair with one hand and pulled his head back. 'Choose,' he said. 'What should I cut?'

Thambi was incoherent.

'Don't,' he kept saying.

'Lift your hands,' said Kari. 'Look down one last time,' he said.

'Sorry,' said Thambi between sobs and they could see his Adam's apple bobbing up and down below the knife's edge. 'I am so sorry,' said Kari. 'I have to do this, say goodbye, quickly.'

Thambi collapsed on the floor.

'If I will let you live, I will have to cut your poolu,' said Kari. 'Can they join it back?' he asked Valiban.

'Yes, they can stitch it.'

Kari looked towards the door. 'Is my hungry dog outside?' he asked.

'Yes,' said Undony.

'Fine, hold him,' said Kari.

'No, no,' pleaded Thambi, struggling to get away. They held him down, Undony and Valiban. Kari leaned forward with the knife and drew patterns on Thambi's abdomen. The boy passed out. They left him there and went out for some fresh air. Moaning sounds came from the room after a while.

'What do you want me to do?' asked Kari. 'Should we report him to Murthy? They will hold him in the station and work on him.'

'The right thing to do,' said Valiban.

Kari sneaked a look in his pocket mirror and adjusted his hair. 'I think he has learnt a lesson,' he said.

'And we get to decide?'

NANBAN

I wasn't weighed down by the grief the kootams were causing all over Tamil Nadu. My brief was – first, visibility. Kootam members refused to pay highway tolls. They blocked lanes leading to queues many kilometres long. They raided newspaper offices when their paper criticised the party. Overenthusiastic Kongu lions smashed their equipment and burnt their records. Two opposition party members disappeared briefly. After a manhunt and three days, they reappeared, looking considerably chastened. They denied they were kidnapped, threatened and then released. The kootams threatened bank officials who prosecuted defaulting farmers. They looted the premises of private moneylenders, decamping with cash and jewellery. Fertiliser storage units were raided, grain silos were looted. The loot was publicly distributed. The bogey was lawlessness, the franchise was Robin Hood.

'The brigand is back, they are saying,' said my political leader. He was being compared to the notorious Veerappan who sat in the forests between Tamil Nadu and Karnataka, sandalwood smuggler, serial kidnapper and ruthless outlaw.

'Is this work in progress,' asked Veerappan, 'or is my image makeover complete?'

'We will make some corrections,' I said.

Each kootam outdid the other and there was outrage in the print media and television. Naysayers, mostly elders from the Gounder community, surrounded Veerappan. The community was on national television for the first time and it wasn't the image they had of themselves. They spread cuttings from language newspapers on a table and summoned him and me. 'Is this our revolution?' they asked.

'Revolution is messy,' I said when Veera looked towards me, 'a bit like growing up.'

They pulled out some photographs. 'Look at these juveniles; look at their expressions. Where did you find them?'

'Puberty is better than menopause,' I said, pointedly. I heard some abuse, purple prose, delivered in an earthy tone.

'You are so badly behaved,' said one octogenarian.

The kootams acquired a reputation and comparisons were made that were unflattering. This wasn't meant to happen in Tamil Nadu, said the newspapers. There were months of turmoil in which I let the gangs loose and they led the state to the edge. The edge was where revolutions happened, where your actions cut through the social fabric. Take no prisoners was my dictum. There were clashes and moments of uncontrolled madness. Importantly, there were victims. A riot happened, followed by looting and arson. Some kootam members were badly hurt. I waited anxiously for a response. Sure enough, the community rose in anger. The families took to the streets and the town of Karur bore the brunt. The police raided our offices and there was a clamour for intervention from the Centre. That never happened.

The high command of the Gounder party met amid infighting. I was the principal target. I was close to being sacked, but I didn't care. 'This is armchair outrage,' I said. 'I wouldn't waste my time with these elderly specimens.' Veera was troubled. 'The party members have ganged up against you,' he said. 'We have to take it seriously.' I scoffed at his attachment to these fossils. 'Your party needs users of Ecstasy, not Viagara,' I said. While the meeting was in progress, Veerappan received a friendly summons from the authorities and he went, against my advice. He had to face civil servants and police officials in a closed room and they interrogated him and, ignoring his denials, they showed him proof. He returned from the meeting looking furious.

'Your shenanigans,' he said.

'What?'

'An IAS officer used that expression against me. For a moment I thought he said shaniyan.'

He expected me to apologise.

'You shouldn't have gone,' I said.

'They would have arrested me if I hadn't,' he said.

'An arrest warrant would have helped,' I said, 'immeasurably. My kootams would have run amok.'

He looked at me with an expression that was hard to divine.

'You won't stop at anything, will you?'

'Will you, Veerappan Gounder? Decide now because there is no looking back after this.'

It was a pertinent and timely question and he had to decide. Decide he did.

He slung an arm around my shoulder and we walked in, together, into the den that held his naysayers. He was a veeran that day. He confronted his party functionaries and he gave them a roasting. He stood tall amidst them and questioned their virility and their ancestry. Two words featured in his questions – maanam and rosham. Both lit a fire because they questioned their pride and virility.

'Do we need an outsider to tell us who we are?' he thundered.

The tide turned. There were shouts of 'Kongu Nadu Veeran' by the time the meeting got over.

I had my hands full with my Chennai foursome. Valiban was depressed. He related what had happened in his kootam. 'I don't belong in this group,' he said.

I promised him an interlude. I got him to help with a small gallery in Chennai, a place you got to by traversing a crowded road called Radhakrishna Salai. We entered a quiet leafy dead-end. We stepped past dug-up cables into a pristine, air-conditioned space. Valiban removed his footwear and gaped at the walls. The hush seemed to affect him. I told him what he had to do. Wear gloves first, I said. He wore new white gloves, held his hands up and smiled. The rest of him stayed slovenly. Soon he was busy packing, unpacking, moving and hanging work. He kept his eyes peeled, as I knew he would – after all this was the boy who read a lot more than people I had seen.

I visited one day and we stood together taking in a show; I knew better than to lecture him or explain what seemed like a very contemporary presentation. Going by his body language, Valiban was dismissive. Then a Bentley drew up, big and cherry red in colour. Two burly barrel-chested men emerged from the front and one from the rear. One of the three opened the other rear door while the other two formed a protective shield. A familiar industrialist emerged. He was wearing an expensive tailored suit that failed to hide his generous specifications. I noticed his coiffure, his pink, fresh-from-a-facial skin, his Cartier wrist and Bvlgari ring finger; I gaped at his shoes as he strode up to the gallery through the open door. The gallery owner and he stood in the middle of the space chatting about making a bronze bust of his father who was a diminutive person, it seemed, but needed to look like a towering personality. After a brief discussion, the industrialist left, leaving behind lingering notes of a limited edition fragrance.

Valiban was profoundly moved. He told me he had never seen anything like it. The naked display of power and wealth had churned his insides. We did not discuss this event. I assumed that such a visitor would dazzle a Velai Illa Pattathari. Valiban was repelled.

He lasted just three months in this part-time job. One day he was thrown out and he came to me with his severance tale, looking gleeful if anything.

THE FOURTH CUT

'I saw this strange piece and they told me it was a sculpture. It was wood, it was misshapen and it was large. It had tendrils but no leaves and was polished to a high degree by the sculptor. The sculptor was a she, five feet and three and very beautiful. Someone came in and asked for the price. "Two lakhs for it," she said. "And if you are writing a cheque please add only at the end."

'They laughed while I raised my eyebrows. Two lakhs only? I thought I should steal it. It was after all a table and quite useful and now I had learnt it was valuable as well. Somebody called a critic, a man with a beard, came and stood next to me. He said, "The distance between art and utility is the distance between form and function."

'Everybody nodded and I said "wotha" instead of "what the fuck". I wondered what I was doing in that place. It was a centre table – that much I had learnt. They had paid me to lift that thing, move it from the van to this hall and then shift it around until they felt the display was right. What if I got caught stealing this thing? I would not be able to run, not with that table in my arms. Inspector Murthy would ask me to put it down. "Do it or else," he would say.

'There was a misshapen rock next to this piece of wood in that strange hall. It was a sculpture and it was precious as well. "Found sculpture," the bearded critic said. "Found sculpture," I would tell the inspector. He would look at me and laugh. "Found thief," he would say.

'In reality, they asked me to move the table once more and I obliged. I lifted the centre table to a height, pretended to stumble and dropped it, and it broke into four unequal pieces. The sound was muted but the silence thereafter was deafening. Finally, the Beard spoke up. "Form has triumphed over function," he said, "thanks to poor engineering."

'"It was precious driftwood," wailed the sculptor. "It was a unique piece," she wept. I could fix it, I said, now that she was crying. It would take a few nails and some adhesive. "You do not understand," she replied. I apologised and I wept, I looked contrite. They allowed me to take it away, asked me to remove it and threatened me with dire consequences because I looked closely at the rock and tested its weight.

'I fixed the broken pieces at home and used it as a table. It was worth something, that driftwood. It taught me there were things to steal inside halls painted white where rich people gathered on evenings and drank wine, made conversation; where the bearded man stood with people around him and they smiled when he spoke, especially when he waved his arms and shared his thoughts. I saw this Beard at every function they called an opening for three months and I saw those young couples who came regularly. They hung on to his every word.

'"You are a good audience," he told them, "such a good audience." They laughed. "You know when to laugh," said the Beard. They laughed some more.

'I loved the young couples, loved what they wore, their careless attitude, their cars, their jewellery, their hairstyles, their watches, their shoes; it was a long list. I loved their conversation. I loved the way they ignored me; when they spoke to me, it was in Tamil and I replied in halting English just to keep up the pretence.

'"My husband is an MBA and he has no idea how to change a light bulb." Really? "I have never seen him do it."

'"Of course I can, she is kidding," said the young banker – he was suited, his tie was fashionably loose and his shirtsleeves rolled up to his elbows.

'"Can you change a CFL bulb?" They laughed.

'Wotha, I said. So young, so rich, and carefree. "My husband is an engineer and he could not open the bonnet of his car," said another. They laughed some more and by this time I was getting dizzy spells watching them stand, holding hands, stroking backs, winking, flirting and thinking God knows what. "What have you bought recently? I believe you bought a huge painting for 40 lakhs?"

'When I told Kari that a painting could fetch so much money, he was genuinely surprised. I took one out overnight and showed it to him. Other ways of making big money, I said. "Take it back before the hall opens again," said Kari. When I did not move, Kari said, "Nobody will buy this from us, you moron – it is not like jewellery or electronics."

'I was crushed. Not even for 50,000? I could get myself a bike with that amount. Kari put his feet up on my precious table. "Wotha," he said.'

NANBAN

Waiting was difficult when there was a road to cross. A small gap in traffic and they ran, risking everything. Then, they stood on the other side and showed the finger to those that had honked. Astride their bikes, the gap game began. A gap appeared between a bus and a car, they swerved into it, accelerated and smelt the paint as the gap closed behind them. Their knees bore bruises. Cars and buses blared, drivers screamed curses. The rest of the day had neither plan nor purpose.

Each of them had Telugu blood pressure. A diet that had a liberal dose of chilli powder and gongura leaves washed down by undiluted alcohol. It was hard to imagine what went on in their bowels. Afternoon was a state of near stupor. Someone sat, someone lay on the sofa, someone stood at the window. Kari watched his listless brood eat up oxygen. Evening he would be manic, wanting to take everybody down with him.

Evenings the four of them came to the bar where they served us at the high table. They stood in the fringe in the company of flies, mosquitoes, roaches and rats. They watched us men, big men in white, hunched, holding booze, and we would be talking all at once, the din reaching the low roof. When the power came back and the lights came on, the truth was searing. In the bright light, they were shown up and they looked like what they were, a crummy group of young nothings.

Things changed within a couple of years of my associating with the Gounder. There was an air of menace bottled up in that bar. It was subtle how this happened but evenings were no longer about drinking alone.

My gang of four stayed together in Kari's room. Staying in cramped conditions was bound to cause friction. My efforts at providing alternate employment had failed. I could sense their anxiety and I could imagine the daily bickering. The weather was hot and muggy; the smell in the room must be unbearable. I made a surprise visit and they were busy swatting flies, killing mosquitos, smoking, spitting, swearing. They reminded me of a herd in a swamp in a hot summer struggling as the water receded.

I had to get them an assignment quickly.

THE FIFTH CUT

An ambulance was parked outside Veerappan's house. The same vehicle was seen outside the trustee's house a day later. Then it disappeared. Nobody mentioned it nor was any enquiry made by anyone on the health of family members. Nanban noticed these things and his antenna was up when the vehicle reappeared. He waited for the right moment and then went up to the vehicle and peeped into the rear. There was a removable stretcher in the centre, cabinets with medicines, seats on the side, a drip stand, two gas cylinders and at the rear were two trunks.

'How was your trip?' he asked the driver, who was seated in the front.

'Very smooth, sir,' he replied. 'Nobody stopped us. The policemen waved us through.'

'And the toll booths?' asked Nanban.

'All okay,' said the driver. 'Only one near Karur asked for payment. A young trainee.'

What was the need to send an ambulance that far, wondered Nanban? Karur was 300 km away, at least.

Later that day the trustee drew him aside. 'No need to ask the driver any questions,' he said. 'We use the ambulance to transport cash. It is a safe and speedy method.' In the political cash economy, the ambulance was playing the familiar role of a lifeline.

Nanban said nothing. The next day it occurred to him that his kootam could handle this. Kari could drive, Valiban could be upfront with him, Antony could be the nurse, Thambi the patient. This would give the boys something to do. This could be their first real assignment after weeks of idle agony.

The next trip was assigned to them. Money was packed into compartments that Nanban had not noticed. Cash money, enough for a few talukas. The destination was Dindigul. It was a day journey. The boys were given some documentation from a small hospital that said Thambi was in remission. A barber shaved his head. Saline bottles, some blood and sundry medicines were placed in the cabinets. They left at 9.00 am, drove past the airport, past the factories. The traffic thinned as they hit the six-lane highway. Soon they gathered speed and at every tollbooth, they switched on the red lights but not the siren. They were allowed to go through without fuss. Kari, who was sweating, leaned back after they crossed Tindivanam, looked across at Valiban and smiled. They were carrying coffee in a thermos.

They reached the outskirts of Trichy where they were told to be careful. There were a few traffic policemen near the bypass junctions. They slowed down and sweat again showed up, dampening their white uniforms. They crossed the city and now they were only 100 km from Dindigul. It was a new highway and the road was in good condition. They relaxed for a while. Valiban turned and looked through the glass towards the rear. Undony and Thambi were playing cards.

It happened well short of Dindigul. Right in front of their eyes. The sound of the crash was sickening. A lorry laden with steel rods was on the left lane, a small car was behind it on the right lane. Without warning the lorry turned right hoping to take a turn. The car braked audibly, some smoke came from its tyres as it began skidding and it smashed into the side of the lorry. There was a loud thud and a screeching sound when the sheet metal skidded on the tarmac as the car bounced right and flipped over. It came to rest with a final thud on the divider where two of its wheels kept spinning. Glass splinters had flown from the windows when the windscreen shattered. For a few seconds, nothing moved. Kari had braked hard and the ambulance halted safely at the side of the road. The tableau stayed still, frozen for a few long seconds. Finally, the front door of the lorry opened, a figure wearing a turban jumped out and ran into the fields nearby. Another man held up his lungi as he ran, following him. The truck had a Haryana number plate.

Kari mumbled something. The road was clear on the left. He looked at Valiban who was staring at the upturned car.

'They must be dead.'

'They? How do you know?'

'You saw it cartwheel, you heard the bloody sound. They must be dead. We should leave.'

'Should we…?'

'No,' shouted Valiban. 'Don't get involved. We will get into trouble.'

They had to get away quickly. They had to speed away before other vehicles arrived on the scene. They peeped out of the window. Some telltale red liquid flowed out onto the road. And a faint sound reached them. It was a groan. They heard the rear door of the ambulance open. To their horror, they saw Undony and Thambi running towards the car.

'Get back,' screamed Valiban.

'What is wrong with them!' shouted Kari.

Undony was in his male nurse uniform and Thambi in a patient's green smock. They wouldn't listen. They tugged at the car door and it opened.

'Get back,' shouted Valiban, again. 'I can smell petrol. It will explode.'

The two reached into the driver's seat and pulled out the driver. He came out screaming, his head covered in blood, one leg at an impossible angle. He tried to stand, he screamed again, an awful sound, and he sagged and the two held him. They left him on the road and rushed back. They opened the other front door and pulled out his wife. She was bleeding badly and they lay her down on the road. Her hands were up in a posture of surrender. She started to plead, ask for her husband and her mother. There was no one else in the car.

'Aaargh,' said Valiban, trying to drown out the noise she was making.

'Now what,' said Kari, rooted to his seat, unable to handle the sight. It was by now a bloody scene. 'Stop the screaming, please.'

Valiban got out and ran. He got hold of Undony turned him around and slapped him hard.

'Come to your senses,' he said. 'Let us leave. They are alive, thank God. But we must leave.'

Vehicles could be seen arriving at the scene. Thambi was cradling the woman in his arms and talking to her, asking her to stay calm. 'We are here,' he said, 'we will help you.'

Kari shouted from the driver's seat but the two would not listen. Undony was on his knees tying a cloth around the man's left leg that was bleeding badly.

'We are not leaving,' he said.

Valiban had to take a quick decision.

'Fine,' he said. 'Take them into the ambulance. Kari, get down, help us.'

Cars arrived and people spilled out and a small crowd collected as they carried both the injured into the ambulance.

'We should wait for the police,' someone said. 'That is the rule.'

'She will die if we wait,' said Thambi. Some people were staring at him since he was wearing a patient's outfit and here he was alert and nimble.

Someone suggested a nearby hospital.

'Where is the truck driver?'

'He ran away into the rice field. The cleaner followed him.'

'Hurry, hurry,' said Valiban. 'We have no time.'

They got into the ambulance knocking the doors with the stretcher and the man almost slid and fell off. The woman they handled carefully and laid her down the best they could. They switched on the siren and the gears clashed as Kari struggled to control the big vehicle.

'The handbrake is on,' said Valiban.

'Shut your bloody mouth,' said Kari.

The ambulance shuddered.

'You are in the wrong gear,' said Valiban.

Kari almost hit him. The first gear wouldn't engage. He found the second gear and they got going. They gathered speed. They kept looking into the rearview mirror to see if they were being followed.

'Nobody.'

A car drew level and they held their breath. Thankfully, it overtook them.

'Bloody good Samaritans,' said Valiban. He was examining his bloodstained hands.

'Who?'

'Those two koodis behind.'

Valiban turned around and looked; Undony was in tears, seated next to the injured woman. He couldn't take his eyes off her. Thambi was using some cotton to stem the blood flow.

The injured man started groaning loudly. 'Is she alive?' he asked, trying to get up. 'Where is she?'

'Right here, don't get up.'

'Let me talk to her, let me speak.'

~~Antony~~ Undony held him down. 'Sir, sir... you will break your bones.'

Thambi started weeping. 'She is going,' he said. 'She is going. I can't stop the bleeding. We need to hurry.'

The woman said something.

'She is feeling cold,' said Thambi. 'I can't do anything. Somebody please.'

He walked up to the partition and banged on it.

They reached a town and soon they reached a hospital. Hearing the siren, two nurses emerged. Kari parked as gently as he could. They flung the doors open.

'We need one more stretcher.'

It took a few minutes to wheel them both inside. It was a small hospital.

'We need names and some id,' said a nurse.

'We don't know anything,' said Valiban. 'It was a highway accident.' He shouted at Thambi. 'You are a patient. Who asked you to get down?' He turned to the nurse. 'Cancer patient. We are taking him to Dindigul.'

But the nurse would not let them leave. Valiban went up to Kari who by now was in the driver's seat. 'What do we do?'

A senior staff member emerged from the hospital. 'I need your names and addresses,' he said.

'Wait,' said Undony. 'I will do it.'

He held the superintendent by the arm and took him back into the building. He returned, went to the rear of the ambulance, and then back inside the building. He came out half an hour later.

'We can leave,' he said.

'How are the patients?' asked Thambi.

'The man is OK, the lady is critical.'

'And we are in trouble,' said Valiban.

Undony smiled. 'We are not.'

It seemed he had disarmed the nurses and the superintendent by donating his blood. He had insisted. Are you related to them, they asked him? He said, no, just check the blood group, quickly. The blood group matched with the critically injured lady. On the way out, he gave them the registration number of the truck and told them to handle the police when they came.

'The superintendent is a Gounder,' said Undony. 'I told him who we work for. I told him Thambi is Veerappan's nephew.'

The bloodstained ambulance reached Karur. Two party men received them, inspected the rear, asked the four to wait inside a room and then disappeared. They returned two hours later.

'We have sanitised it. You can leave.'

They handed them some money. 'Please call your seniors, quickly.'

They called a number. Perumal answered. 'Good job,' he said, 'you made the delivery, doesn't matter how. I will ensure you are safe from the traffic police. There will be no investigation.'

Nanban waited for them in Chennai and he welcomed them warmly on their return, shook each hand and left in each a cash reward. He heard them relate what had happened. He patted them on the shoulder. 'Drink?' They hesitated then said yes. They drank with him and soon they found the whole episode funny, I mean here they were driving a fraudulent ambulance on a national highway and guess who showed up? Patients.

'What did you learn from this episode?' asked Nanban, when it was time to leave.

Valiban looked at Kari who in turn looked at Undony and Thambi. 'A lot,' he said, 'but don't ask me exactly what.'

Nanban left them with a promise of more meaningful engagement and set off to meet Narsimhan at the bar.

'You look excited,' said Narsimhan. He sat in his corner with his measure of Old Monk.

'I am,' I said. 'There is a kootam in every other village now. We have feet on the ground; mostly dissatisfied people, data entry slaves, call centre sore throats, tired delivery boys, girls handling garbage, workers suffering in cracker factories and teenagers being exploited in matchbox units. And we have the unemployed. We have placed them in small outposts that have a table and some banners. Mostly they are out trying to help the locals, willing to take on anything and anybody. At periodic intervals, we synchronise events. Then the whole state comes to life and every street bears our name.'

The editor of *Dai Tamizha* swirled his drink, the ice clinked and the dark rum rose to the surface.

'When will something useful happen?'

'I cannot force the pace,' I said. 'I can set the stage and hook the audience to our narrative. We govern the narrative in Tamil Nadu; that is the key. Tell me, why does the rain use thunder and lightning? Do you know?'

'You tell me,' said Narsimhan.

'To get people hooked to the sound and light show. So when the rain arrives, the audience is ready to receive it as a blessing and a reason to rejoice.'

'You are using a rain metaphor?' said Narsimhan.

'Yes,' I said.

The bastard laughed. 'I have seen your thunder and lightning. What is your rain?'

'Melas and mass gatherings where we distribute largesse, where we speak to them about our common roots and our vision. Gounders now dream of a new city for themselves and a political party that is forceful, that has an agenda and the will to achieve it.'

'Sounds credible,' said Narsimhan. He was drinking steadily and that made him more agreeable, I thought. 'What if nothing happens?'

'Look at Indian history,' I said, 'at what has happened. Disorder and chaos, and then the moment of magic when everything fell in place. How many times has a random sequence of events produced an epiphany?'

My audience of one heard me without blinking.

'You are hanging the prospects of Veerappan on this slender thread?'

'Mr. Narsimhan, every significant happening in India is a low probability event,' I said. 'That is the beauty of it all. Life wins over mathematics.'

Narsimhan sniffed. 'Hope is so durable in north India,' he said. 'Out here, life is less sublime.'

I understood what he was up to. 'You are egging me on, aren't you?'

He would not look at me. 'From the beginning,' he said.

'Why?'

He spoke with feeling. 'This state has under-achieved. I cannot bear to see the polity we are left with, that drags us down to our feudal past. I am fed up with my fellow Tamils. They are birds, born in a cage, who think flying is an illness.'

I wanted his approval because he was an old hand and a seasoned observer. 'What do you think of my approach?'

He paused, searching for something pithy to say. 'You are suffering from a severe case of intuition,' he said.

DELHI

He kept away from the bar for a couple of days. Withdrawn, he sat at home, twitchy and restless. Past the twilight hour, doubts assailed him. His ideas seemed less brilliant.

Some traditional pickle arrived from Veerappan's village. 'Made by Veeran's mother,' said Veera's driver as he handed over an ochre ceramic jadi covered with a white cloth. Nanban handed it to his mother.

'You could have smiled at him,' she said. 'At least call Veerappan and thank him.'

Nanban grunted.

'What is biting you?'

His mother was impatient with his mood swings.

'Don't play ~~the~~ victim in my house,' she said. 'Better you play dead.'

She said this so loudly, he dropped whatever he was holding.

'Sorry?' said Nanban.

'Are you?'

'Don't speak in riddles, mother,' he said.

She threw up her hands. He went up to her but she turned away. They were in the veranda, it was evening and yet again clouds had gathered and given way to rain. The unseasonal showers had unearthed a fragrance, a sense of renewal after three turgid months. His mother was stroking Mayandi's neck, his ears, ruffling the hair on his back and finally holding his paws one at a time. The need to be loved was simply expressed. Mayandi gurgled and rolled over on his back with his eyes closed.

'Tell me,' said Nanban, 'what is bothering you?'

'You.'

Nanban waited. His mother counted up to three with her fingers.

'High blood pressure, diabetes and ulcers. Add to that sleeplessness and an eating disorder.'

'Eating disorder?'

'What was your weight in Mumbai?' she said. 'What is it now?'

'Must be your cooking,' he said. 'If you made the things I liked, I wouldn't have gone out so often.'

'And drinking?' she said. 'Every day at some dirty bar? Why? What are you doing sitting in Chennai? You think I am stupid?'

He could tell her why they were in Chennai. Right now, he was the trigger in a movement; soon, he would function as a catalyst in an uncontrolled experiment. When the time was nigh, he hoped to be a wondrous spectator watching the endgame play out. The personal cost was mounting but the pay-off would be thrilling.

'You think you are a good actor,' she said, 'but you cannot fool me.'

They moved to the kitchen. Insects entered through the open windows and slapped against the warm yellow ceiling light. He began chopping vegetables. She placed some pasta in boiling water.

'Why are you going to Delhi?'

He had a ready reply. His mother heard him and said nothing. She spiked the pasta with salt and chillies and when he coughed and sputtered at the dining table, she smiled. The next afternoon he left for Delhi. He tried to sneak out of the house but his mother was up, siesta over, waiting. She made him some coffee and sat with him as he sipped it. Yesterday was forgotten, or so it seemed.

'You can plant a kiss on my cheek,' she said, 'like you care.' He hugged her. 'Say the local word now.' He smiled. 'Poyito-varein,' he said. I will return. 'Poyitovaa,' she replied, delighted that it sounded right.

He revelled in his mother's simple confrontations. She understood so much more than she let on. She could not exorcise his inner demons but she could goad him into confronting them now and then. He was afraid and she knew it. He would never admit it. In the game of unequal forces, what drew him in was not just the thrill but fear. He dreamt often of being in a small boat with a paddle facing a dark swell the size of a mountain.

Delhi was hot and dusty, the roads well-lit, the gardens well-maintained. The ride to Connaught Place was in an Ambassador car, a government vehicle that had a red light on top. As they reached a small nondescript building, the power supply went on the blink. The driver used his cell phone torch to guide Nanban to a side entrance where they frisked him. They switched off his cell phones and let him through.

CENTRAL INTELLIGENCE BUREAU,
NEW DELHI
(Read and Delete)
MEMO
Author: Raghavan
Operative: Nanban

We met in complete darkness in our Connaught Place office. There was a power cut and I saw him open the door, peep in and wave. He walked up to my table and extended his hand. The grip was firm and dry. He swivelled, stumbled and fell into the visitor's chair. 'Just the two of us?' he asked, turning this way and that. And our shadows, I said. I asked him if he had brought his cell phones with him. I took possession of them.

'I hate Delhi,' he said.

We sat for a while waiting for the power to come back. He began speaking.

'The state is on the boil,' he said.

'Tamil Nadu is simmering,' I said. 'You have to escalate matters. We don't have much time.'

He smarted at my tone and I realised I had been too abrupt. However, with outside agents like Nanban it was better to be cut and dried. Asking him a simple question like 'How are you?' was a risk.

'The tentative election schedule is out,' I said. 'We need to work backwards.'

He sat hunched. It is worth recounting the first time he came to this office. He was under a cloud in Mumbai at the time, in considerable distress. Yet, when he walked in, he looked me in the eye and said, 'An ordinary man in an ordinary office.' I was taken aback but I did not respond. 'You are a proud man,' he told me. 'Are you happy that all your achievements will remain anonymous?'

I kept quiet.

'Do you have a separate department for small talk?' he asked.

He was uncomfortable, sitting, waiting for me to take the lead. I did nothing. 'Mr. Secret Agent,' he said, finally. 'Strong. Silent. Just like I guessed you would be.'

After a few minutes, he spoke again. 'Are we waiting for someone?'

I said, 'No.'

Then he leaned across the table and rolled up his shirtsleeves. 'I am in your hands,' he said. 'I am in the kind of trouble that drove me to this.' He showed me his wrists that bore ugly stitch marks.

I made him an offer then. He heard me out and he accepted it. Just like that. Later, he asked a question that was nagging him. 'Sir, what exactly do you do in this department?' he said.

'What do we do? We write history,' I said. I realised I shouldn't have said that.

'What a fucked-up job you have done so far,' he said.

Our department has kept its side of the bargain since. Nanban has received no summons and no show-cause notices in the last three years. His Economic Offences case is in cold storage. Now he is back to see me for the second time, for a review.

The power supply returned and the lights came on.

'How are you?' I asked, despite myself.

'If you were my analyst I would have told you how I really am,' he said.

He has added weight and his skin looks splotchy. There are circles under his eyes. Thankfully, he is under medical supervision.

'I am being polite,' I said.

'Yes, of course.'

He was distracted and itching to get away. He handed me a two-page note, which I have read since. It is a unique read of the political situation in Tamil Nadu. He has spelt out what he has done to revive the fortunes of the Gounder political party.

'What are you planning to do now?' I asked.

He gave me a breathless plan that was open-ended. He was anxious. He need not have worried. He has no idea of the social interventions we do, which are as open-ended, because large-scale change cannot be otherwise. We can at best provide direction and momentum. The kootam structure has been beautifully set up. The situation is a tinderbox and Nanban is driving these youngsters to the very edge. Things can get ugly very soon. I support his firm belief that from this aggression and chaos, an enabling incident can be triggered.

Nanban has the potential to be one of our most successful operatives. He is a provocateur par excellence, a change agent with an uncanny sensibility. He is a natural. I have no doubts he will produce results.

I recommend we extend his protection.

III

NANBAN

I met Raman at Chinna Tasmac. He had lofty notions and he ran a small-scale unit. 'Two things I cannot do at home,' he said. 'Eat eggs and drink whisky.' Three evenings a week, he tanked up at Thangabalu's establishment, other days he knocked it back at the T Nagar Social Club, a friendly dive where they served cut fruit with hard liquor. Raman was gregarious, intelligent and a little woolly-headed. He would down two large pegs quickly, knock his temples with his knuckles, mutter a prayer and then talk a lot. A Brahmin, he bore the marks of temple and prayer on his forehead and that, juxtaposed with his drinking in this lowly bar, was delightful.

'I have a fatal flaw,' he told me. 'That is why I drink.'

I thought he must have some medical issue.

'I went for a medical check-up,' he said. 'I spent half a day on a treadmill wearing probes. They gave me a sheaf of printouts. Two results in the periphery, the rest were in range.'

'So what is this fatal flaw?'

'It won't show up in medical reports,' he said.

'Are you depressed?'

He nodded. He spread his hands wide, enveloping Thangabalu's bar. 'What am I doing here?' he said.

'We don't come here for tourism,' I said.

'A thing of beauty,' he said.

'This place?'

He smiled. 'When did we last produce one?

'I happen to know a little bit about art,' I said. 'Contemporary art, mind you.'

'Hah,' he said. 'It does not measure up. It does not deserve to be in the same room as, say, a Chola bronze. No art gallery of yours can compete with our ancient temples and monuments.'

A humid cloud settled around us. I asked for a pedestal fan. Raman knocked his fist on the bar table.

'My work has no aesthetic, babu,' he said. 'I have a mechanised unit that produces identical items. I sit in my glass cabin in the factory and watch it make widgets. So much activity that does nothing for my pride.'

'Swallow your pride, Raman,' I said. 'You are a small businessman.'

'I am having hallucinations,' he said. 'I have difficulty sleeping. I went to a psychiatrist, a friend, for some advice. He told me I was restless.'

'Did he charge you for that?'

He snickered. 'Well-settled people get restless in middle age. It is an ordinary syndrome.'

'Raman,' I said. 'You are not ordinary.'

He laughed, genuinely happy at my quip. 'You are my friend,' he said. 'The only one who really understands me.'

His friend asked him to travel, which he did, visiting exotic locales, watching seasons change, something that never happened in Chennai. The unease persisted.

'When I got tired of natural wonders, I travelled to all the manmade marvels, engineering feats, great architecture, historical cities. I was happy for a while.'

'How is your business doing?' I asked.

'My customers love me,' he said, smiling again. 'I make the perfect product. Every unit we produce, we lose money.'

Aha!

'I employed consultants to help me out. They told me perfect products are unaffordable. Software crashes often, they said. Even spacecraft crash sometimes. Learn, they said, from NASA and Microsoft. They allow failure, you know why.'

'Because nobody can afford perfection?'

'Exactly,' he said. 'But I did not listen. I find perfection irresistible.'

He went through another peg and finished what was left of a whole packet of peanuts.

'I was moved to make something more challenging than moulded plastic. I set up a second unit in the spare land that I had, and this was new technology and a daring product.'

'And?'

'Again a commercial failure. The product found very few buyers. It was too expensive.' He looked gloomy. 'I had borrowed money to fund this project and I ended up defaulting. The bank has invoked my personal guarantee and they have threatened to come for my house.'

It was time to get away. I tut-tutted, asked for the bill, patted him on the shoulder and quickly left.

Something about Raman was strangely appealing. I felt I should help him because he was in some ways a kindred soul. Without his knowing, I organised a cash loan for him, enough to repay most of the loan. It seems he repaid a few instalments and then stopped.

A couple of years elapsed and we lost touch. Then I heard he was in trouble again. This time I was asked to meet him. I dropped in at the bar when he would be around. We met again, like old acquaintances. After some pleasantries and two large pegs, déjà vu. Raman was back to unloading on me. I noticed changes. He had grown a beard and he was completely out of sorts.

'I owe money to people,' he began, sounding like he had committed a crime. 'I am overdue, babu. The lenders have been hounding me. I have to look over my shoulder, like this.' He looked. 'They come at night and tell me they will teach me a lesson.'

'I see.'

'What can they teach me?' he said. 'Bloody illiterates. Scum they are, sitting on illegal cash.'

'Is it a large sum?' I asked.

'For me, it is a large amount,' he said. 'But the real problem is that the money came from a politician. I did not know. How was I to know? This is terrible. Politicians are ruthless people, I am told. Is it true?' He looked at me.

'I have no idea,' I said.

'I asked the Sindhi financier, the one who comes here,' he said. 'He knew everything. He said in the cash market default news travels quickly. He told me I was in big trouble.'

He leaned closer and dropped his voice. 'It seems last month, a businessman who could not repay political money checked into a hotel with his wife and they both drank rat poison.'

'What?' I said. 'Seriously?'

He nodded. He was distinctly nervous.

'They sent some boys after me,' he said. 'Ruffians. They told me, "You are a Brahmin, which is why boss lent you money. He thinks Brahmins are honest and will not cheat." I asked them about their boss. Who was he? They did not reply. They gave me some rat poison in a bottle. They told me I had a week's time to get my effects in order. I fled the city. For three days, I stayed in lodges that rented by the hour. I could not sleep. They threatened my family and I had to return. Within hours, they were back. They rang my bell, stood there and said "Four more days".'

I allowed him to stew a little. 'What happened to the money, Raman?' I asked softly.

He was high and a little careless.

'I made a big mistake,' he said. 'I squandered some of the money. I feel ashamed to tell you, but I spent half of it on a Chola bronze.'

'I see.' I needed a strong drink. I had helped a true dodo borrow money from my politician friend.

'It was cruel fate,' said Raman. 'Someone in the family had some antiques, remarkable pieces. They needed money for a wedding and for expanding their house.

They had no choice. By chance, I glanced at what they were selling. I saw this Chola bronze piece and I fell in love. There were two seated figures and one small standing figure on a single pedestal. It was Somaskanda, a representation of Shiva with Uma and Skanda. I had seen an image of the one in the Metropolitan Museum. This was as good. It blew me away. In a flash, I knew this wasn't a coincidence. Such things happened for a reason.'

He was looking up at the ceiling beyond which was heaven where the gods had mulled over his destiny.

'It so happened I had the money with me, that too hard currency.'

'So now you have a Chola bronze and some overdue debt,' I said. 'Was it worth it?'

'I kept it with me for one glorious month and you cannot believe the joy it gave me to wake up every day and see it in my possession. I had seen great bronzes in the Madras Museum and this was as good as any there. That bronze carved the space around it.'

'And then?'

He knocked his temples with his fists, asking forgiveness for a grievous sin. 'I sold it in the informal market. I had to. It was horrifying that I had to sell it and that too to an ignoramus who asked me who is Uma and who is Skanda? I got a fraction of what I paid.'

This was now turning out to be a horror story.

'So now you have only the debt? To whom did you sell it? Someone in Chennai I hope. We should not allow Pallava heritage out of the state.'

He wouldn't tell me anything more. In fact, he suddenly became tight-lipped about the matter.

'Why the beard, Raman?' I asked him, a little lightly. He looked even gloomier.

'I surrendered to the police after foisting a case on myself. The stupid bank wouldn't put me in prison so I became a self-accused cheat and that bought me a year. I spent a year in Central Jail, away from that politician. It was a terrible price to pay. I faced abuse – by men, by the poor conditions, poor hygiene; what kept me going was my family. They did not give up on me and came visiting. When they released me, I asked that they release me at night. They refused. It happened in broad daylight and I was terrified. I have grown a beard and worn clothes that are now loose-fitting.' He looked into his glass tumbler. 'It is a poor disguise,' he said.

He thought he was safe in that bar not knowing that Veerappan was the lender and he was nearby, watching the proceedings. Veerappan had a look at that moment that I did not like.

I had some information but more was needed and, unfortunately, the only way it could be obtained quickly was by really scaring Raman. There would have to be some violence or the very real threat of it. I was personally responsible for this disaster and I had to make amends. I had to recover that bronze. I knew more than most about the purity of form and timelessness of the

Chola bronze sculpture. According to an expert, this example was truly stunning. I planned to acquire it and pay the amount due to Veerappan myself.

I had to keep Veerappan informed. I asked him to give me a couple of days. 'Let me meet Raman once again,' I said.

THE SIXTH CUT

Valiban entered Veerappan's house, crossing the threshold with his right leg – an old habit. He left his footwear at the gate and it seemed from his gait that he was walking on coals. The house had a veranda that faced south and it had a few scattered cane chairs and one security camera. He stood next to a chair and looked into the camera. Veerappan entered the veranda, dusted a chair with his thundu and sank into it.

'Thimiru,' he said, loudly.

'Sir?' said Valiban.

'The Thimiru Kootam,' said Veerappan. 'I hear your leader Kari is a thimiru pudichavan?'

'Sir,' said Valiban, 'we will do anything for you.'

Why had the big boss called him? Initially, he had thought he should inform Nanban. He realised in time it would have been his last mistake.

'Will you do anything for Nanban?' said Veerappan.

'No, sir,' said Valiban, without hesitation. Now there was no going back.

'Good,' said Veerappan. 'Listen carefully, I will not repeat myself. Perumal will give you instructions about a man called Raman. He comes to the bar; you must have seen him. Perumal will call you from time to time. Do not call me. You hear?'

'Yes, sir.'

Veerappan rose from his chair, stood like a feudal lord. Valiban bowed before him as he had seen people do. He could hardly contain his excitement.

'I have given your mother some money,' said the new boss.

'Sir, there was no need,' said Valiban.

He got the stare. He mumbled a hurried thanks and left, walking backwards until Veerappan disappeared. At the gate, the two watchmen looked at him with contempt. He raised himself to his medium height and stared back insolently. 'Dai security,' he said. 'Mind it.'

The Thimiru Kootam annals started with a kidnapping. The man the kootam hijacked from his car was Raman, the small-scale industrialist who had a unit in Ambattur that made moulded plastic items. He had a wife and two high school-going children, a fact that he kept spluttering to them repeatedly. He was balding and he had a small belly. He was wearing what he wore every day, a white shirt, grey pants and brown shoes. He also wore a leather belt that they used to tie his hands behind him as they had seen in films. His socks went into his mouth. After a while, he puked and they removed them. He was a normal coward and the moment they took him out of the car that they had parked in an enclosed garage, he looked around wildly. He needed to see something familiar and unfortunately, he saw Kari with his scattered locks and half-mast veshti, standing with the light behind him, holding an aruvaal. It was laughably filmy, but Raman did not see such films. He took it to heart. He started pleading. In a couple of minutes, they knew what he had of any value and it was all theirs as long as he escaped in one piece. The sound of his pleading resembled an animal whine. It set the jumpy kootam on edge.

'Stop it or I will cut your tongue,' said Kari.

The whining continued at a lower key. 'Someone kill him,' said Kari. Raman tried to reason with them after an hour had passed. The gang was sitting on nails, waiting for a phone call.

'Harming me is not in your best interest,' said Raman.

'Why?' said Kari.

'Sir,' said Raman. 'My first cousin is an IG Police. He will surely come after you.'

Nobody responded. 'It is not too late,' said Raman.

An hour later, the waiting got to him again and he had been imagining a lot by then. He tried to tell them that nobody he knew would want to harm him. He had no enemies so this must be a random occurrence and looking at them he felt they were doing this on their own and he understood they needed money because where were the jobs? So he would give them money and damn it some advice as well as long as they all sat in a civil atmosphere without that aruvaal and preferably without his being alone and tied.

'How do you want to die?' asked Kari.

Raman lost it for a while and the gang cringed at his breakdown. He looked like what he was, an ordinary man who had never harmed and yet had come into this nightmare. He needed a way out and he had to think a way out of this. Suddenly, what he had was not very valuable, not enough perhaps. He made loud promises. There were people he could contact, those with wealth, related to him. They stuffed his mouth again, this time using a rag from his car. He made some strange sounds and his eyes bulged. Undony laughed for some reason. He had come to life like never before. The sight of a Brahmin at his mercy seemed to tickle him. He made faces at Raman, who was turning blue by now. Thambi looked concerned and moved towards Raman, wanting to take the rag out, just in case. Kari said no, with a slight shake of his head. The waiting was getting to him as well. He kept looking at his phone. Was this a mistake? This man did not seem worth kidnapping. What was the motive? It could not be money. Then?

Raman was a pitiable Brahmin by now, his shirt was splotchy with sweat and his poonal thread showed through. His clothes were plain, his protestations were above average. He was by now a cornered rat, a man climbing the gallows. He twisted around, shook his legs violently and kicked a tyre hard. His arms were bleeding and, while his face had recovered some colour, some fluid was leaking from the sides of his mouth. He made muffled sounds; he started coughing and choking. Thambi could not handle it. He pulled out the rag. Raman gasped, retched a couple of times and tried to speak. Only sobs emerged. He took in gulps of air, looking around, then at each of them. They stared at him wordlessly. He was a fish out of water. They could have done anything to him.

They killed him.

He had it coming. He did not want harm but there were ways of saying it that were humane. Squealing like a pig tied by the legs was not the way. Flapping like a hen, when its body was held in one hand and its neck in the other, was not the way. Goats and sheep went quietly. It was eerie to watch them at an army slaughterhouse, grazing uselessly at the abattoir's door. Why graze with your head in the grass when a door away your kin were lying, bleeding, and you were next? Valiban cringed. He wasn't a vegetarian, he had seen death, washed his father's body when he died. The process had taken ten minutes, each minute an eternity. His father lay naked, demeaned, thankfully dead, but surely he must have gone with the knowledge that one day his strange son would bathe him. The scriptures prescribed it – to bathe, dry and clothe the dead body, but why have the son do it? He shook his head free of such thoughts.

Raman was demented by now. His veins stood out near his temples and those in his forearms were like pylons coursing with electricity. He had not lived fully. The will to live was inside him, and it fought its way out. The foursome looked at each other, surprised at the lengths this man was going to save himself from perceived demise. They were not even threatening him seriously.

Six hours in that oppressive garage, dark, humid, the temperature climbing – some of them were having doubts and Raman was hallucinating. He was close to death and every minute that elapsed was driving him insane. He looked so disturbed Valiban expected him to burst a vein. He untied his hands.

'Speak,' said Kari, finally. 'Tell us.'

'Krishnaveni,' said Raman, uttering the first thing that came to his mind, perhaps his wife's name. It had to be; it was a Brahmin-wife kind of name. 'Krishnaveni,' said Raman again, a little louder, looking around, hoping to see her.

'Not Seethai? What about Sivagami?' asked Kari, leering at him and they all laughed. 'Do you know any Sivagami?'

Despite threats, Raman refused to say anything else.

'Where is the idol?' asked Kari, suddenly.

Raman sat bolt upright and his eyes widened. He finally understood. 'What idol?' he said.

Kari walked up to him, leaned down and looked into his eyes. 'Where is that Chola bronze statue that you paid so much money for?'

The evening made sense at last to the others.

'Will you let me go if I tell you?'

Kari shrugged. Raman confessed. He gave a name and a location. He had sold the beautiful precious idol for a fraction of what he had paid for it, he said. After sobbing for a while, he looked up.

'Can I have a glass of water? Please?'

Kari nodded and Undony filled a steel glass with some water from the tap and brought it to him. He stood in front of Raman, deliberately sipped from the the glass himself and then held it out to him.

'Here, drink it.'

Raman watched this small performance. He shook his head. 'It is okay,' he said.

'Take it,' said Undony again, thrusting the glass now into Raman's hands.

'No, no,' said Raman. 'I am not thirsty.'

'You are dying of thirst,' said Undony, stuffing the glass into Raman's face.

Raman struggled and turned his face away. 'I will not drink it,' he shouted.

'Why?" said Undony, his voice rising. 'Because I have touched it?'

'Obviously,' said Raman with a snicker.

Undony tried to pour the water into Raman's mouth. Raman flailed and his hand hit the tumbler. It flew away and fell with a loud clatter. Undony laughed. 'I knew, I knew,' he said. 'You bloody Brahmin.'

Someone switched on the car's headlights. Raman held up his hand to shield his eyes. His shadow loomed on the wall and as he started struggling, it exaggerated his movements. He started shouting at them. He cursed the small man first, the boy Undony. He cursed him using simple curses like madaiyan and muttaal. Next, Raman went after Thambi, the weak link. He appealed to his good sense, his good nature, to his good upbringing. Thambi asked him to shut up, more than once, but he wouldn't listen and he went on like a stuck record praising Thambi until he could take it no more; Thambi shut his ears and started shouting back.

Valiban stood and watched, not intervening yet, and Kari looked at him and raised an eyebrow. A mishap was taking shape and the two began to sense it. Raman leapt free. Undony held him down. Raman threw him away. Undony fell. 'Antony!' shouted Kari. Undony wasn't listening. He shot up and seized Raman's hand and then slapped him a few times, each slap sounded louder. Ugly welts formed. Undony stood over the cowering Raman, his exaggerated shadow towered over him. Raman was on his knees, pleading. Undony got hold of the aruvaal and swished the air with it. Raman should have stayed down. Kari should have intervened. Valiban stood rooted, caught in this unfolding nightmare. Raman rose and hit Undony. He surprised himself. He looked at his hand and smiled. Even as he raised his hand again, the aruvaal cut his throat, his blood sprang free and drenched Valiban's shirt, and as he fell, Valiban screamed and Kari extended his hand. He had finally stepped up, trying to get hold of Undony. 'Aaaaahhh!' Thambi said as if it was he they had killed. 'Wotha,' breathed Undony; 'Chuthmarika,' shouted Kari and in all this, Raman merely looked surprised. He fell like a tree log and it sounded ugly. He lay there awkward and careless with his legs splayed impossibly; his blood gushed, a line beneath the car and then a thick puddle. Undony's face froze in a leer.

'Bloody Brahmin hit me,' he said.

A sob escaped Valiban and Kari stood staring at him, surprised that something had finally moved him. He asked him to pick up his phone that lay on the cement floor near the stool. 'Call somebody,' he said. Who? Valiban ran out of the garage and gulped air till his head cleared. When he returned to the garage, nobody had moved an inch.

The four stood around and stared disbelievingly. They had killed a man. It was chilling, the realisation that they were a party to this mishap. Each looked at the other. What were they to do now?

It was raining hard; there was thunder and lightning. They opened the garage doors and a window and let the cool air in. Water seeped in from a gutter and took out some red and some grease. They watched for a while, stunned. The spirit of Raman was still around. Thambi was convinced it was hovering in his periphery – he was the one who had stepped up and caught Raman as he fell. He saw him die. They were looking at each other and Raman tried to tell him something. His hands were clutching at his throat because he couldn't breathe. He made some choking sounds, a guttural cry for help emerged, some bubbles formed. He was drowning in red foam. Thambi was horrified and helpless. A long guttural rasp and then Raman went limp, his eyes still open. Thambi sank by his side and tried to pump his chest; he slapped his cheeks. Undony had turned his back on them and he was looking into the distance. Kari kept looking at him without expression, trying to divine something. 'Dai koodi,' he said, finally. 'Bloody useless fool. You stupid ass. Why?' Undony shrugged his shoulders. He had no answer. The bluster was gone and the mindless jabber had died. There was a hollow feeling, a mixture of fear and horror.

'Minor, don't just stand around,' said Kari. 'Think da. What is the way out?'

Valiban moaned. The sound surprised everybody. 'We are in big trouble,' he shouted.

'We have to call people,' said Kari. He looked towards Valiban. 'Can you? Please?'

Months later Narsimhan recorded this incident in his private diary. 'This incident triggered others,' he wrote, 'and together they changed the course of Gounder history. The courses of movements and revolutions are like the paths that rivers take. Mighty rivers owe their origins to a momentary drop in air pressure and a small change in wind direction. This was the day in the month of Aadi that Kongu Nadu was born.'

Valiban called Veerappan but he did not answer. Just as well. He had dialled the wrong number. He called Perumal. 'Pick up, pick up.' Perumal did and he said 'Yes?' 'Sir, hello, sorry sir,' said Valiban, incoherent. Perumal peered at the name of the caller. 'Sorry?' Valiban said 'Sorry.' 'For what?' 'Goinda sir, goinda. We are in trouble.' 'Calm down,' said Perumal. He held the phone to his ear while he got off the bed and washed his face. Valiban was sputtering the details. 'Everything was going fine. We were in control, but that Undony, he is really mad.'

'Calm down,' said Perumal.

'Sir, what should we do? If the police come…' Valiban was panicking.

'Stay where you are; whatever happens, do not run away,' said Perumal.

He called Nanban. Bad news was best shared, quickly. Nanban was livid. What had Veerappan engineered without his knowing? The phones kept ringing, calls were on hold.

Veerappan called Valiban. 'Perumal spoke to you? Do what he says.'

'Stay for how long, sir?' said Valiban. 'I don't want to be found here.'

'Perumal will give you instructions,' said Veerappan. 'Just wait.'

Nanban's number kept flashing on Veera's screen. Three missed calls. Nanban was fuming and he sounded like he wanted to kill somebody.

'Veerappan Gounder, if you think you can go behind my back…'

'I did not order the killing,' said Veerappan, trying to stem the anger.

'What? Then who did?' said Nanban.

'You are sitting at home and asking me questions?' said Veera. 'Who are you to question me?'

Both men were on the verge of saying something irascible. Veera spoke first, his voice had changed. 'Wait for me,' he said. It was an order.

A few minutes later, his Scorpio pulled up outside Nanban's building. A jeep that followed stopped right behind it and two burly men alighted. Veera entered Nanban's house, the two men stood at the door.

'You started this,' said Veera as he entered.

'Sit down,' said Nanban.

He sat next to Nanban. Both barely held their tongue.

'Did you or did you not have Raman kidnapped?' said Nanban.

'We held him for questioning,' said Veera. 'He overreacted.' He poked Nanban's chest with his finger. 'And then your kootam took over. Your kootam.'

'They followed your orders, Veera.'

'You should have trained them better. Damn it, you should have chosen better people. It is your fault, now you handle this mess.'

Nanban got up and stepped away. 'I will not.'

They stared at each other for the longest time. 'Fine,' said Veera. 'We will do it my way then. From now on, you will not speak to anyone about this or ask me anything. Is that clear?'

Nanban shrugged.

'Meet me later tonight,' said Veera and he left in a hurry.

He called Kari from his car. Kari was relieved to hear from Veera. 'Here is what you have to do,' Veera told Kari. 'Before the night is over, you understand?'

Kari demurred.

'This is how it has to be handled,' shouted Veera. 'There is only one way.'

Kari refused to listen. 'I am not responsible,' he said. 'I cannot do what you are asking me to.'

Veera's blood boiled. But there was no time for threats. 'Give the bloody phone to Valiban,' he said.

'He wants to speak to you,' said Kari, thrusting the phone into Valiban's hands.

'Sir,' said Valiban, suddenly alert. The fact that the leader was turning to him sent a rush of blood to his head. His fear and his diffidence disappeared.

'Are you willing to do something I ask you to?' said Veera.

'Sir,' said Valiban, 'I will do anything.'

'Good,' said Veera. 'I knew I could count on you. Perumal will call you.'

'I will call him, sir,' said Valiban.

Two cleaners who worked in a hospital morgue arrived at the garage. They wore white clothes and a plastic coat. They ignored the boys. The gory nature of the setting had no effect on them whatsoever. Wordlessly, they set about sanitising the place.

Perumal called Valiban. 'Did Raman speak about a bronze?'

'Yes,' said Valiban. 'I know the location.'

He gave him the location and the name of the man in Delhi.

'Sir,' he said. 'Two men are cleaning the place. But the body is a problem. It is stiffening and it is smelling. There are flies all over the place. There are rats.'

'The body is a problem,' said Perumal. 'Where is Antony?'

'He has disappeared. But I know where he has gone.'

'Antony is also a problem,' said Perumal.

'I understand,' said Valiban. 'Don't worry.'

Nanban arrived at Veera's place looking out of sorts, driven perhaps by guilt. He had decided that he would help Veera get hold of the bronze. He had spoken to Kari, the trained burglar, and asked him to show up at the airport at 5.00 am. They would leave on the first flight to Delhi. They would get the bronze. When Nanban spelt out his plan to Veera, the latter's anger subsided. He held Nanban's hands with his own. 'At times like these I know my true friends,' he said.

'That's all that I will do for you,' Nanban told him. 'This kidnapping and killing is not what I ever want to get involved in. I hope you understand.'

'Just get the bronze and hide it,' said Veera. 'The money is less important.'

Perumal called Valiban later that night.

'The place has been cleaned, sir. The body has been wrapped in gunny and plastic,' said Valiban. 'Sir, I plan to use it.'

'Use the body? For what? Hello, are you okay? Is something wrong?' Perumal asked.

The boy paused for a moment. 'Nothing is right or wrong, sir. I am just doing my job,' he said.

THE SEVENTH CUT

There is no stock footage in the city of what happens in the dark. There are night crawlers aplenty. Petty crime thrives, addicts search for dealers, mobs move their material and garbage sifters hunt through the day's debris.

Early the next morning, something happened. Without preface. While it was still dark.

Undony was in a 'kallu arrack' haze. He stepped out, and, in a moment etched in his private archive, he took a piece of chalk and sketched on the pavement. The finished work was eight feet by six. From two storeys high, it looked like a vision. For walkers who would arrive in the next two hours, it would be erasure.

Undony left his kolam sketch, stumbled to a wall and stood, leaning against it. He focused on getting his wits together. He knew that if he survived this night, he would live. A man wearing a tracksuit with a hood arrived and held out his hand. Undony sobbed. The man gripped him firmly. They left.

They tied him and dragged him, along with a deadweight. It was a tar road. Undony was certain it was tar because it felt soft and uneven and it leaned to a side. He had been blindfolded and his hands were wrapped around something really heavy, his wrists were tied together and a gunny sack had been pulled over his head and torso. He knew it was gunny because the rough texture was jute and it was moving along his cheeks; under his nose, he could smell it. He lost balance as they leant to the left suddenly; the deadweight almost pulled him down. Righting took some effort. He was on his feet but he could barely walk; his feet were not tied but they were cramped in the gunny sacking. He stumbled and he fell, again and again, but he was being pulled along. He scraped his toes and ankles badly and he could feel his blood ooze. What was he hugging? The question was at the back of his head and it hurt.

All around him, no one paid any attention to his murmurs. There was a tea kadai that had three stools and two dogs. The stall owner averted his eyes. The murmuring sound from the gunny bag would disturb him for a day or two.

There was dark loam in the Adyar Estuary. It was a broad estuary helmed by a bridge, and the black swollen flow that came up to the bridge took the smallest of pauses as it confronted the mighty Bay of Bengal. From the bridge, the bay looked vast and everyone paused. Every one who confronted the ocean stood and stared at the water. The smell could kill those who had a clear nose. Undony did not. The back of his neck was hurting, burnt by the friction, and his insides felt rotten. He felt himself falling. He heard a loud splat and he felt a smack. The black sludge of Adyar entered his throat. Undony gurgled but no bubbles formed. His brain screamed. A pedestrian heard the loud splash and turned to see two men walk away without turning back.

Nanban learnt about Antony as he was leaving for the airport. He was scared like he had never been. Things were out of his control, for one night the gang's activities were outside his remit. He called Veera as he was checking in for the Delhi flight. Veera sounded fresh and alert.

'You have shown your true colours, my friend,' said Nanban.

'Sorry?' said Veera.

'Till now I thought you were different from other politicians,' said Nanban.

Veera looked out of the window where his people were gathering, waiting to meet him. 'I have disappointed you?'

'No,' said Nanban. 'You have not. I should have known better.'

'Are you on your way to the airport?' Veera asked. He arose and went out of the door. His party men raised a cheer, drumbeats sounded and crackers went off; the noise was deafening. Veera loved pre-poll rallies, the adrenaline and the unreasonable optimism.

'I never thought you would do what you did,' said Nanban, shouting above the din.

'Hah! I wish you were here right now – see me as I stand before my people. We are warriors. We are Kshatriyas again.'

Veera was on a high as he accepted flowers, garlands, gifts and greetings from people who had travelled to Chennai from the length and breadth of the state. He held the cell phone away from his ear, towards his people, their loud slogans and their cheers.

He placed his cell phone back against his ear. 'You still there? Did you hear our party people?'

'I did,' said Nanban. 'I am happy for you.'

'Listen, my friend,' said Veera. 'Listen to this coincidence. My name is Veerappan. Your name is

Nanban. This happens for a reason. Let us forget everything else.'

'How can I forget all that has happened?' said Nanban.

'You can,' said Veera. 'You have taught me how to forget. There is not much that I can teach you Nanban. My father had a small homily that helped us samalchify. He said – cut your quarrels first, it is better than counting your losses later.'

THE EIGHTH CUT

Inspector Murthy's plate was full of local savouries. The arrival of a Delhi cop, a Punjabi called Khurana, was a welcome change.

Inspector Khurana arrived in Chennai like the Siberian crane; he took the short route to Kotturpuram, alighted at the brick-red police station, a few short steps and he grabbed the chair opposite Inspector Murthy. 'Saar,' he said. Murthy blinked. Delhi Police in his modest constabulary? 'To what do I owe this honour?' Khurana asked for coffee and while they waited, he placed his cap on the table, ran his fingers through his hair and looked around. 'Promotion?' Murthy nodded. It was hard moving up the hierarchy when all that came his way was a petty crime. There were times he wished the low life he chased had more ambition. A gang like Kari's provided some respite. They were worthy adversaries.

Khurana turned out to be a soulmate and this discovery delighted them both. The two shared contempt for their superiors, their colleagues and the rascals that kept them busy. Khurana brought with him a gem of a case, one he called 'The Case of the Gourmet Thief'. He said that this thief and his accomplice/s could be from Chennai, in fact, he was sure they were. Murthy tried to tell him that, in retail terms, the Chennai thief was a petty shopkeeper who sat in his small pottu kadai, just like the kiraana vyapaaris up North. Khurana waved away the suggestion. Over the next couple of hours, he related his story.

It seems the owners of a mansion in Sunder Nagar, a posh Delhi colony that houses the arriviste, were on a long vacation and the help had left for their annual visit to their hometowns. Nobody was inside the house. The two household canines were in their kennel, drugged. The watchman was with them in a similar state. The burglars, who had raided their house and its kitchen, had stayed the night, behaving for all purposes like cultured guests. They prepared a meal, ate it with finesse, saw a film, tidied up and smoked cigars in the veranda while consuming half a bottle of Amarone, a dark and dusky red wine from Italy. The other half was sealed and placed in the chiller. Seemingly, they took away nothing.

At 6.00 am that Monday morning the alarms went off in the house and in the Sunder Nagar police outpost. The clanging siren woke up the cretins in the neighbourhood. They added to the clamour. The household canines were fighting sleep, the watchman was dreaming of life as an alias. The first posse arrived at 6.15 am; they came in a jeep with a swirling red light and a blaring horn, alerting all the petty thieves in the vicinity. This was the night shift, the weary brigade.

They trampled the lawn and the flowerbed and rang the bell. Wet earth clung to their shoes and formed clumps behind them. Nobody answered the bell. They looked around. The grounds were clean and empty and there were no signs of a break-in.

'False alarm,' they squawked into the black police radio.

They leaned on the front door and it opened.

'Oh teri!' said one.

They walked into the house, unhindered, when it struck them. Why wasn't the front door locked? At the rear, the kitchen door was open.

'Could be a break-in,' they squawked into the wireless.

Inside the house, everything was in its place. There were no signs of a search or struggle. No strewn objects, no broken glass.

'Nothing missing, sir,' they said into their radio.

'Your fathers are missing,' shouted Inspector Khurana as he wore his shoes then washed his face at the police station.

There was liquor on the sideboard – a bottle of Blue Label, its seal intact. A wine chiller hummed in a corner; many bottles lay inside, untouched, save one that was half full.

Both constables were nervous by now. They were used to crude crime scenes with broken doors, shattered windows and pillaged almirahs. This puzzle confounded them.

The bedrooms were locked. They broke in and looked around. Flat TV, DVD player, Bose speakers, some jewellery, some cash, some foreign currency, expensive bags and some art. Neat and tidy. The bosses kept calling them and they had no answers. They examined the burglar alarm console.

'Sir, some people came in.'

'Came in? Did they take anything?'

'No, sir. But they stayed the night, eating, drinking, and smoking like it was their house.'

'And the alarms? Why did they go off?'

'Sir, the same people set them off before leaving.'

'So you could arrive there and look like fools?'

Rummaging a crime scene was Inspector Khurana's speciality. It featured high on his list of things he liked to do – a notch below Black Label, a step above sex. This scene should have taken him to the nearby basti behind a sniffing Dobermann that would have threatened a migrant from the heartland. The fellow would have cowered and revealed the whereabouts of his no-good son and his friends who had decamped to Manesar with the loot to impress their girlfriends. But no. The Dobermann lost his scent in the dining room itself, where he stood like a rock, his tongue askew.

The dining room had a ten-seater table with high-backed chairs. The chair at the head of the table had a deep depression indicating the weight of the person who used it and the time spent there every day. A chandelier hung over the table like an omen, with gargoyles baring their teeth amidst slinky light bulbs. A service table with wheels was at the side; it had a medicine box with pills in compartments.

Subordinates came up to Khurana every now and then and their litany added to his woes. What the chhod was this? Could this be a bunch of rich kids high on substances, who had done this for a dare? Near the large entrance door, Khurana spotted a sign. Someone had scraped the wall with a knife and left a mark that looked like a Y. That rang a bell. Khurana had read about some thieves in Chennai who left a symbol wherever they looted and he had seen an image that looked like this.

'Inspector Khurana, what is your summary assessment? Is this a burglary or is this a false alarm?'

His boss wanted him to write down his opinion.

'Both,' replied Khurana. 'It is a burglary with red herrings.'

Why does uncommon intelligence reside in common places? Why, for instance, should a honest Delhi cop – who lived in Lajpat Nagar, who went to the club every evening to play badminton but sat in the bar instead, whose father ran a tent house business that collapsed, whose closest friend was a yappy brain-dead Pomeranian, who fought with his neighbours every day for parking and water – have this insight?

It happens. That too in the week when Khurana went on the wagon. From four or five drinks a day, he was down to zero. His mind travelled to every watering hole. His hand held a soda. He was disoriented. He roamed around Najafgarh looking for his mother's place. His last visit was more than a year ago. The suburb of Najafgarh was a hardy dump where a bulb factory belched during the day. Fumes survived while water bled.

He stood at his mother's door, hesitant. She had sworn to him that she would outlive him. They had fought. 'Join a Treatment Centre,' she had shouted. 'Kick the habit. Don't show me your pain.' He rang the bell and she let him in without drama. They shared what she had cooked for herself.

Khurana had no idea why he drank so hard. His wife stayed with her mother along with their two children. She did not miss him.

'You have no idea what I go through,' he told his mother, trying hard not to bleat. 'Can you imagine what I go through, day-in, day-out, in the company of kameenas, crooked humans, bloody scum at their worst behaviour?'

He was tugging at an ingrown toenail and worrying it. His mother slapped his hand away from his leg without thinking. An old gesture. They looked at each other and remembered when she had done this before. She laughed first. Then he did. He was at peace and it was time to leave. She walked him down and showed him out.

'Why does my life have to be so hard?'

She knew the answer. She repeated a line she had heard repeatedly in the movies she saw.

'In India, the smart get tortured and the stupid are dead. Which side are you on?'

Late at night, his boss called and pleaded with him. 'Tell us what is missing.' Khurana told him to go back and study the arrangement in the puja room. It was obvious that one item was missing because the pedestal outline showed clearly among the dust. Khurana had questioned the house owner relentlessly and the latter had finally admitted that he had made cash acquisition that he had not declared for tax purposes. He had acquired an ancient Southern deity and that was the only item that was missing. Was it very valuable, this item? When Khurana came to know how much had been paid for it and how much it was worth, he let out a low whistle. When he was told that the seller had mysteriously disappeared in Chennai recently, he was intrigued.

While Khurana was interrogating the house owner, Nanban and Kari were at Terminal 2, New Delhi, boarding the flight to Chennai. They were nervous, expecting trouble. When frisked, they jumped; when someone dropped a bag and the clatter echoed, they almost jumped out of their skin. Every uniformed officer seemed to be looking at them suspiciously. Nanban's ulcers were bleeding. He was sure they were. Kari looked like he had swallowed a frog; his face was red and his eyes bulged. Once the plane was airborne, they permitted themselves a smile.

'Where is it?' Nanban asked. Kari gestured towards the baggage hold above. Nanban began laughing and Kari joined in slowly. Soon, they were barely in control of themselves. In the course of the next two and a half hours, they chatted about everything that came to mind. Kari was on a high but as the aircraft descended, his mood dropped. He looked more and more morose.

'What happened now?' Nanban asked

'I am stuck in the wrong company, in the wrong job,' he said. 'Every day, it gets worse.'

The plane descended through clouds, the wing flaps moved. Nanban had been bowled over by Kari's performance in the Sunder Nagar bungalow. The youngster had shown poise, alacrity and finesse. He had opened a bottle of Amarone as expertly as he had disabled the electronic alarms and then picked the house locks. He had neutralised the two canines and the security detail. He had thoroughly covered their tracks. Kari had done enough to qualify for a Bond film.

'Leave it to me,' said Nanban.

'Sir,' said Kari.

Nanban laid a hand on the young man's shoulder. 'I have ignored you for too long,' he said.

'Sir,' said Kari, seizing the moment, 'Valiban is intelligent. But he is a Brahmin. He will never rule this land.'

'And you can?' said Nanban.

'I can surprise you, sir,' said Kari. 'Between a street dog and a pedigree dog which stands a chance in this country?'

Nanban laughed. 'You have a point,' he said.

'Sir,' said Kari, 'what do you have in mind for me?'

Nanban saw Kari for who he was – a potent, unpredictable, handsome hulk. Men would emulate him and women would vote for him. In a flash, it came to him that the next generation was sitting right next to him. 'I will take you for a screen test,' he said. 'Have you acted before?'

The police raided many places the day after Khurana arrived in Chennai. These included Chinna Tasmac, Kari's small room and the offices of Veerappan, and while they made no arrests, they conveyed the clear message that they knew Raman owed money to Veerappan and the amount was overdue. This was the primary motive. No ransom calls had come in and that was worrying. When the raids were in progress, Kari and Valiban were in the Kotturpuram Police Station sitting in Inspector Murthy's cabin filing a missing person report. They looked anxious, their eyes were bloodshot and to Murthy they looked guilty. The two left photographs of Antony with the inspector as well as their contact numbers. A couple of days later, a potential murder weapon, an aruvaal, was found near Antony's hutment. It bore Raman's blood type and it carried some fingerprints. Police records had Antony's fingerprints and it was a perfect match. Inspector Murthy looked more puzzled than happy. 'You have found the killer?' asked his boss. 'No, he is missing. And so is the victim.' Kari, Valiban and Thambi were called in for questioning. 'There is a bad smell,' Inspector Murthy said. 'Should I look up your backsides?' The three had only each other for alibis.

They claimed they had not seen Undony for a couple of days. The police could not glean anything more from them. Murthy was itching to have a go at them but his boss was rule-bound. He had to let them go without the overnight treatment.

The Raman incident shattered Kari's Kootam, splinters flew and each one was hurt in different ways. Without actually saying so, they took time off to repair themselves. It made sense to lie low knowing the police would be sniffing around them for the next few weeks. There was no evidence yet but if any of them had to spend a night or two in the station lock-up…

Thambi, a potential weak link, disappeared from the city and only Kari had an inkling of where he was – in southern Tamil Nadu, visiting relatives. Kari decided to move from his room to the resettlement in the kuppam, vacated for him after the Timur incident. The place suited him because there were families nearby that served as distraction and distraction was what he needed. The freeze-frame of Raman being sliced by Undony refused to fade. He imagined the plop sound that Undony must have made as he sank into the Adyar River. Valiban's deadpan retelling of events had not helped matters.

The family opposite his new quarter in the kuppam was complete and wholesome. Three generations stayed together. The new grandparents hovered around their grandson and every day was precious. The grandfather's behaviour mirrored that of the infant. Both made gurgling sounds, had no teeth to speak of and looked at the world around them in wonder. Such happiness was a welcome balm for Kari. Then, the first fever came and the grandfather was mortified. It was a common flu but he flapped around the small bundle. Kari offered to help. He lifted the crying infant and to the dismay of the parents, he nuzzled the child with his unkempt beard, his attempts at friendliness frightening for the family.

Valiban called every evening and they chatted for a while. What was he up to? 'I am looking,' said Valiban. 'Wotha,' said Kari, 'looking at what?'

Valiban had fled to a suburban hideout on the way to Elysium. He stayed next to a vast lakebed fed by salty backwaters. The lake had started to dry and with the water retreating, the land began to stretch up to the horizon. What remained was a small pond. In a few weeks, the rains would arrive. In the meanwhile, the white encrusted soil began to bake by the day. A layer rose, leavened like the local bread, and cracked. This stretch between Old Mahabalipuram Road and the East Coast Road looked desolate and uninviting. A link road ran behind Valiban's house and traffic zipped up and down, screeching to a halt at a hump of a speed breaker. The speed breaker wasn't painted. Vehicles flew over it and landed with a thump. Two-wheelers skidded and fell. Life was tiresome staying in this urban miasma where a flock of goats came every day hunting for blades in the baked bed, a couple of cows joined them in the afternoon, and two boys herded them when evening arrived.

A few days later, he paid a visit to Elysium. The complex was away from the sea. No villa had sold – all thirty were ready and none occupied. He paid some money to a security guard and quietly shifted into a villa at the rear. Someone had left a window open in the villa and two birds had flown in; they must have tried to fly out after exploring the house. They hammered the glass windows until their feathers fell, their muscles tore and they bled to death.

'Bird brains,' said Valiban.

'Stupid birds,' said the stout security guard.

Valiban moved in at night into the bloodied villa. The room was warm and airless and he undressed in stages until he stood in his striped underpants. Strange noises filtered through the windows. He tossed and turned on his jamakalam, a thin colourful rug. His sleep was shallow. Occasionally, he mumbled something.

At 5.00 am, he opened an eyelid. His phone was ringing, shattering the silence.

'Where are you?' Kari asked.

'Why? What happened?'

'Nanban sir lost his mother last night,' said Kari. 'She died in her sleep.'

NANBAN

It was a good time to flee from land. We had to beat the tide, the sea's first line of defence. We took what looked like a flimsy boat, a catamaran, a set of seasoned logs tied together with rope. We had to find an opening, breach the tide and ride the current. My boatman was a grizzly thug who had taken half my money. I should have given him all of it because in that deep blue, I was at his mercy. He hummed a song that was out of tune, smiled at my discomfort as we forded the tide. We reached an impossible calm. Far from the shoreline was an alcove shaped by ~~the~~ wind.

A deep swell sent subtle signals to my legs. I was powerless, faced by the sheer magnitude. Occasionally, the swell moved, like tectonic plates did, reducing me to a sweaty heap. Things could change in that shelter, the grizzly said. Right then, a light breeze swirled gently around us. No sound carried from shore and the light remained constant. I could hear only my breath and once that settled, nothing.

I was carrying my mother's ashes. It was a small vessel, a container like her body was. I was supposed to stand in the boat and throw the ashes over my left shoulder and then my right. I would return alone. I stood in the alcove. The boatman nodded and I let her go. I sat quietly while we navigated to the shore. I cried a little.

Later, in moments that would come unannounced, I would weep.

Sharada moved into my place after my mother died. She lent a shoulder. People I never knew cared showed up at home. And grief. Veera behaved like my elder brother. He stayed close to me. The kootam boys hoisted her and we went to the Besant Nagar cemetery without noise or fuss. There were no other pyres that day. There were flowers. There were more than a thousand people. Most of them did not know my mother's name. Veera and I stood together. A wave of emotion swept over us as the furnace door opened. A lever went down and she moved. A collective intake of breath as she caught fire. An involuntary keening sound. Death was an uncommon denominator.

'So your nuclear family is down to one?' Veera did not acknowledge Sharada as part of the family.

'Yes,' I said.

'Your mother should have experienced this gathering,' he said.

'In a city she never considered her own,' I said.

'It doesn't matter,' said Veera. 'These people are here because she was your mother. They care for you. They know what you are doing for them. All that matters is this moment. Remember it.'

Yesterday was like a bad dream. People kept calling, my phone kept blinking. I sat around unable to do anything. I needed to get away from it all – from Veerappan, the kootam, the TASMAC Bar and the city. I needed to head back one more time to Mumbai and to Muskaan.

We returned to the shore when the wind changed, the tide rose and we bobbed to the edge where the sand rose to ground us. I headed to the airport and to that tube in the sky, my alcove at 30,000 feet. The touchdown at Mumbai was smooth and she arrived, just as I exited, in her car. She drove. I could not look at her for a while. She said nothing but she glanced in my direction every now and then. She waited for me to find my way.

'It happened in her sleep,' I said. 'Peaceful, unexpected. She probably wasn't aware.'

She drove south without a destination in mind.

'She always liked you,' I said.

'I know,' she said. 'But Mumbai was her first love.'

We were in Dadar. I expressed the first thing that came to mind and it was the need to eat. I had not touched a morsel the whole of yesterday. We went to a restaurant that served seafood. There was my favourite, that delicious fish called Bombay Duck. I had a craving for the thin almost flaky fried 'bangda'. It tasted like cardboard. I drank a beer. It was warm and we sweated. I recovered somewhat by the time I announced my pet peeve.

'I have been diagnosed with middle age,' I said.

She put a hand through mine. 'It is an inevitable affliction,' she said.

Another beer arrived and it was colder.

'I am now officially dissatisfied with most things. I fight with my friends, I treat my kootam badly and when left alone, I watch pornography till my eyes burst.'

'That's it?'

'I shave on alternate days, stand on the road and stare at public hoardings, and when people walk by, I walk behind them and eavesdrop on their conversations. Nothing works for me. I call telephone call centres and complain bitterly. I have started listening to old Hindi songs, you know, what my mother listened to.'

It wasn't the time to go into these things.

'I am glad you came to Bombay,' she said. 'Saved me a trip to Chennai.'

'It is her home,' I said. 'I came to meet you too.'

She smiled and squeezed my arm. She looked into my face. 'Something is missing, isn't it?'

She was right. That is how I felt. A thing without a name – gone missing – that made me flit between Chennai and Mumbai.

'Trouble in Chennai?' she said. 'Something you want to tell me?'

'Too much is happening together, but I can't discuss it.'

She was upset, quietly so.

'Something happened other than this,' I said. 'Something bad happened. I am out of my depth for once.'

She waited for me to say more. I had to decide.

'You made a mistake?'

'I wouldn't call it that.'

'You will never admit a mistake, will you sweets?' she said.

I was on the verge of telling her everything and she sensed it. 'Don't,' she said. When I insisted, she said, 'Wait till you get over this. Then talk to me.'

I asked Muskaan to take me to that landscape that she had described, the place where her portrait was painted – that bleak place that held the studio of Azmi. Show me the ants, I said, and the shit they made, the red soil climbing trees, the baked earth, where the sky was a roof and dust was pollen that made you sneeze. Once we reached the place, I sat her down and said I was ready to listen, for that is what I came to meet her for, the chance to get away, to escape from my own narrative and listen to her speak. She was the one that introduced me to art, to a different language, to a beautiful world that was a distraction at its worst, but so much more when it questioned the obvious and connected the unlikely.

I called Raghavan while I sat at the airport. He was expecting my call. I had no idea how he kept abreast of my doings without my telling him, but he did.

'Something happened,' I said. 'Something ugly.'

'I know.'

'I wasn't involved,' I said.

'I know.'

I felt I was at a confessional. I felt better having spoken to him. As an unofficial agent for a spooky arm of the government, involved in an assignment whose sponsors and motives were unclear, I felt vulnerable. The uncertainties were too many even for me.

'Am I a poor leader?' I asked.

'You have your own methods and they work,' he said. I wished he would elaborate.

I was about to disconnect when he said, 'You have created agency. The boys are in neck-deep. Isn't that what you wanted?'

'Yes. But the killing and the burglary were not in my script.'

He stayed quiet for a while. 'Things are falling in place,' he said. 'But we have just one year to go.'

One year seemed a long time. Twelve whole months. A leap year that too.

IV

TWELVE MONTHS TO ELECTIONS

'Off Season Sale' was emblazoned on hoardings all over the city. Every store advertised 'The Last Sale'. A little later, 'The Final Last Sale'. Newspapers carried inserts promising free toppings with pizzas. Pedestrians looked up past the hoardings at the sky. The sweat capital of the country waited, patiently, for rain.

In a small room behind high walls, Valiban lay tossing and turning. The sheets were wet and his pillow had salty residue. 'Go to sleep, kanna,' said his mother, Mrs. Ramanathan. His mind was taut, tightly sprung, seeking a way out of a well-imagined situation. Thunder followed lightning followed by the first summer shower accompanied by a swirling wind that swept the dust off the streets. Large drops gathered and washed the city roads. An exultant Mrs. Ramanathan faced the rain and closed her eyes. She was close to dancing. She took a few steps and turned on a toe as she used to in Kalakshetra. A few drops splattered the floor near Valiban. 'Wotha,' he said. He remembered simple things in his delirium – a paper boat, a small stream, a kite that ran colour on a tree.

The fever was climbing, his legs felt weak, his shoulders shuddered. The seasonal pox was virulent. It coursed through the air, water and his veins. His mother fanned the air with her sari pallu. Get up, Valiban told himself, be a man. He wanted to run into the rain as he used to. He could not. The local doctor arrived and he planted his stethoscope on Valiban's chest and back. He felt his pulse and frowned. 'The fever will run its course, Mrs. Ramanathan,' he said. He shook the thermometer. 'Say aaaa.' He turned his face away. 'Your mouth smells like your armpit.'

The fever camped for a week, in which time his mother consulted another doctor. 'Very poor habits, Anni,' he said, looking around the room. 'And the very bad company he is keeping.' Valiban half arose and fell back. 'Get him away from me,' he shouted. 'He looks like a capitation fee doctor.'

'His friend Kari has become an actor,' said Mrs. Ramanathan. 'You should see the girls who come to his room every day.' The quack said, 'Aha.' That explained a few things, especially the scabs on Valiban. 'Venereal disease is so ugly,' he said. 'Anni, could you please leave the room?' She left hurriedly as the quack pulled down Valiban's shorts.

'Turn away boy.'

Valiban resisted. 'What is in that syringe?'

'Arsenic,' said the doctor.

'That's poison,' shouted Valiban, 'you are trying to kill me?' They arm-wrestled for a while but Valiban was too weak. 'Help,' he said.

'This will hurt,' said the doctor.

'My eyes hurt,' said Valiban.

'So wear dark glasses,' said the doctor, 'like our political leaders do.' He sent the medicine on its way. 'What did you say?'

'What day is it?' repeated Valiban.

There was a calendar on the wall, one with auspicious days and festivals clearly marked. The two turned and looked at it. Valiban's mother had circled the beginning of Aadi maasam. The month had just begun.

'One year to election time,' said Veerappan to Perumal as they added up the numbers. The grand total was good news. They had the money.

It was time for puja. The bare-chested priests were busy, hurtling down city roads on their motorcycles, their pigtails bobbing, their veshtis funnelling, their knees showing. Sanskrit rent the air in ~~the~~ temple and tavern. Gods were in short supply.

Nanban rolled out of bed and headed to the window. Rain was imminent. The clear day was gone; the blue sky had left for Pondicherry. He scratched his head. What was he supposed to do today? He consulted his desktop. The screensaver blinked and Muskaan appeared. How did that happen? 'What the flying fuck,' he said. The sequence was all wrong. 'Attention,' said an electronic voice. 'This car is backing out.' He remembered and he ran for the door. He was supposed to take Sharada to the temple. The car left the gate just as he reached the entrance door. He waved his arms in vain. Exhaust fumes found their way to his nose. He sneezed all the way to the washroom where he hit his head against the door…

Nanban wanted to protect his kootam. He felt responsible. Veerappan got him Inspector Murthy's number. He called him at the close of office hours, on his cell phone.

'We are supposed to meet someone today at 8.30 pm,' he said.

Murthy looked at his screen. Unknown number.

'Meet whom?' he said.

'I can't say.'

'And you sir, who speaks so well, what is your good name?'

'Forget my name, just call me Nanban.'

Murthy leaned back in his chair and searched for a toothpick. He had long fingers and they dug around in his pockets that held cigarettes, a matchbox, a pocketknife and a few keys. He found a safety pin.

'I know who you are,' he said.

They met in a car on a small road near the seashore. Veerappan held out his hand ceremoniously; Murthy ignored it.

'How is the case going?' said Veerappan.

'Which one? There are two cases,' said Murthy.

'You have a good reputation,' said Veerappan. 'Who do you work for?'

The inspector cracked the digits of his fingers one by one. He said nothing.

'A free agent?' said Veerappan. 'I respect that.'

'I don't have time for all this,' said Murthy.

'Why have you come then?' said Nanban.

'To see what you looked like,' said Murthy.

'You could have called me to the station,' said Nanban.

The inspector grimaced. 'I have been asked not to touch you,' he said. It obviously hurt him that he had to comply with this unusual order.

Veerappan looked puzzled but he did not pursue this mystery. 'Inspector Murthy,' he said. 'We all know something unfortunate happened. It was a grievous mistake, a mistake all the same. The punishment has been delivered. Why don't we get along with other important things?'

Murthy shrugged. 'With all due respect...' he began.

'Are you the same third-degree Murthy that people talk about?' said Nanban.

Murthy got out of the car.

'Don't you do any honest police work?' said Nanban. 'I believe you sit in your dark cell and torture people. Have you heard of legwork?'

Murthy laughed. It was an ugly laugh. He was pleased that his reputation had travelled and that people feared what was to come.

'I don't do ~~the~~ legwork,' he said. 'I prefer doing nails, and hands. I find that more effective.'

'A pity we cannot agree,' said Veerappan. 'You are a practical person, just like us.'

Inspector Murthy was being polite because that was his nature. Doing things to people did not change that. He saw in these two something he did not get to see every day. Naked power, killer instinct and keen intellect. He wanted to impress them. He even considered confessing. I like interrogations, he wanted to say. I conduct them in the company of two constables, one young and one old. The interrogation room smells of stale incense. We use joss sticks but we are unable to camouflage the ugly smell of fear.

'How is the Thimiru Kootam?' he asked Nanban. 'Actually, where is it?'

'What do you mean?' said Nanban.

'Where is Kari?' said Murthy.

'He is in a kuppam hiding from you,' said Nanban. 'Have you located Raman?'

'No,' said Murthy. 'Where is Valiban?'

'He is unwell I believe, poor boy,' said Nanban. 'Have you located Antony?'

'Don't play games with me, sir,' said Murthy. 'Where is Thambi?'

Nanban had enough of this. 'Sir,' he said. 'I am not their caretaker. Do some legwork for a change.'

'Please be worried,' said Inspector Murthy, addressing Nanban pointedly. 'You don't belong to this group of people; I know that. Please call me, sir, whenever you feel like.'

Veerappan coughed, feeling a little left out. After the inspector left in his jeep, he turned towards Nanban. 'Is he trying to divide us?'

'The situation is a fucking time bomb,' said Nanban.

He had no illusions about the situation. Very soon, FIRs would get prepared, police custody would happen, the boys would go into Murthy's horror chamber and emerge having confessed. How would this affect the political journey? That was his only concern.

'The inspector has a severe headache,' said Nanban. 'Without bodies, there is no established crime. They cannot establish the motive. We have closed ranks, but his famed interrogations will prise us apart. He needs warrants and warrants take time.'

Murthy was busy over the next few days preparing the paperwork. He called Nanban from time to time.

'They call you mapillai,' he said. 'You know why?'

'I can guess,' said Nanban. 'They watch too many films?'

'Is it true that you are to marry Veerappan's youngest sister?'

'I have not met her yet,' said Nanban. He had imagined what she looked like.

The inspector turned towards the wall in his cabin and examined it closely. The resident spider was near the ceiling. Another Murthy that preyed on flybys.

As he hung up, Nanban received a call from the movie studio where Narsimhan sat listless, depressed by a weak script. He had started calling Nanban frequently.

'After stall comes free fall,' he had said the previous night. He sounded drunk. 'I am having trouble staying erect.'

'Come home,' said Nanban, 'right now. Have dinner with us.'

He came within the hour.

'Narsimhan sir, meet my partner, Sharada,' said Nanban.

Narsimhan was wearing a traditional white jibba and a dhoti and his camera hung around his neck. His forehead was polished and his naamam etched in the middle. He was reasonably high. 'Namaskaram,' he said, removing his sandals with some difficulty. The moment he entered Sharada said, 'A proper Brahmin. Please come in.'

Nanban offered him a drink, which he thankfully declined. Sharada was surprised. 'No drink?' She had heard about his drinking. She headed to the kitchen and heated dinner.

'You are from Mylapore?' she asked through the doorway.

'Yes. From an original agraharam,' said Narsimhan.

'I have made some archavittu sambar from fresh ingredients,' she said. 'Just for you. You don't mind spice, I hope?'

'I don't eat spicy food,' said Narsimhan.

'No spice?' She served the rice and sambar on his plate and brought out some fresh curd. 'Then what do you do for excitement in this city?'

'I go to the High Court in Parry's Corner,' said Narsimhan as he massaged the rice with his fingers. 'I fight cases.'

'Your own?' asked Nanban.

Narsimhan nodded. He chewed a drumstick piece and licked his fingers. 'I have three defamation cases and one sedition case against *Dai Tamizha*. I cannot afford a good lawyer.'

There was silence after this announcement. Narsimhan hiccupped, drank some water and hiccupped again. Nanban looked at his auteur and wondered what else this man was going through.

'Now there is an income tax hearing as well.'

'What? They are harassing you?'

'No.' Hiccup. 'My mistake. Veerappan paid for the documentary in cash, which I deposited into my bank account. I paid the tax but the IT commissioner wants to know the source. Obviously, I cannot tell him.'

Nanban clucked in exasperation. 'Why did you deposit the cash?'

Narsimhan suppressed a burp. 'Because there was a spate of burglaries in Brahmin houses in Chennai,' he said.

'Only elderly Brahmins were burgled, Mr. Narsimhan,' said Sharada as she cleared up. 'You are not that old.'

Narsimhan laughed uproariously, throwing his head back and bringing the roof down. Tears ran down his cheeks. Sharada liked him, especially his laugh.

'How old are you?' she said.

'You shouldn't ask,' said Nanban.

She looked at the camera, the long-snouted DSLR. 'Will you take a snap? I will pose for you.'

Narsimhan fiddled with the settings, looking at her all the time as she moved around and the camera clicked before she could pose. They crowded around the small viewing screen. It was a portrait in black and white. She looked stunning.

'How did you manage that?' said Nanban, ducking, as Sharada took a swipe at him.

Later, when they sat for a cognac, Nanban promised him a potential hero. The next day, he took Kari for a screen test partly to fulfil the promise he had made to the young man. The effect on Narsimhan was magical. He couldn't take his eyes off the tall strapping lad.

'Who is he? What is his real name?'

'Everyone calls him Kari.'

'Who are his parents?'

'He is an orphan.'

'Adopted?'

'Never.'

'Is he a Gounder?'

'Nobody knows. Could be Muslim.'

'Ohh, I see. How does it matter? He is one of us. Just look at him.'

Kari was being himself. He wandered among the props, the cameras, the lighting equipment and the extras, making faces. The girls on the set were hopelessly distracted.

'Do you want a screen test?' asked Nanban.

'Just look at the undertone of menace he carries so effortlessly,' said Narsimhan. 'He could be my hero, our hero. He has a mysterious origin, a criminal record and he journeys through present and past to seek out who he really is. And he comes under the tutelage of a political leader and is reformed.'

'Sounds like a plot,' said Nanban.

'A real-life urban orphan, a big and handsome hulk who keeps seeking answers, a quest that takes this adopted son of Veerappan through the cities and villages of Tamil Nadu questioning not just his own origin but that of Gounders, of the state and its politics. Kari could be the narrative thread that binds the story together and his unfulfilled quest could drive the film.'

'Do you want a screen test?' Nanban asked again.

'No,' said Narsimhan. 'He will fail it.'

'Then?'

'I have found the right pitch,' said Narsimhan. 'The film has found a voice. We need to change his name.'

'How about Karivardan?' asked Veera.

'That sounds classic,' said Nanban, getting a little excited.

'The name belongs to my community as well,' said Veera.

'There you are,' said Narsimhan. 'We have the title for the film.'

'Veera Gounder Karivardan?' said Veera, echoing the Kattabomman film.

'No, please no,' said Narsimhan. 'Just Karivardan. Tell me his story, his real story.'

Nanban related what he knew. He asked Valiban to pitch in as well. Over the next two days, Narsimhan rewrote the screenplay. He wove Kari's real life story into the film.

'This young man will be the future,' said Narsimhan.

'This maramandai?' said Veera.

'Once I am done with this film, your history will be rewritten,' said Narsimhan.

'I see,' said Veera.

There was a short silence. Nanban looked at Veerappan for a reaction. He wasn't singing paeans yet. This was not a natural succession plan. What was the succession plan?

'I can say now with certainty we have a film, sir,' said Narsimhan. 'Trust me, it will be electric.'

'Begin the shooting,' said Veera. This filmmaker had a cinematic vision he liked, but his script sounded a little too revolutionary.

'Karivardan, come here,' called out Narsimhan. 'Come see the earlier film.'

They sat in a small preview theatre on TTK Road.

'Where did you shoot this?' asked Kari.

The crew had travelled to Karur where they had identified a location. It was semi-rural. For the next hour, an anxious Narsimhan observed Kari as he watched the documentary. Mosquitoes buzzed around the theatre and the air-conditioning struggled to cool the place. It did not seem to matter; the magic of cinema was at work on the small audience.

NINE MONTHS TO THE ELECTION

Veerappan went to work touring the state with a cartographer's diligence. He made speeches, he made friends and he developed a sore throat. A masseur travelled with him sharing a car with a speechwriter, a psephologist and an actor. Nanban joined them for a week. His stomach rumbled on the third day after a parotta orgy and on the fifth day, a tamarind fish curry gave him the runs. He sat in a 3-star hotel and observed pigeons make a nest using sticks. He spoke to Muskaan. 'Electioneering is an activity where there is a lot of song and dance,' he said. 'And Tamil actresses know better English than I do.'

Sharada called. She was watching the local news channel. 'I haven't seen you yet,' she said. 'But Veerappan was on the 9.00 pm news.'

'Good news on both fronts,' said Nanban.

'Why haven't you called me since you left?' she said.

'I am sorry,' said Nanban. 'I am not used to… to your being in my place.'

'You are sleeping with me, right?' she said.

'What?' said Nanban.

'If you are sleeping with me, you should occasionally talk to me as well,' she said.

'I see,' said Nanban, 'and then we should get married?' He regretted it the moment he said it. It was too late. She hung up before he could apologise. She ignored his subsequent calls.

People were noticing Veerappan's speeches. He unveiled portraits of Gounder leaders and legends at every rally. These were life-size portraits painted by Azmi. Veera spoke about them using homespun tales and folklore and he rekindled memories. He spoke of his initiatives in his farm, his village and his community. He also spoke of his vision of a Gounder heartland, of a frontier spirit.

By now, he had an image of being 'different'. Good for the classes, said Narsimhan of this image, but not one with the masses yet.

He had the 'look'. When politicians went to the people asking for votes, they adopted it. A smile, folded hands, attentiveness, a hand over the shoulder, a hug (careful), a confident demeanour and the occasional fist that was raised to show power. The hangers-on had to have the correct composition and the correct collective geometry.

Every now and then, there were surprises – some heartening and some ugly. Nanban had to call Muskaan after one such surprise.

'People are smarter than you think,' he said.

'Are you distributing freebies?'

'Freebies are a part of Tamil culture,' said Nanban. 'By the way, Azmi showed up here in the Tamil heartland.'

'What was he doing there? Did you call him?'

'No. He came with his own TV crew. It was quite a tamasha. Veerappan was happy. He got a portrait of himself, free.'

Women attended rallies in large numbers. In one rally, Kari appeared for the first time as Karivardan, introduced as an upcoming actor. There was a rush towards him and a small touchy, feely, selfie riot ensued.

Nanban was enthused. There was work to do. His online team asked him to change the orientation of his kootams. First, tone down the rhetoric, he was told. Then, issue instructions to the kootams to get involved in digging wells, planting trees, constructing toilets, conducting medical camps, distributing footwear to women working in the fields and other similar social activities for the next nine months. Importantly, Nanban was ordered (by an increasingly assertive Veera) to sort out the police cases. 'They are cancerous and malignant,' Veera told him. 'Whatever happens, bury them.'

Nanban called Valiban to Chinna Tasmac, parked his car under a tree, sidestepped a fruit vendor and walked up to the bar. Flies floated in slow motion in the afternoon haze. A dog lay curled inside a car tire. An old woman uttered a plea as he passed her and he gave her some money. The place was otherwise deserted.

Valiban was late for the meeting. When Thangabalu raised an eyebrow, Nanban shrugged then nodded. He got a quarter of dark rum with water, no ice. The barman made a gruff noise that was a complaint of sorts. An old film song was playing. Nanban drank steadily. He slanted the small bottle and tipped the last drop into his mouth. Thangabalu heaved himself up and brought him another.

'Can you play a song by Chandrababu?' said Nanban.

Thangabalu smiled. The two shared a deep love for this singer-actor who was light on his feet, quick with a smile and had a body made of India rubber. He could dance, he could sing and, above all, live a lie that you believed in.

Nanban had tanked up by the time Valiban arrived. The latter slipped in quietly and stood near the high table.

'You should have taken me for the election tour, sir,' he said, sounding hurt. 'You took Kari instead.'

'He has charisma,' said Nanban. 'You should see how crowds respond to him.'

There was an awkward silence.

'One day, I will make speeches,' said Valiban.

'I am sure you will,' said Nanban. 'Where were you?'

'I have been reading,' said Valiban. He looked at what Nanban was having. His lips glistened in the dark.

'Tell me what you have read,' said Nanban.

Valiban kept staring at the booze. 'Give him a quarter,' said Nanban.

Thangabalu was reluctant. 'Not here,' he said. 'This porikki doesn't belong here.'

'Why? He is a Brahmin,' said Nanban.

'Then, he shouldn't be drinking,' said the barman.

Valiban got his quarter but he had to drink it standing. He unscrewed the cap, raised the bottle to his lips and emptied it without a pause, looking at Thangabalu all the time. He raised a finger as the politicos did and asked for another. Thangabalu ground his teeth audibly as he slapped another quarter on the counter. Valiban drank it without fuss. He had that look that Nanban had seen a million times in Tamil Nadu when drinkers tippled hard, then looked inward, and waited for the 'kick'.

'Are you done with Shri Ambedkar?' said Nanban.

Valiban nodded. 'Caste is cancer, sir,' said Valiban. 'In sum, that is what I have read and understood.'

'I have read what you have read,' said Nanban.

'And yet, sir?' said Valiban.

'I don't feel what you are feeling,' said Nanban. 'I am caught in the middle. I have been told by intellectuals that my position is privileged, my pain is less valid and my truths are not self-evident.'

Valiban twirled his empty bottle on the counter, spoiling for a fight. His nervous energy was palpable. Nanban asked for two more quarters. They drank some more.

'Nothing short of a revolution will do,' said Valiban.

'Of course,' said Nanban. 'Because the ill is deep-rooted, the cure has to be… what do you youngsters call it?'

'Epic,' said Valiban.

'And who is the enemy?'

'Besides caste? People like you, sir,' said Valiban.

Nanban laughed. 'I was an enemy of the state and now I am an enemy of the people,' he said.

'Don't treat this lightly, sir,' said Valiban. 'There is a strong undercurrent against people like you.'

'I belong to the capitalist philosophy,' said Nanban. 'Unashamedly. I take no prisoners. I do not play victim. The state taxes me and practises socialism for people that need redistribution. They are passengers, I am the engine.' He took another sip. 'What about you?'

'Where do I begin?' said Valiban, now a little unsteady.

'Take small steps,' said Nanban. 'Because you are drunk and you are not Babasaheb.'

'Communism appeals to me, sir,' said Valiban. 'There must be a reason it survives in India.'

Nanban snorted loudly.

'Sir?' said Valiban.

'Nothing,' said Nanban, suddenly dropping his head. 'All this comes to nothing.' He looked tired all of a sudden. 'I am just a bloody manager,' he said.

'You are getting old, sir,' said Valiban. 'And so is capitalism.'

'The world is failing,' said Nanban. 'This bar is a good place to be.'

'Sir, you keep telling us time will tell and time will heal,' said Valiban. 'Should we keep waiting?'

Thangabalu heaved himself up again and laid a hand on Valiban. 'Do you want me to throw him out?' he said.

'No,' said Nanban. He headed to Narsimhan's corner and Valiban followed him.

'There is no space in politics for political correctness,' said Nanban. He sat down. 'Those who practise it, wear halos. They are intellectual cowards.' A rat emerged from a dark corner and ran along the wall. It disappeared with a squeak. 'This is the land of the Mahabharata and Khajuraho, my mother said. Grow up, she told me, take your stand and confront. Don't sit on your arse and judge others.'

Valiban's head was swimming.

'I cannot even sit,' he said.

'I know what you want,' said Nanban.

'We want a real revolution,' said Valiban. 'The Adi Dravidas have to rise and tear this society apart.'

'Easily said. Our society is durable. Do you know why? Because it is a mongrel,' said Nanban. 'So is our country.'

'Join me, sir,' said Valiban, 'we will annihilate caste. You and I. If you set your mind to it, we can do it.'

'Some day,' said Nanban, holding his head. 'Till then let us dream. A casteless society, a nation of orphans.'

They sat for a while holding the table between them. Waves of nausea came and went.

'Has Ambedkar's time come?' said Nanban. 'Did you check?'

'It has come, sir,' said Valiban, smiling. 'We have erected his statues, named roads after him and named some nagars after him. Like Gandhi, he now has a jayanti.'

'Jai ho!' said Nanban.

'Sir, I need to use the toilet,' said Valiban, rising with difficulty. He stumbled to the washroom and poured water over his head. He stood there for a few minutes until the nausea subsided. The drink stayed inside, barely. When he felt better, he returned to the bar. Nanban had recovered from his temporary gloom.

'Did Inspector Murthy call you?' said Nanban.

'Yes, sir,' said Valiban. 'I am coming from the police station. Inspector Murthy questioned me. He asked me to produce an alibi, which I have done.'

'What did you tell him?'

'I told him that in the morning I visited my aunt – the one who is not mentally stable,' he said. 'Then I went to Valsarvakkam to my mother's place. After that Kari and I went to the zoo in Vandalur and late in the evening we went to Elliots Beach.'

Nanban laughed. 'So your mental aunt, your doting mother and some monkeys in the zoo are your alibi?'

Valiban smiled. 'The autorickshaw driver who took us around is our alibi. That very night, they picked up Ramesh and dragged him to the station. Inspector Murthy kept him in his pickle room for a night. Poor Ramesh, he was so frightened. They asked him what fare I paid for each trip. Then, they asked me. The figures matched. Murthy said we were lying. He said I would have paid exact change, not round figures.'

'This name Ramesh sounds familiar,' said Nanban.

'They are checking the fare tomorrow, sir,' said Valiban. 'They have seized Ramesh's rickshaw. They are travelling with him on the same route to check out our round numbers.'

Nanban called Kari after Valiban left.

'I think Valiban has bought himself time. He has given them the Kaanum Pongal story. The bad news is you are up next.'

'What are they planning for me?' Kari asked, sounding anxious.

Nanban paused but there was no way he could soften the blow. 'I hear they have a warrant for police custody. I am sorry, we could not stop it. You are a history-sheeter with a past murder rap. The magistrate ruled against you.'

Kari was quiet for a while.

'Murthy will come down hard on you,' said Nanban. 'Once you go into that room, anything can happen.'

'Sir, I can take it,' said Kari. 'Let that myrandi do his worst.'

'Karivardan, you are not thinking clearly,' said Nanban. 'There is a fine line that separates a Kshatriya from a chuthiya.'

Nanban knew that the police were after him and Veera. This tamasha needed to be short-circuited and quickly. There was one plausible sacrificial lamb. Nanban took his name.

'Sir,' said Kari. 'It would be cowardly on my part to feed a kootam member to the cops.'

'No,' said Nanban. 'It would be cowardly if you didn't.'

Despite himself, Kari shivered.

'I will be waiting outside the police station after you go in,' said Nanban. 'I will count your nails when you come out.'

THAMBI

Growing-up stories in Chennai were predictable and boring. Nobody bloomed in their teens because boys and girls wore braces and specs and buried their noses in books published by the Textbook Society. Father was usually a hard-working bore and mother was a teacher or a peachy homemaker. The divorce courts were empty and analysts were underemployed. In this land that produced techies, bureaucrats and bankers, how could childhood be vivacious?

Thambi had imagined his teens as the best phase of his life. He had had a disconsolate childhood. His father had literally run away. He wasn't a drunkard or a wife-beater, neither was he a wastrel. Yet he made his wife miserable. His biggest crime was that he was not interested in anything.

One day, Thambi's mother saw a film by K Balachander, a director who created strong female characters who rebelled in domestic situations; homemakers loved his version of middle-class redemption. She was moved enough to ask her husband to get off his perch for once, switch the television off and help her in the kitchen. 'Dai moodevi,' shouted her husband, 'know your place.' He threw the TV remote at her. She returned to the kitchen, considered the pestle and settled for the bread knife. There was blood in her eyes and she wasn't thinking clearly. Her husband was in his permanent seat. He saw her coming at him, bread knife at the ready and he fled, never to be seen again.

Thambi was naturally awkward. When puberty arrived, his voice broke, hair sprouted here and there. He started looking at himself in mirrors and windows. 'A cactus in bloom,' said his mother. She was no desert rose, clumsy and a terrible cook.

'I should have been a girl,' he told her one day.

She laughed. For a while, she looked normal. Then, she waddled away to the kitchen where her disinterest played havoc with taste.

Thambi roamed the streets on his bike. Cops stopped him at every check-post and harassed him.

'Who are you? Give your name and address. Proof. Where is the bloody proof?'

Policemen came home, ever so often, looking for his father. His father had turned to crime and surfaced every month in a different state. So he dropped his father's name.

His mother taught him how to introduce himself. He wrote down who he was. 'I am Thambi. I am a Kongu Nadu veeran. I belong to the Vellayan Kootam. My ancestors stayed near a temple near Karur. My Kulaideivam is Solli Amman.'

THE NINTH CUT

The pickle room in the police station smelt antiseptic. Thambi stood in the dark corner. He moved his hand. It floated away from him, disembodied. For a while, he heard himself breathe. His chest rose and fell. He was powerless. It was beyond his will, this life. He took a deep breath, held it inside him and let it out slowly. He heard them speak.

'What were you doing in the Public Library in the evening?'

'I was planning to meet my friends.'

'What are their names?'

'Kari sir and Valiban.'

'What are their real names?'

'I don't know.'

He had to stay conscious. He did not trust the dark, not in a police station, not when the cop facing him had nail extractors.

'Where were you later that day?'

'I was in Kari sir's house, his room. Valiban and Kari were out the whole day. They returned in the evening. We were there the whole night.'

'Do you know someone called Raman?'

'Which Raman, sir?'

'Was there a Raman in the TASMAC Bar you kept going to?'

'Yes sir, there was.'

'What does he look like?'

'Sir, I don't remember.'

'Where was Antony? When did you last see him?'

Thambi hesitated for a moment. He was sweating badly by now and he kept licking his lips, clasping and unclasping his hands, looking all the time at the nail extractor.

'Sir, he came for some time and left in the evening. He told us he had to meet someone.'

Murthy laughed loudly. He picked up Thambi's right hand and laughed again. He turned the hand over, palm facing down, and placed it flat on the table. He ran his fingers over Thambi's nails. 'So smooth,' he said. 'Like a young girl's.'

'Sir,' said Thambi looking around in panic. There was nobody to help him. There was no good cop, just this one, and he was looking very dangerous.

'Your leader Kari was here yesterday. You knew that?'

Thambi looked surprised. 'No, sir,' he said.

'He told us you did it,' said Murthy. 'He told us you stole the Chola statue. Where have you kept it?'

Thambi's head swam and Kari's face came into view. He felt sick.

'Sir,' he said. 'Kari is a murderer; everybody knows. He killed Timur, sir; I saw it with my own eyes.' He was stammering by now. 'Antony was my friend, sir, why would I hurt him? That Kari, he likes to kill, sir. He did it. I heard him getting orders.'

Murthy looked at the shivering lad. His eyes were wide with fright. Asked about Raman, he was singing about Kari. He would probably say anything to save his skin.

'Who gave the orders? And where did they dispose of the bodies?'

'I don't know, sir,' said Thambi. He realised he had spoken too much already. To reveal anything more would be to sign his death warrant. Veerappan and his kootams would finish him.

'What shall we do, Thambi?' said Murthy. 'Should I send you back to your mother in one piece? Or should I send her your pieces?'

'Sir, sir, I need to go to the toilet,' said Thambi. He tried to pull his hand away but Murthy's grip was firm.

'Look who has come.' Murthy said. Thambi turned and in a swift move, Murthy pulled a nail out. He unclasped the extractor, the nail fell. It looked like a bloodied insect. Thambi screamed. He went cold in shock and then feeling returned and he screamed again and he tried to get up but a man who had come in quietly shoved him down.

'Normally, I do one at a time,' said Murthy, cleaning the extractor, readying it afresh. He then lit a cigarette and watched the matchstick burn, bend and fall. The process took a minute, which gave Thambi time to clutch his hand and stare at his bloodied finger. Murthy stubbed the cigarette out on Thambi's arm – on the inside of his elbow. Thambi screamed again and his head jerked back as Murthy pulled out the second nail. This time the nail stuck and Murthy had to wrestle with it and some flesh came loose.

Thambi passed out briefly. The room smelt of the piss that was running down his legs. The man behind him poured some water onto his face and, when he came to again, Murthy was relentless. Thambi began speaking and the cops smiled, thinking they had broken him. They leaned close to his mouth because he was mumbling.

'Note down what he is saying,' said Murthy.

'Kongu Nadu veeran,' said Thambi.

'What?' said Murthy.

'Vellayan Kootam,' said Thambi, his voice rising.

'Dai rascal,' said Murthy, holding him by the collar.

'Karur mavattam,' shouted Thambi.

'I will kill you,' shouted Murthy.

'Solli Amman Kulaideivam,' screamed Thambi.

It said something about the boy that he spilled nothing; not another word about the Raman episode escaped his lips. Three nails were Murthy's limit and that passed by without reward. They fed him some sweet sugary tea and biscuits before they released him and he puked all over the floor. A constable raised him by the armpits, led him out onto the road and released him. He fell onto a tree stump in front of a tea stall and gagged again. The world swam into view. A passer-by tried to lift him up.

'Who are you?' he asked him.

'Kongu Nadu veeran,' said the delirious boy.

'Where are you from, boy?'

'Vellayan Kootam. Karur mavattam,' said Thambi through clenched teeth. 'My mother, get my mother.'

'Where is she? What is her name?'

'Solli Amman,' said Thambi, holding on to the stranger as he tried to get up. He was behaving like a drunk. 'She is my Kulaideivam.'

He staggered home to his mother's place. He received calls from Kari and Valiban, repeatedly, for an hour, but he did not answer them. His mother nursed him the best she could and took him to a clinic to protect him from shock and infection. He spent an hour smoking hash while his mother watched. The throbbing pain subsided. They spent half the night holding each other. Early the next morning, before daybreak, he left for Egmore Station and caught a train to Rameswaram; from there, he skipped across the sea to Sri Lanka's northern reaches where his mother's family stayed. After a week, he had recuperated enough to give form to his hate. He joined a young Tamil group that was undergoing a self-inflicted regimen, best described as martial training. When he was done with that, he learnt how to use a gun, how to assemble and dismantle a crude bomb.

The Thambi episode disturbed Valiban deeply. He knew he was next. He couldn't bear to look at his fingers. He decided to take matters into his own hands. He met up with an A-grade history-sheeter. The man was plain-looking but he carried a knife. It was shiny, handmade and quite good-looking. There were three nicks in the handle. Each had a name, he said. The man baulked when he got to know the target was a policeman.

'What is the police kaaran's name?' he asked.

'First, tell me if you will do it,' said Valiban.

'Let me think about it,' he said.

Valiban began doubting him. 'Are you even capable?'

'If I decide, yes,' said the killer.

The next day, Valiban was asked to help at a family meeting chaired by Veerappan. He turned up, hoping to get a private audience at some point. The clan gathered for a traditional repast, eaten by hand. After, they washed up and cleared the plantain leaves and paper cups. The caterer and his men disappeared. The family members spoke in turn. Valiban stood at a distance noting the hierarchy, based partly on age and partly on results achieved. Nanban had told him – family means blood, relations are relations, and while he himself may be close to Veerappan, the family echelons would always exclude him.

'Yes,' said Veerappan, when they had some time together, 'you have two minutes.' When he heard of the target, he said, 'No. You have to learn some simple rules. We do not take down policemen.'

'But, sir,' said Valiban, 'he is an animal. He is the only one who knows what happened. Some day, he will be a nuisance to you.'

Veerappan stood firm. 'I cannot allow it,' he said. 'But I will handle it.'

He looked once more at the young man who was surprising him every day.

'Sir, Thambi is missing,' said Valiban. 'I don't know if you remember him. He is a Gounder boy. But I don't trust him.'

'Does Nanban know?'

'Yes, sir,' said Valiban. 'Sir, if I may say so, Nanban sir is not a Veeran. He is not a commander. He cannot lead us from the front.'

'What would you do?' said Veerappan. 'What do you think Thambi will do?'

'Sir, if Thambi has any feelings, the first thing he will do is hurt you.'

Veerappan was shaken by the boy's conviction. 'What am I missing in all this?' he asked.

'Sir, I say this respectfully,' said Valiban, 'you let us down when Raman got killed. Poor Antony, he ended up dead. Then Thambi. He was thrown to the wolves. You sir, Nanban sir, you should have protected him from that animal, Murthy.'

Veerappan shrugged.

'Sir, the inspector did things to Thambi. I cannot describe it. Sir, I cannot describe the hate we have for him.'

'I see,' said Veerappan.

'Sir, I hold Nanban responsible but Thambi is a Gounder. He holds you responsible.'

There was no way they could track Thambi down. He had no public record. The police had issued notices with his photographs. These, like the scent of a man, stopped at the shores of Rameswaram from where saltwater was shared with the Lankan island. In the straits, fishermen got lost when shoals came by, and gunboats traded arms and equipment and diesel and drugs.

Two boats set sail that night, choosing the new moon quarter; they carried enough contraband that would help loosen tongues. They returned with information. Thambi, it seems, was on the island with a renegade group that trained youngsters in the use of explosives. It seemed he had enough money for the training and for a new passport. He would need a new identity on his return.

'Who did he last speak to?' asked Veerappan.

'He spoke to Kari, once, when he was busy filming. In between shots, Kari's mood changed. I asked him but he did not tell me what was said.'

'Why?'

'Sir, I don't know,' said Valiban.

'I could force him to,' said Veerappan. 'Ask him to meet me.'

They had to ask Nanban because he was controlling the actor's schedule. Kari had a tight timeline and shooting was proceeding at breakneck speed.

'Do not disturb him,' Nanban requested. 'Unless it is life and death.'

Veerappan laughed. 'Don't be so dramatic,' he said.

SIX MONTHS TO ELECTIONS

Narsimhan and his team had completed a three-month shooting stint with Kari. They shot in his crummy room and the orphanage where he grew up. They covered his quest for his origins, journeying through interior Tamil Nadu. Then some scenes with Veerappan. A couple of flirtations, a developing love interest and one bloody fight in his kuppam. Two haunting numbers that they had recorded kept playing in the background. Kari learnt kalaripayattu, a martial art from Kerala, to help loosen his body language. The unit kept goading him until he lost his temper. That helped with his expression.

In one important sequence, Karivardan stalked the land of the Dravidas. He travelled south and he stood before the biggest temple in South India – the Brihadeeswara. The Big Temple was imposing, in some sense impregnable, and its crowning glory was a huge single rock cupola. To arrive at the temple entrance, he had to get past a massive Nandi bull sculpture hewed out of impenetrable black stone. Kari stood before it, looking for a way past. Veerappan joined him. It would seem they were up against the Dravidian movement, which was a stable, well-grounded silo. It would also seem that in their political quest, they needed divine intervention.

The narration switched to the historical tract, to actual footage of an incident on Mount Road, Madras, many years past. A small procession walked down the road carrying framed pictures of gods, principally Rama. Chappals, not flowers, bedeck the pictures. The camera zoomed in on the footwear slapping the glass frame and it moved on to the leader of the procession, the man called Periyar E V Ramaswamy.

'A man who had Rama and Swamy in his name and was an atheist,' said Veerappan to Karivardan. 'He encouraged his followers when they abused the Hindu gods that granted Brahmins their higher caste status.

'The parties had such nice names at the time,' said Karivardan. 'Self-Respect Party. Justice Party. Why did they have to change them?'

'To reflect the "movement". They became Dravida Kazhagam and Dravida Munetra Kazhagam; short form DK and DMK,' says Veera. 'Then the splintering started and we had ADMK, AIADMK and the MDMK.'

'So many kings and kingdoms in Tamil land. Where are the monuments?'

Veera laughed. 'Students of history have to learn from daily life,' he said. 'Pandian is a train, Pallavan is a bus corporation, Cheran is a train and a bus corporation, and Chalukya is a hotel. These are our monuments.'

Nanban was thoughtful after watching the rushes. 'When and where did the Dravidian parties and the movement diverge?'

Veera shrugged. 'The historians will tell us after twenty or thirty years. All I know is the time is ripe for these parties to be challenged.'

The enormity of what they were attempting struck them. Studying the Dravidian movement was not helping Nanban beyond a point because so much happened for them that was not pre-planned.

'The one thing I have confirmation of is that large-scale movements are mysterious phenomena. All you can really do is set things in motion and the rest isn't up to us.'

He saw Narsimhan smiling. 'What? Something I said?'

'What you said we call Poyyamozhi,' said Narsimhan. 'A statement devoid of untruth.'

Sharada left on a five-day temple tour with her friends.

A day later, Muskaan arrived in Chennai. Nanban waited for her at the arrival hall in the airport; she floated down the escalator in a red dress. She looked at his modest car, his simple shirt-pant-sandals outfit and smiled. They drove directly to Adyar. Nanban introduced her to Narsimhan and they set off to Kalakshetra for a dance performance after which they walked along Elliots Beach smoking cigarettes; by then Muskaan and Narsimhan were already chattering about truth and historical fiction.

'Where have you been hiding her?' asked Narsimhan.

'He is the one who is hiding,' said Muskaan.

They headed to Vadapalani, to a film studio where a Gounder wedding was being filmed.

'It isn't the usual wedding scene, is it?' said Muskaan.

It was not. So much was different in a Gounder wedding. 'So far removed from the mainstream Brahmin wedding,' said Nanban.

Narsimhan laughed. 'Mainstream and Brahmin? The Gounder population is 100 lakh people. What do you think the Brahmin population is?'

Muskaan and Nanban roamed the beaches of Chennai. They visited Mahabalipuram and Pondicherry. The sun was strong and despite sun hats and sunblock, they tanned. They drank beer, smoked grass; they checked into a star hotel and lay in its vast swimming pool while live music serenaded the trees. On the third day, he took her to Mylapore where they trawled the temple, sari shops, vegetarian eateries and shops called 'Fancy Store' and 'Cut-piece Matching Centre'. They walked through small lanes to San Thome, to the historic white church where a service was being performed.

'Happy?'

'And sad,' she said.

'Have I changed?'

'In this place you are different,' she said. 'So yes, you have changed.'

'I am the same person,' said Nanban. 'No place can change me.'

She smiled. 'A strange language, a strange culture, a different pace, a different people and yet you look like you could belong,' she said. 'Not what you wanted to hear from me?'

Nanban took her home. It was late and the colony was asleep. Muskaan walked in warily; she wandered around instead of sitting. The place was clean, everything was well-organised; there were fresh flowers on the dining table, small plants in the windowsill, water for birds in the balcony and a large floral shopping bag.

'I thought you stayed alone,' she said.

Nanban coughed and looked awkward. Bringing her home was a mistake. 'Chennai is just a sabbatical,' he said. 'Clearly, I cannot be here for long.'

'Really? You want me to believe that?' She picked up a photograph that had Nanban and Sharada in it.

'Yes,' said Nanban. It was his only refuge, this belief.

'I spoke to your mother a week before she passed away,' said Muskaan.

His eyebrows rose. His mind was awhirl. What could they have discussed?

'She told me you cannot leave this place and she did not know why. But she could guess.' Before Nanban could say anything, she asked, 'Who is Sharada?'

'She is a good friend,' he said.

'Don't play games with me,' she said.

He pointed to the photograph she had picked up. 'That's her.'

'I see.' They had reached an impasse.

'I have a problem,' he said, trying to deflect.

She put her hands on her hips. 'So let's discuss it,' she said.

'Now?'

'Now,' she shouted. She pointed to the door. 'Or I will leave.'

'Don't leave,' he said, trying to hold her hand.

She stepped back. 'If you have a problem, you should discuss it. That is part of the solution.' She waited. 'Didn't they teach you that in business school?'

He tried to hold her, but she broke free.

'There is something that I meant to tell you,' he said. 'But…'

'But what?' she said. She waited. It was hopeless. She realised he wasn't going to tell her.

'Are you in love?'

'Yes, I am,' he said.

'With whom?' she asked. 'With yourself?'

He hesitated. 'With you,' he said, sounding lame. He stood there confused, now wishing she would just go away. She was raising questions that he had buried. She kept looking at him, trying to understand his confusion.

'Lust is a season, you stupid fuck!' she said. 'Haven't you figured that out yet?'

'It's not about Sharada,' he said.

'Really?' she said. 'And you will tell her that?'

He said nothing.

'You are alone now my friend, truly alone. Is it worth it? For God's sake, what is so precious that you are holding on to?'

He had no answer and he was running out of time. He had to decide right now. Should he give up his fight against the authorities? Half his life he had wasted fighting to save his reputation. He realised that the fight was all that he was left with. The fight was the fix that held him together.

'I have enough money, sweets,' she said, 'for both of us.'

'Give me some time,' he said. 'Please. I will be back. That's a promise. Please trust me and…'

'Fuck you!' She screamed. 'You think I am going to sit and wait in Mumbai? For a miserable loser like you? Rot here for all I care.'

She knocked over something and almost fell. She left.

He called her that night, again and again.

He called Raghavan.

Neither answered.

Sharada returned the next day. She noticed a photograph was missing.

THREE MONTHS TO ELECTIONS

Some temple prasadam arrived from Veerappan's village. 'Sweet,' said Sharada opening the cloth bag. Two bananas, some betel leaves, a coconut, three small supari packets and in a silver box, there was some sweet Pongal.

Nanban looked up from the morning newspaper. 'Veerappan must be praying,' he said.

Sharada was busy examining the silver box. The Pongal inside was homemade.

'They all pray and they consult astrologers,' said Nanban. 'Even some Dravidian party members. It makes sense. Elections are so random.'

'What happens to you if he loses the election?'

'Ha ha,' said Nanban. 'Ha, ha, ha.' He had stopped caring. 'What else is left to lose?'

Sharada was exasperated. 'Seriously, isn't he paying you for all this?'

Nanban folded the newspaper neatly and finished his coffee. 'He has given me some land. If he wins, he will be generous, I have no doubt about it, but this is not about his generosity, you know that.'

'There are so many things I do not know,' she said. She went into the puja room with the prasadam and returned a while later. 'I found a mobile phone in the medicine cabinet,' she said. 'An old Nokia that belongs in a museum. I have put it on charge, in case you need to use it.'

'God!' said Nanban. 'You are worse than my mother. Why do you have to peek into everything?'

She laughed and wagged her finger. 'I *am* worse than your mother. Where are you going today?'

It was the day of 'The Speech'. For the first time, Veerappan would broach the topic of a separate state for the Gounders. There would be fireworks at the rally and mayhem in the state for the next two days.

'Get me the phone, please,' he told Sharada.

'Get it yourself,' she said. He shook himself loose from his throne.

He called Delhi.

'We have an intelligence report that says that the fellow called Thambi is back in India,' said Raghavan. 'We don't know where he is and under what name he is travelling. Ask the kootam members if they have heard from him.'

'Is there a problem?' said Nanban.

There was a pause. 'We don't have enough information to issue an alert or beef up security,' said Raghavan. 'But we both know the possible target. So stay off this rally.'

THE TENTH CUT

Thambi returned to India after six months. He had aged visibly and there was a hard edge to his hands, the outline of his jaw and the expression in his eyes. His passport photograph captured none of these and he looked like a shaggy pup in his new Sri Lankan passport, with his hair all grown. His name had changed too. He was now Tamil Selvan, a common name that occurred on every database. He came back the way he had left, using the same route, but he stopped at a temple on the way, a temple that belonged to his family on the outskirts of Karur and it had the deity of Solli Amman. He smeared himself with the red dust on offer and spent an hour seated there in the open looking at his people come and go.

In a studio in Kodambakkam, Narsimhan was giving finishing touches to the film. He had shot the crucial Dheeran scenes. There were two important days and each was a sizable segment. They covered the prelude and the hanging of the valiant warrior. Both days were in the month of Aadi.

More than two hundred years later, not far from Kodambakkam, on approximately the same day of the year, preparations were on for 'The Speech'. Another Kongu lion would soon have his moment.

Thambi held a ticking bomb in his hands.

He still had a few minutes and they seemed to be getting longer. His breath turned shallow. He placed the attaché case between his legs. It was a good quality suitcase made of genuine leather. He had spent time stealing it; he wanted the real thing – a deep tan leather case with rich veins and made to look old. He had marvelled at the soft lining, the cloth partition and the small pocket with a smooth zip. He loved the handmade feel. It was seductive. He gripped the sides of the wicker basket and pulled out its cover. There were purple brinjals inside. He took out some of them and made a rectangular well; he placed the attaché case inside and covered it with the vegetables. He shut the basket and tied it loosely with some rope.

He checked out of the lodge at 2.00 am. He had cleaned the room carefully, sanitised the washroom and then, as a familiar gesture, he had left some change on the windowsill. He had seen his errant father do this once. 'Keeps the police away,' he had said. Thambi's escape route was unresolved when he left the hotel; by the time he arrived at the wholesale vegetable market in Koyambedu he knew what he had to do.

The old woman stood beside him, chewing betel leaves. She crouched as he hoisted the basket on her head. He held it as she straightened and felt the load. She complained. Right through the last hour – from the time they had caught a bus to the Beach – she had complained about this and that. It was difficult to ignore her.

Traffic was light at this hour. He rubbed his eyes and shook his head. His mind was clean now of names and numbers, places and faces. It frightened him sometimes, this complete lack of record after an incident, especially when he had prepared by memorising every small detail. He had not willed this deletion; it happened. He could not retain any detail once it had no use for him. If interrogated, he would die protesting, spilling nothing more than sweat and blood.

They got off at the beach bus stop and sat waiting in the bus shelter. The sun rose over the waves and lit up the morning sky. Soon it was 10.00 am, time to move. The address at the election rally would be at 10.30 am; people had arrived in trucks, waving flags and buntings. Party workers were distributing packets of biryani and in one corner, there was a surreptitious group distributing quarter bottles of alcohol. An old woman stood near the Anna Memorial entrance, begging, her eyes hopeful, her torn clothes assembled in layers from different sources. He noted every piece of cloth she wore, the colour, the weave and its possible origin. Detail was like his breath. It came and went ceaselessly.

The last number was four digits – the time. The last co-ordinate was the placement of the basket near the election lectern. The old woman he had brought with him sat on the sand with the basket next to her. He had to remember to leave quickly but without showing haste. This was practised, a manoeuvre that he had mastered, the non-theatrical exit when he merged with the people and props and disappeared backstage. He spoke to the old woman and asked her to leave the place after a while. When she protested, he gave her some money and pointed her towards a distant eatery. After the speech begins, go there and eat, he said. She would live, hopefully she would, but he wasn't sure. The way she sat next to her trusted basket. For a moment, just a brief moment, he looked at those in the vicinity of the lectern and reconsidered what he was doing. Then, he left.

There was a huge crowd by the time Veerappan got onto the stage. Along with him were Kari and Valiban. Perumal was handling the crowds; Nanban was not present. After the preliminary speeches and introductions, his party men presented a gold shawl to Veerappan. A few women brought flowers after which he got down to business. The television crews gave their thumbs up and the cameras started rolling.

'The Dravidian ship is floundering on freebies,' thundered Veerappan. 'Everything is free or subsidised. Look what it has done to the Tamizhan. The Tamizhan is lazy, so lazy that labour comes from other states.'

There was an angry chorus.

'We are Tamizhans. We are not dhandasorus. Look at what we have achieved under the Dravidian rule. Is this how civilisation will be remembered five hundred years later?'

'No,' shouted the crowd.

'What do we have to show for the last thirty years?'

'Nothing,' shouted the crowd.

'I disagree. You are wrong. Look around you. We have 'katchis' and 'kazhagams'. So much song and dance; no wonder they are called parties.'

The crowd laughed and roared.

'DK, DMK, ADMK, AIDMK, PMK, MDMK. Do you want any more political parties?'

'No,' shouted the crowd.

'We don't need katchis and kazhagams. We need kshatriyas.'

'Yes,' shouted some in the crowd.

Veerappan wrapped his shawl around him. It had a lion painted on it. His voice dropped.

'Gounders are meant to be warriors. Two hundred years ago, we fought the British. We defeated the mighty English Army not once or twice but thrice. Have you heard of Dheeran Chinnamalai?'

The crowd roared his name. 'Veeran, Veeran, Veeran.' Dheeran was the only Veeran.

'Are we the descendants of the Veeran?'

'Yes.'

'No,' said Veerappan. 'Look at us today. We are quiet farmers, quiet exporters. We are social nobodies and political zeroes.' His voice rose. 'Do you want to be warriors again?'

'Yes!' The crowd screamed.

'Today, your vote is your weapon. Your vote has the power of battleships and battle tanks. If we vote together, we can defeat anybody.'

Would he mention who was to be defeated?

'You have been defeated in every election in the last thirty years. Do you know that? No? Of course not. You thought the katchis and kazhagams would take care of you.'

Veera laughed loudly, sounding bitter, echoing the feeling of each person at the meeting.

'What do they care about Gounders? Nobody will care for you unless you rise together. That is your power.

That is how you will be noticed. That is how people will come to you.'

A loud roar threatened to drown Veerappan's voice.

'Are we Dravidians?'

He had used the D-word.

'Who is a Dravidian? Do you know who is a Dravidian? Let me tell you the truth. Nobody knows. Dravidian is a katchi, it is a kazhagam. It is not a party for all Tamils. Where were these parties when Tamils were slaughtered in Sri Lanka? Where was Tamil pride? Where were the kshatriyas?'

The crowd was silent now.

'Nobody respects us anymore. When I go to Delhi, they make faces; they call me corrupt because I am from Tamil Nadu. What are your katchis doing? They are filing cases against each other. They have nothing to fight for, or against, so they are fighting each other. There are only two of them so they take turns to rule. I don't know who wins in all of this but I know who loses. What should we do?'

The crowd murmured.

'What should we do?' shouted Veerappan.

The murmuring increased.

'Should we fight them?'

The crowd was confused.

'Or should we make our own Nadu? Don't you want a Kongu Nadu?'

All hell broke loose. As if on cue, some katchi members in the crowd surged towards the podium, even as others tried to hold them back. Slogans rent the air, chairs got broken and ropes that had been strung to hold back people were cut loose. A stampede was in the making. Out of nowhere, there was a bright flash followed by a deafening sound near the dais. In the ensuing silence, flames leapt into the air. The smoke formed, curdled and dark fumes funnelled into the sky. A few people screamed, the shouting returned. People lay bleeding, some sat shell-shocked and others tried to walk away. When the smoke cleared, Veerappan was still on the dais, looking up at the sky, still holding the mike, bleeding, his lips moving. 'Wotha,' said somebody from a channel. His headphones were on and his camera was still rolling.

For the next three months, parts of the state continued to burn. Vandals set fire to buses, blocked highways, pelted stones. The state police was stretched to its limits but the army was not called in. The Gounder party held rallies and there were several meetings at all key constituencies. Slogans echoed across the rallies and the meetings. 'Kongu Nadu vazhga, Veerappan Gounder vazhga.' The community rallied around their leader.

The leader was in a hospital in Chennai. Out of danger, said the medical team. In coma but responding to some stimuli. Perumal had taken over the running of the party but Nanban had seen the rushes of the film and at his insistence, Karivardan became the new face of the party.

Nanban was glad he had chosen Narsimhan. There was a barely hidden excitement on the sets in the closing stages of shooting; in the editing room, there were broad grins. There were two parallel tracks in the film. A historical track that dovetailed smoothly with the other, the quest of the young Karivardan. The film spoke about the dream that Veerappan and other Gounders had – the creation of a new state called Kongu Nadu. It was a radical premise. Based on Nanban's suggestions the party had abandoned its target of winning the state elections and settled instead for statehood. It was a much more believable target.

'I don't think the Censor Board has realised what they have cleared,' said Nanban. Kongu Nadu had seemed a fiction and a farfetched premise. But no one had foreseen the groundswell of support after the speech and the explosion. The film aroused sentiment, instilled pride and got the Gounder community on its feet. Importantly, excerpts from the impassioned speech by Veerappan and live footage of the blast had been included. Call it divine intervention or a strange coincidence, it did not matter. The movement had its momentum and the film had its epiphany.

Nanban took some time off in the run-up to the elections. He drove around aimlessly, past an old age home on Greenways Road. He arrived at his house and it hit him. 'Fuck,' he said, 'this is my middle age home.'

Sharada pushed him around that whole day. 'Let us use this time,' she said. She wanted to go trekking.

'Where?'

'Faraway places,' she said. Till then? They went to a bookstore and bought books that promised to teach them Malayalam and Hindi in sixty days. This was her strategy to stave off dementia, Alzheimer's and other local forms of paithyam. 'Middle age is a delicate decade,' she said.

The next day, Nanban headed to Chinna Tasmac. He had not been there for a while. Thangabalu was there, glimmering in the gloom in his freshly pressed white shirt. 'Fresh fish,' said Thangabalu, announcing the attraction of the day. That was a treat because the place now had a native chef who treated flesh with respect. Nanban's mood lifted as he grabbed a quarter and emptied it into the glass. Three cubes of ice fell in with a splash and he licked his wet fingers and tasted the dark caramel. Who was in today? Damn, it felt good to be back there. Not a woman in sight or within shouting distance, just some burly men who had drawn borders around themselves. The inmates nodded at each other, each spilling nuts, smearing sauce, dropping pretence. Thangabalu slapped the chokras and the rest adjusted their underwear.

At 9.00 pm, the place emptied and the select few remained. Thangabalu twirled his moustache and looked content. Here he was the host of the mighty who left their cares outside and repaired to this den. Today he broke every rule and he spoke up aloud, looking at Nanban. 'How is Veerappan?'

Nanban walked up to him; he placed his phone on the counter and showed him the video of the speech. Everybody crowded around and watched.

'One million hits on YouTube,' said Nanban when it was over. The video had gone viral. Then Nanban flipped through some photographs that he had taken. Thangabalu's face darkened while looking at the damning evidence of a man laid low in hospital.

'His head is facing north,' he said. 'These hospital people are careless. The head should not face north.'

'I see,' said Nanban.

'Next time you go there, please change the locks on the door,' he said.

Were there locks on hospital doors? Nanban had no idea. 'Why?' he asked, just in case.

Thangabalu shrugged his massive shoulders. 'Not all visitors are welcome in hospitals,' he said.

Valiban arrived looking disoriented. He had been trying to get in touch with Nanban without success. Nanban took him to Narsimhan's corner.

'Where were you on the day of the speech?' he asked.

Valiban's posture changed, his eyes wandered.

'You were supposed to be on the podium,' said Nanban.

'And Karivardan was supposed to be sitting next to Veerappan sir on the podium,' said Valiban. 'Have you asked him why he wasn't?'

'Let me ask the questions,' said Nanban. 'Where were you when it happened?'

'Why are you asking me, sir?' said Valiban.

'Because nothing happened to you. Not even a scratch.'

Valiban shifted in his seat. He was a young fellow and a long way from being able to pretend.

'You knew Thambi was in town, right?' said Nanban.

Valiban nodded, not trusting himself to speak.

'Did Kari know?'

'No,' he said, quickly and firmly.

'And did you know what Thambi…'

'No sir,' he said, softly. This time he looked Nanban in the eye. 'We did not know, sir.'

'I am sorry,' said Nanban.

'For what, sir?'

'They are coming. And I cannot help you this time.'

A few minutes later, a police team descended on the bar. They got hold of Valiban, grabbed him by the arms, stood him up, slapped on handcuffs, cuffed him when he protested and dragged him out. Valiban kept looking at Nanban who sat motionless as they took his young ward away.

VALIBAN

THE ELEVENTH CUT

It is so dark I have lost ~~the~~ sense of time. I cannot stand the bloody pain. Somebody is standing there. Chuthmarika, it is that black belt Murthy. He surprised me. How he hides his rough hands in his office? He towers over me, in this devil's chamber.

'There is no day like today,' he says. He sits beside me.

'Sir,' I call him and cringe. What has happened to my voice?

'Yes, kanna,' he says softly, the bloody pretender.

Yesterday, his posse got hold of me at Chinna Tasmac. The way they held me I realised this was different. They called Thangabalu to make sure I was there and they came in two jeeps, sweeping gravel. They wore uniforms, the bloody jokers; their boss wore polished shoes. They held me leaving marks, searched me physically. Let go, I must have said. They laughed. I could not walk so they dragged me. Gone were my laptop, my phone and my books. Strike one, said Murthy, feeling my fingers. In the jeep, they broke one.

They took me to an unknown station, kept me on ice for hours till I couldn't count. The light was constant and a drop of water kept falling till my ears ached. It was mental, the rude silence, it was breaking my ears. After that the glare – the door opened. Murthy, tall, grew taller as he came up to me. He smiled and patted my shoulder.

'All a mistake,' he said. 'We have a few questions. Just answer them and we will let you go.'

'What do you want to hear?' I asked.

He smiled again as he took me to a washroom. 'Freshen up,' he said. 'Try not to smell.'

I came out and they hit me. Two of them took turns. The blows kept coming, a steady rain. I moved between them, drunk and unsteady, the salt of blood, the hurt of bone. Dear God, I said. I stood, barely. I stood tall once before I fell. I was light-headed, shivering. They watched me until he raised his hand.

'He is ready,' he said.

They squeezed some more tears out of me. The pain was a thrum and it would not ebb. Everything was hurting. They fed me some drink and it burned my throat. I coughed and spat out blood. I stood up and they dragged me to another room. A shaft of light bisected me. Came Murthy the interrogator. This time a folded sheet, its cutting edge. Three cuts he made and blood seeped again. I almost laughed; I was so light-headed. The drops gathered and darkened. The paper caressed my neck.

'Who got you here?'

'You,' I said.

'Who taught you to lie?'

'Books,' I said.

'Who is your teacher?'

'A thevadiya called Nanban.'

'Describe your gang, your so-called kootam.'

'Together we are nothing, sir. One sothai, one loose and one lollu. We are underage.'

'You are going to die underage. Any regrets?'

'Just the knowledge, sir,' I said.

These were cops, I told myself. They will not kill you. Rile them and soon you will be senseless. Do it quickly.

'Are you into substances?'

'Yes,' I said.

'Why won't you tell us what you did, or who did? Just point the finger and we will let you go.'

'I cannot,' I said.

'You can. What did you do?'

'Nothing,' I said.

He hit me, personally. His touch was lighter. I was weakening by now, cowering for no reason. I was hungry; I felt I hadn't eaten for the longest time.

'We have Ramesh, that auto-driver. He is next. He will crumble and he will confess. Then you will be in a cage and we will poke rods through the bars. Keep your ass covered or don't if you like it there.'

They stood me up and knuckled me in the face. I fell once more. Someone counted to ten and I began blurting. Murthy had to bend low so he could hear.

'We hated Raman from the start,' I heard myself saying. 'He was whimpering and afraid but the bugger was a thimiruu pudichavan. Antony was buzzing around him with a strange energy that day. He wasn't in control around him. This Raman, he was thirsty but he wouldn't drink water because Antony was giving it. He was in trouble, but his Brahmin thimiru wouldn't go away. That was his downfall.'

'Why did you kill him?'

'Antony did it. Why won't you believe us, sir? He used the aruvaal. One cut did it. The Brahmin fell like a tree.'

I was down to wheedling by now. 'Sir, sir, you are a principled officer, sir,' I said. He laughed and straightened his collar.

'Are you doing this for the government, sir?' I asked. 'Beating me like this?'

'No,' he said, sounding nasal, 'I am working for the families of the two cops who died in that explosion.'

Chuthmarika. That was it. He was out to eke revenge and no one would stop him. I was at the mercy of this animal. I knew I wouldn't last. My mind was made up. I hated what I was about to do but I had to stay alive.

'You are intelligent,' said Murthy. 'Why put up a show when no one is watching? Confess quickly.'

I spoke up. 'Thambi triggered the bomb,' I said.

Murthy looked hard at me and I fought to hold his gaze. 'Tell us where he is and you can leave,' he said. I told them. They left me as if I did not exist anymore. They dropped me like I was a burnt-out cinder. They would get hold of Thambi before dawn. Where could he hide?

Thambi was never seen again, but I saw him in my dreams. He looked at me long and hard; he said nothing.

It took three months for my wounds to heal. I hid in a room in the Valsarvakkam house and refused to emerge. I was bleeding inside. After much prodding, I emerged into the sunshine wearing a beard.

'Feeling better, kanna?' asked my mother.

'No,' I said. The hurt remained and that would be fuel.

'What are you writing on these sheets of paper?' my mother asked. She saw me writing ceaselessly. Just one word, hundred to a page. Nanban. She looked into my face. 'Kanna, he is still your hero?' I shook my head. I would have laughed if it didn't hurt that much.

Nanban sir was also being manipulated but he did not know. He thought he was in control but Veerappan Gounder made me do the small things.

'Small interventions,' he said, echoing Nanban sir. 'Do them quietly.'

The first time he asked me to do something – it was a minor task – I shivered. There was no room for failure. Each succeeding task was trickier but I managed. Then, came the Raman episode. It is true that Raman was not to be killed. He was to be taught a lesson.

'Nobody in politics will accept a financial default. It is an unwritten rule that Nanban understands but does not want to implement.' That is what Veerappan told me.

Undony had no business killing Raman. When it happened, Perumal said, 'Let him be, he has made a mistake.'

I said, 'No, he has to pay.'

I still remember the look Veerappan gave me when he heard my tone.

'Antony has to go,' I said. 'The principle of Omerta – he cannot be trusted.'

'What do you mean?' asked Perumal.

'He has to be killed,' I said.

'Let us not be hasty,' said Perumal.

'We have no time,' I said.

'And who will do it?' Veerappan asked, softly.

'I will do it,' I said.

I drugged him using chloroform and stuffed his head into a sock until he choked and went blue. I had to slap his cheeks to keep him alive. Then, I tied him up to Raman, his two-tumbler nemesis. Feet to feet, face to face. He came to, just for a while, and when he did, I walked him then dragged him then leant the two over the Adyar Bridge. I saw them disappear.

'You are my lieutenant now,' said Veerappan.

He asked Perumal to meet me. He gave me a small plot of land near Elysium.

I needed money to build a house on my plot of land. I had thought of asking Veerappan but I hesitated because he might have given me another gory task. The next time we met, he was in a good mood and I was planning to pop the question but there was no need to. For a change, he was not drinking. He was eating a fruit we call nongu, one that Nanban sir calls thadgola. It was a hard purple ball that when broken yielded three soft white fleshy portions with sweet nectar inside. You had to be careful while peeling the thin eggshell-like cover otherwise the nectar would spill. I was peeling them and I was concentrating.

'I need Nanban,' said Veerappan.

'You want him to stay in Chennai?'

'Yes,' he said. 'He is in love with a girl in Mumbai and he wants to get back. That city is also pulling him back but I need him here.'

I peeled another nongu. It was soft and it quivered in my palm and just as I peeled the last of the shell, the knife broke through and the nectar spilled.

'I know how to keep Nanban in Chennai,' I said, looking at my wet hands.

Veerappan was surprised that I had a quick solution. 'How?'

'Sir, I buy household groceries for him, his personal care products and his protection,' I said.

'Protection from what?' said Veerappan.

'Sir, his condoms,' I said. 'I could do something to them that would serve your purpose.'

'I see,' said Veerappan. 'Actually, I don't. Just do the job, we will reward you.'

A few months later, sometime after Veerappan got hurt, I received money from Perumal for building my house. Perumal was friendly because I was close to Nanban sir. They were rivals. Perumal confided in me after he saw me getting instructions directly from Veerappan.

'The day Nanban learns how to handle cash, I will be out of a job,' he said.

'Start sending sacks of currency to Nanban sir's house,' I said. 'Put him in charge of party money. I know him very well. He will not be able to sleep. And he will realise he cannot replace you.'

Now Undony was gone and Thambi was a goner too. Kari we had lost to films. Others had come in their place. I located two youngsters. Scary fellows. They were visibly out of control. Twice a week, we met in a garage in MIG Colony, Besant Nagar. The place had blackened windows and in that cave, we could smoke, drink and perform. I was the Anti-Caste, inheritor of simple prejudice, a thread-cut Brahmin, who stared at women and fell in love with men. I was obsessed, just like Nanban sir, but with different things. Like the cruel accident of birth. I dreamt of a simple upheaval that would begin in the ward where the babies would go into a common pool, parents would be drawn by lot and caste would die.

Caste marks make me livid. The blood boils over, causing an occasional nosebleed. Only the Brahmin has caste marks. This is my blind spot. As an anti-caste fighting the entrenched majority, I have no choice but to behave like a vigilante, with an agenda that precludes nothing.

I stay now near Elysium in a small house. My land is the other world, a back of beyond called the boondocks. Ramesh, the rickshaw driver, needs convincing and the incentive of a return fare to take me there. One day, we were standing near a bush and a mongoose slinked by followed by a cobra. Ramesh's mouth opened and closed, he lost his tongue.

'Stop pointing,' I told him, softly. 'Don't move.'

He was shivering from head to toe. 'Kill it,' he whispered.

'Which one?'

He pointed to the snake; it had its hood up by now, looking regal and quite extraordinary. I did nothing but I was rooting for the cobra. The dance of death began; never would it be as beautiful as this – the darting mongoose, the hissing cobra, the circling, the feinting, the quick strike and finally the clinch, each biting the other. In the end, the mongoose killed the snake. Ramesh was happy.

'Just watch,' I said.

In a short while, the venom took effect and the mongoose breathed its last.

'Wasn't it beautiful?' I said.

'It was horrible,' said Ramesh. He sat on the ground staring at me, wondering what I was made of.

'It is ugly when men do it,' I said.

NANBAN

My beachside plot looked barren. I built a boundary wall and I fixed a gate. I planted a row of casuarina trees. Perumal said I had made one mistake. He took me to the edge of my plot and we stood facing the sea. He pointed to an irregular five-yard stretch between my boundary wall and the beach that was covered with shrubs and debris. 'This is called porambokku land,' he said. 'Nobody owns it because at one time it belonged to the sea.'

'And since the sea has retreated?' I asked.

He grinned. 'It belongs to you.'

I stepped onto it and my feet disappeared.

'People call you a porambokku person,' said Perumal, happy to highlight my outsider status.

I would like to leave this city but Sharada is pregnant. She stood before me one day holding a test result. It was blue in colour. Her cheeks were flushed; I had never seen her so happy. I was sad, sad beyond measure. I mean how old were we? How would she give birth at this age and who would live to see the grandchildren?

Do I have a blistered mind? Why does it think of such things and not the joy of what has escaped us thus far, the chance of living again with a third, a small bundle that we could nurture, that would one day take flight and give us wind beneath our wings?

'What?' I said.

'Yes,' she said, looking anxiously at me. She looked so vulnerable I could have held her, run my hands through her hair, kissed her and murmured something in her ears.

'Are you sure? I mean is this test final?'

Her eyes narrowed and tears formed. I moved quickly and hugged her but she held me off and searched my face. I was confused and I was a poor liar. We were standing in her balcony. We held hands instead of the railing.

'Sorry, this is so sudden.'

She nodded. She was happy to wait for my thoughts to coalesce. They did; something that I never expected occurred and I smiled. That was enough and we hooped and we hugged again, we looked at each other, felt different, walked to the beach, held hands and looked at the waves.

I drove carefully to the clinic. Inside the clinic, the lady doctor and Sharada disappeared for a while.

'Wait here, don't go outside and roam.'

I read a magazine called *Femina*. The clinic had a fresh smell of canned spray and it was spotless. Nobody else was there this early. They returned beaming and I shot up and stood awkwardly.

'Congratulations. I am so happy for both of you.'

'Thanks,' I said.

'What a courageous decision,' said the doctor.

'Yes, yes, what the hell...'

'Age is just a number, ha ha,' said the doctor.

She gave us some printouts on late pregnancies, some do's and don'ts, and a paper on how to prepare ourselves. The drive home was quiet. How did this happen? I was the one who used protection, and no, we were not careless. I figured a poor quality condom had trumped us.

'A gift from the gods,' I said. 'My mother would have been pleased.'

My mother had an enduring image of the life I would lead when things slowed down. A quiet and solitary old age in the suburb of Juhu in Mumbai. Enough time to write a memoir.

'A new chapter,' said Sharada. 'A new life.' She was glowing. 'Come here,' she said, patting the bed. I approached and sat down gingerly. She leaned back. 'I am not made of glass,' she said. 'But learn to be gentle.'

The next day, she sent me out on a walk. 'Be brisk,' Sharada told me. In the evening, I joined a gym for some light workouts and I bought a hair dye at the department store. I had committed myself to three uses. Then, we would see. I promised her I would use the dye that evening and dressed up as best as I could. She wore a red and blue Kanjeevaram. She looked stunning. We drove carefully down a small inner road. She was thoughtful and I was distracted. She held my left hand at a signal and placed it on her baby bump.

We sat in our favourite seats in Kalakshetra. The dancer tucked her half-sari into her petite waist, carved the air and planted a toe. The percussionist used a small hammer and tuned his mridangam. It was dusk and while we waited, grains of sand rose to greet the blustery winds of margazhi. A flock of birds flew past in the skies above and their calls retreated. Finally, the seated singer cleared her throat, nodded at the dancer and her accompanists and slapped her thigh. The performance began and soon I was truly lost. Life at its very best was a kutcheri where others performed and my world changed.

KONGU NADU

Nanban, Kari and Valiban drove one last time in Nanban's car. They parked at the roadside and walked up the stairs to a new eatery. They sat in a secluded corner and stared at the menu.

'I had to drag him here,' said Kari, pointing at Valiban. 'He hates your guts.'

'Brain fry?' asked Valiban, ignoring the introduction. He did not look Nanban in the eye.

'No, I cannot eat brain,' said Nanban. 'You know why.'

'Chicken legs?' asked Kari, rolling up his sleeves.

'You go ahead,' Nanban said. 'I am done with plump thighs. They look manufactured.'

The other two looked puzzled.

'Quail?' asked Valiban. 'It is a small bird, totally natural.'

'No, not for me,' Nanban said. He rustled through the menu and pointed to the vegetarian section.

They waited for the stuff to arrive. Things were downbeat thanks to Nanban's mood. It turned out to be an awful meal. They left the place, walked silently down the stairs, sat in the car and held their stomachs. It was too late to go anywhere else. They parked near Elliots Beach, rolled down the glass windows and felt the city's sweaty embrace. A cop car sidled up, a cop leaned out and he stared at each of them. They waited for his attention to wane. Finally, he moved on.

'Kari visited Veerappan,' said Valiban.

Nanban looked towards Kari who could barely hide his triumphant air.

'Within half an hour of my being there, Veerappan began to move around,' said Karivardan. 'He tried to break his straps and pull out each tube and they had to hold him down and remove all the tubes. He sat up and within minutes he was on the phone.'

'You should have seen it,' said Valiban. 'It was like a miracle. It was like he had woken up from sleep.'

'And?'

Valiban stayed silent. 'Tell him,' said Kari.

'He asked for you,' said Valiban. His insides had churned when the first thing the Gounder leader asked was, 'Where is Nanban? Why hasn't he come with you?'

'I was there yesterday,' said Nanban. 'Sorry, I should have told you. I met up with the doctor as usual and he told me the unpredictable had happened. "Your leader has started moving," he said. We went in and he asked me to speak to him. He came to life.'

Nanban would never forget the moment. He realised how much he had grown to like Veerappan Gounder.

His first sentences were in Tamil. 'Where am I? What has happened to me?'

The medical team brought him abreast gently, showing him his room, his tubes and explained to him his medical condition. 'What brought me here?' He was woozy. You are fine, they kept telling him, repeatedly.

The family came in. There was a spontaneous outpouring of joy. It was as if the head of the family had taken birth again. Nanban sensed the heartfelt relief, tempered by the unasked question, 'Can we assume he will wake up after he sleeps next?' Veera tended to drop off even while speaking.

Nanban left the room for a while. He met him again in the afternoon, alone. 'Why don't you sit down,' said Veera. Nanban could not. 'You look awkward,' said Veera. 'I have never seen you look awkward.'

Nanban apologised. Veera brushed it aside. 'Not your fault,' he said. 'I haven't heard all the details but why should you apologise?'

Nanban briefed him on what had happened. He wanted to cry off his assignment. 'You don't need me anymore,' he said.

'Let me decide,' said Veera.

They promised to meet again after 2–3 days. Veera looked tired. He asked for a calendar. He wanted a day-wise summary of all that had happened.

'Finally, he was so tired they had to put him to sleep for the night,' Nanban told the other two. 'He wouldn't sleep because he was nervous about waking up. He had lost faith in the simple instinct that we all have; we just wake up.'

'He is a true veeran,' said Kari.

An uneasy quiet followed. The two youngsters seemed impatient and restless and Nanban could sense an undercurrent.

'Sir,' said Valiban, looking awkward and sounding strange. 'Kari wants us to part as friends. I have a problem with that.'

'Dai minor,' said Kari. He placed a hand on Valiban's shoulder but the latter brushed it off.

'Don't touch me,' he said. He got up abruptly, breathing hard.

'You want to say something more?' asked Nanban.

'You don't know what I am capable of,' shouted Valiban.

'I don't,' said Nanban. He looked unperturbed. 'But I know what I can do to you.'

Kari held Valiban by the shoulders and forced him to sit down. He sat next to him. 'What is wrong with you?' he said.

Valiban sat, coiled, his muscles tense.

'He wants to be an ugrawadi,' said Nanban. 'This hothead wants to take on everybody, including me.'

'First, I need to teach a cop a lesson,' said Valiban, through clenched teeth. He had imagined Murthy's death at his own hands. He had imagined a trail of revenge that included his mentor. There were waves of rage that consumed him at odd hours and they left him sweating. 'Sir, I cannot help it. One day I might come after you.'

'Why give me time?' said Nanban.

Nanban looked thoughtful. He tapped his fingers on the table as if arriving at a decision.

'There is only one way to resolve this,' he said. He looked at Valiban and Kari. He had discussed this with them before as a solution for disputes that were intractable. The water would decide.

'Shall we?'

The three left for Elliots Beach. It was deserted and they removed their footwear and walked, their feet throwing up sand behind them. The wind picked up as they approached the shoreline. They stood abreast at the water's edge. They looked at each other through windswept hair; each was ready.

Valiban spoke first. 'Eye to eye and head to head,' he shouted, 'this shall end when one is dead.'

Nanban smiled, happy the protégé was well-read. He spread his arms wide as if he wished to take wing. 'Turn for turn and twist for twist,' he shouted, 'hah, the hooded Death shall miss.'

They walked into the water. There was no turning back now until one had succumbed. It was high tide and the unruly sea came at them; crashing waves, swirling foam and, at every retreat, the deadly undercurrent. The earth sank and sloped, the sea rose. Nobody missed a step; none looked back. The force surprised them and they were thrown off their feet. But they recovered, splashing wildly, stood again, laughed, shouted at each other and continued forward, answering the call of the wild. By now it was perilous and the sound was deafening. The salty water stung their eyes, the current began to pull at their feet. Nanban was the first to cough, the first to splutter and the first to bob around before he began to sink. He was losing the battle, visibly. Valiban was swimming expertly away from the shore, fording each wave. Kari was still standing, his nose barely above the water. He began swimming as well, his powerful shoulders holding him in place.

'Don't,' shouted Valiban.

Kari wouldn't listen. He swam up to Nanban, bent a hand around his neck, held him up and swam ashore. They laid him on the ground and pumped his chest. After a while, he coughed and retched. He was incoherent and couldn't see very clearly.

They took him home where Sharada opened the door. Her eyes widened in disbelief and fear. They sat him on a sofa where he collapsed, his head falling onto his chest, his eyes climbing their sockets. 'Is he drunk?' she asked. 'Why are his clothes wet?' They thought they would spin a story but looking at her, they could not.

'Are all of you mad?' she shouted. 'Just look at him.'

'He cannot swim,' she said. 'I hope you know that.'

The two youngsters left abruptly without saying anything. Sharada led Nanban to his room, removed his wet clothes, wiped him with a towel and laid him down on the bed. She sat next to him while he slept most of the next twenty-four hours. She kept staring at him. There were questions. She held Nanban's hands in her own and ran her fingers over the cuts on his wrists. There was one big question mark.

When Nanban awoke, he had no recollection of what had happened. Was he pretending? 'Was I drunk?' he asked. 'I must have been.' He had a long bath revelling in the hot water from the overhead tank. He emerged refreshed; his face red, his eyes bright, for all purposes a new man. 'I am so hungry,' he said. He ate a whole meal, stood up, stretched his hands wide and burped.

'Sorry,' he said.

He walked down to a gent's parlour, a swish outfit with a hoarding outside that showed youngsters with sculpted hair. He asked for the senior stylist and he turned out to be a young man with tattooed hands, two studs and a ring on his lip. He ran his fingers through Nanban's hair.

'Colour?' he said.

'I hope you mean black,' said Nanban. The stylist nodded.

'Could you give me a long-lasting dye?' said Nanban. 'I don't care if it is expensive.'

The stylist laughed. 'First time here, sir?' he said.

Nanban nodded.

'It doesn't matter how permanent your dye is,' said the young stylist. 'Your hair will grow and your grey will show.'

After an hour of patient study of glossy magazines, Nanban emerged from the parlour looking younger and smelling of a zany shampoo. He peered into every mirror he came across. He rang the bell at home so Sharada could open the door as if to a stranger. 'Look at you,' she said. 'Just look at you.' He did look again, standing next to her. 'I wish we could take a photograph,' she said. He took one after she was ready. 'Can you feel the excitement?' she said. Duhhh? She hit him on the back of his head to jolt him out of his fugue. 'Go meet your friends,' she said. 'There is so much to celebrate.'

He headed off to Chinna Tasmac. Thangabalu looked agile and he unveiled new malt. He raised the bottle from its round cask and peeled its cover. They opened the cork and Nanban got the first sniff. It was peaty, just as he liked it, the smell of smoke from unlit coal. He sat alone at his usual place and waited for Narsimhan to show up. He did not. Nanban drank that evening, alone, just him and a distant Thangabalu.

He raised his glass many a time mouthing toasts to his missing friends.

'Bloody buggers,' he said.

'They will be back soon,' said Thangabalu.

A glass sat heavily and broke. The drinking continued.

'I haven't enjoyed an evening as much in a while,' said Nanban.

The barman smiled broadly. He waved a fat arm, stunning a drowsy mosquito. Halfway through the bottle, Nanban was toasting distant acquaintances. It was late when his solo performance tapered. He stood up and he stumbled. 'Final,' he said. 'Last and final.' He looked solemn as he raised a thimble. 'To my unborn child,' he said.

SODA MUDI

For the first time, the Nokia phone was on display, out in the open in the living room. Nanban called the Delhi number every day for a week. Nobody picked up. He was at a loss. This was the only way he could get in touch with Raghavan. Other than landing up in Delhi. Should he?

'Go,' said Sharda.

He waited another week, the phone heavy in his pocket. No call came and his messages remained unanswered. Shortly thereafter the sim card died.

'Go, and be done with it,' said Sharda.

'I am not that desperate,' said Nanban. 'They should be calling me.'

'To thank you?'

'Why not? Why this silence? I am a little hurt.'

He hung around at home.

'I don't know where I stand,' he said.

The thought crossed his mind of a boat adrift, a catamaran marooned by listless tides.

He landed up at Chinna Tasmac. He drank two quarters without blinking. Thangabalu refused him a third.

Kari in his newfound prosperity rented a small office for Valiban. It had cement floors, steel furniture, posters on the wall, newsletters and amateur videos. Evenings it was busy. A small group of young educated men and women gathered in the veranda to hear his views. When Valiban spoke, they listened. He was well-read and he had the life experience of a kind they had never seen. Where would this lead to? He had a vague idea.

Kari dropped in at night carrying a couple of quarters. The two licked their lips and watched the dark outside.

'Nanban is at a loose end,' said Valiban.

'How do you know?'

'I follow him.'

'How?'

'On foot.'

'Why?'

'I cannot get him off my mind.'

Kari laughed. 'Minor, you are still a puppy dog and he is still your guru.'

Valiban snorted. He stumbled into the pantry and pulled out a crate. He returned with a soda bottle. He found a rusty opener and popped it. The metal cap lost shape and fell on the floor.

'Pick it up,' said Kari. 'It could hurt someone.'

Valiban stared at it and didn't move. 'That is Nanban sir,' he said, his voice slurring.

'That soda mudi?'

'Yes. He is useless now. A week ago, I followed him to the airport. He caught a flight to Delhi and he returned the same evening. It looks like he was turned away by his masters. You should have seen the look on his face the next few days.'

Valiban was right and Kari was amazed at how much his friend had gleaned from a distance. Kari had met Nanban on his return from the capital. The latter had spoken at length on how his efforts had not been appreciated. He had gone expecting a welcoming committee, at the very least a thank you speech, and a handshake of some kind. Instead, Raghavan had met him at the entrance with a barely disguised air of impatience. 'Why have you come?' his manner implied. 'It's over,' he said.

'That's it?'

'All recordings have been erased, files have been deleted and the team has moved on.' Raghavan pointed towards the building. 'Nobody here knows who you are.'

'I see.' It was disorienting.

'It is better this way,' Raghavan had said.

Valiban drank the soda and burped.

'Why do you drink that stuff?'

Valiban burped again. 'It is good for my acidity,' he said.

The soda eased his insides, repressed the bile that rose in his throat on most days.

Kari picked up the bottle cap. 'I must leave,' he said. He rose to his height and looked down at Valiban. 'I have a gift for you from Nanban. A Nokia phone. He asked me to give it to you.'

Valiban was unsure. 'This is a gift?'

'He said so,' said Kari. They looked at the outdated model. 'Such a small screen. It looks like a museum piece.'

Valiban switched it on.

'It works,' he said.

The phone stayed on the office table and blinked through the night. It rang in the morning at 10.00 am. Valiban peered at the 011 number.

'Landline,' he said.

It was a call from Delhi.

ACKNOWLEDGEMENTS

This book was on the drawing board for a few years. My thanks to Sucharita Dutta-Asane and Minakshi Thakur for their feedback on earlier versions. I'm grateful to Indira Chandrasekhar who published an extract from this work in *Out of Print* and Chitra Viraraghavan and Krishna Shastri for publishing an extract in their collection on Madras.

My publishing journey began some years ago with Nandita Aggarwal, and I'm grateful for it. Her acquiring *A Tamil Month* for Bloomsbury meant a lot. Nandita left this book in great hands with Faiza Khan. It's been wonderful working with Faiza and team Bloomsbury.

And finally, all my thanks to Priya Doraswamy, my literary agent, for being there at every stage.

CREDITS

The work of Valay Shende, referenced in the narrative (dining table with chairs et al.), is titled *Farmer Suicide 2009*. Dimensions variable.

'Art is Elsewhere' is an engraving on a block of marble. It is an editioned work by the artist NS Harsha.

Four lines (with a minor change) have been extracted from Rudyard Kipling's *The Jungle Book*, Chapter 5, titled 'Rikki-Tikki-Tavi'.

A few sentences of Jorge Luis Borges have been modified and used in the narrative.

'Daylight Moon', an extract from an early version, was published as a short story in a collection titled *Madras on My Mind*, publisher HarperCollins India, June 2017.

'Karivardan', an extract from an early version, was published online by *Out of Print* magazine in March 2016.

A line about birds in a cage is taken from a quote by Alejandro Jodorowsky.